Crashing

Upwards

By S.C. Wynne

Chapter One

Harper

The unmistakable tang of blood filled my mouth. My brain was fuzzy as I tried to open my eyes, but it was like they were superglued shut. My shoulder throbbed as if jammed in a wood chipper, and I couldn't seem to move, no matter how much I wanted to.

"Can you hear me?" a gentle voice asked. Fingers gripped my wrist, and I groaned. "I'm so, so, *so* sorry." A definite loss of control wobbled thorough that same male voice. "Please be okay."

Someone smoothed the hair off my forehead. It felt kind of nice. The hands were soft, and they touched me like I was fragile. Valuable.

I'm neither.

Sirens, blaring horns, and raised voices surrounded me in a swirl of confusion, and still I found it impossible to move.

"I saw the whole thing," a nasally voice announced. "He rode right in front of you. There was no way you could have stopped in time."

"That isn't really the point right now, is it?" the gentle voice snapped back.

A loud, raw groan erupted from my tight throat. My bones and flesh ached so horribly I thought I might even cry. Oh, God. How embarrassing. I wasn't a crier. But then I'd never been in the kind of pain I was in at the moment either.

"It's okay. It's going to be all right," the soft voice reassured me. "I'll take care of you. I promise."

People grabbed under my arms and lifted me. That's when the real torture started. I wanted to yell for them to put me back down. Leave me where I was. But I couldn't seem to form the words needed to beg them to stop. But then none of that mattered because everything went black.

****

When I opened my eyes, the light above me was so white and harsh I slammed my lids shut again. I wasn't out on the street anymore. I was in a room, and the only sound was a high-pitched beep off to the side of my bed. Instinctively I knew better than to try and move. My body still ached, but there was a warm layer of something blurring the pain. It was like someone had inserted a barrier of cotton between my nerve endings and my injuries.

My injuries.

I popped my eyes open again and scoped the room as best I could without moving my head. There was someone sitting near me. I couldn't make out who it was because I was terrified of actually engaging my muscles enough to look properly. The memory of my earlier pain was still very much etched in my brain, and I really didn't want it to return.

"You're awake." I recognized that gentle voice from the street, and a chair creaked as someone stood and came closer. A guy about my age appeared above me. He had jet-black hair and moss-colored eyes. I'd never seen eyes so green. Who was he, and why did he look so guilty?

I licked my dry lips, noticing that my lower lip felt swollen. "Where?" I attempted to speak. My throat was bone-dry, and I sounded like I was in *Citizen Kane* about to share the name of my childhood sled.

"You're at Dallas County Hospital. I don't want you to worry about a thing. My dad's paying for everything, absolutely everything, and you really, really don't need to be concerned." He swallowed and his Adam's apple bobbed in his slender throat.

Paying for what exactly? I still wasn't sure what had happened.

I guess he could see the question in my eyes because he said, "I hit you with my car." He winced and then held up his hands quickly. "Nothing's broken. Well, on *you*. Your bike is toast."

Now it was coming back: the screech of tires, the slamming onto the pavement. I frowned and even that hurt. "Who are you?" I did another husky Rosebud impersonation.

"I'm Sam. Sam Foster." He started to hold out his hand and then shoved it in his jeans pocket. "I saw from your license your name is Harper."

I just stared because I wasn't really able to do much more than that very well.

"My dad will buy you a new bike. I don't want you to worry about a thing." He grimaced. "I know that's easy for me to say, when you're the one lying in a hospital bed. But I mean it. It was all my fault, and I'm going to see to it that you're taken care of."

"Right." I was too tired to argue, and I still felt disconnected from reality. Was this actually happening? Judging by how banged up my body felt, it was. But it was hard to believe I'd have been that careless. I'd been riding for years and no one had ever hit me. Sure I'd had some close calls. The streets were packed with cars at rush hour, but I was careful. No way I'd let someone plow into me. I was quick. I was professional. I was fucked.

He approached the bed and leaned over to gently squeeze my arm. I wasn't accustomed to people I didn't know touching me, but a pleasant shiver rolled through me and I sighed. There was something about his touch that made me feel better. I remembered that from earlier. His smile was warm, and my chest tightened as his sincere gaze held mine. Nobody smiled at me that way usually. Nobody wasted time trying to charm me. As thrashed as I felt, the heat of his smile wiggled through me. Why was he being so nice? Was he afraid I'd sue him? I wouldn't be surprised if that was his motivation. If there was one thing I was certain of, it was that most people were self-serving.

He shared another beguiling smile. "Like I said, no bones are broken. But your shoulder was dislocated, and your leg was sliced open and bruised pretty badly. They gave you like twenty stitches. You're going to have to stay off your bike for a few weeks."

I widened my eyes in horror, and he flinched.

"What's wrong?"

I did something very stupid: I attempted to sit up. The screech I let loose didn't sound like me. He cowered briefly, and I fell back against the bed as agonizing pain radiated through my shoulder and shot down my arm. I gasped for breath and tried to stay perfectly still as the excruciating, stabbing pains in my shoulder and arm slowly began to fade.

"You shouldn't get up." He sounded almost angry. "What are you doing?"

I licked my lips again and gritted out, "My job. I'll lose my job."

He shook his head. "No." His voice was sharp. "I'll make arrangements. I'll figure something out. You will most definitely not lose your job."

I gave a short, bitter laugh, making sure not to jolt my shoulder. I worked as a bicycle courier. There were no desk jobs at my place of employment. My boss, Jack, already didn't love me, and he didn't tolerate fuckups of any kind. Not being able to ride for weeks would definitely qualify as a fireable offence. What the hell was I going to do? I could barely make rent as it was on my one-bedroom apartment. I wasn't soft or weak, but I didn't know that I could survive being homeless. The very thought of that made me feel sick. Hopeless.

Sam still hovered. His eyes were bright, and his mouth drooped. "I didn't see you, and by the time I did it was too late." He paled. "I feel horrible."

I knew he wanted me to forgive him. I wasn't sure I had it in me at the moment.

I cleared my throat. "Water?"

He straightened and grabbed a plastic pitcher on a tray nearby. Then he poured some water into a little pink cup with a bendy straw. He held the cup near my lips, and I sipped from the straw. I was embarrassed when some of the cool water dribbled down my chin. He surprised me when he wiped the drops away with his thumb, as if it was no big deal to wipe away a stranger's drool.

"Is there someone I can call for you? Maybe your parents? Your cell was smashed." He swallowed hard. "I'll replace that too."

My throat felt much better now that I'd had some water. "No. I don't have anyone to call."

He frowned as if he couldn't imagine that would be true. "No one?"

I thought about some of the riders at my company. *Maybe* I could have reached out to them if I were a reaching-out type of guy. We were a tight-knit group while on the clock, and we'd occasionally drink together after work. But we didn't spend holidays together or hang out at each other's houses. Besides, my fellow employees were already riding their asses off trying to make a living. They couldn't cover for me without blowing out their legs. There was no way they could risk that just to help me.

I closed my eyes and tried to keep back the tsunami of fear that hurtled toward me. I didn't know what to do. I usually had a plan, but I couldn't think my way out of this at the moment. I'd known the possibility existed that I might get hurt one day, but I'd never really believed it would happen.

"You can probably claim disability insurance."

"My boss doesn't exactly do things legally," I whispered. "I'm not sure what I can claim."

A line appeared between his perfect brows. "Oh. Well, either way you'll be okay. My family will take care of things."

He sounded so self-assured. He obviously had great faith in his family's willingness to help me. I didn't have any such faith. Not in his father and not in anyone. I'd been on my own since I was sixteen, and depending on someone else to save me wasn't in my DNA.

An older man with a fluffy salt-and-pepper mustache strode into the room. He looked vaguely familiar, and his wide shoulders and palpable self-importance shrunk the room immediately. Instinctively I wilted from his aggressive energy, pressing back against the soft pillows.

"Dad, what are you doing here?" Sam's surprise was evident. "I told you I could handle this."

The older man approached the bed and observed me with steely gray eyes. "You're far too trusting. I wanted to meet your new buddy Harper myself."

I was taken aback that he knew my name, and I stared at him wordlessly.

Mr. Foster tilted his head studying me as if I was an amoeba on a glass slide. "The nurse at the desk said nothing's broken, so that's good." He rubbed his chin.

"Why are you here?" Sam repeated. "Don't you think I can do anything on my own?"

"It's my money. Am I not allowed to assess the situation?" The older man sounded patient when he spoke to his son. His tone changed when he addressed me. "Sam believes in the goodness of others." His tone implied he thought his son was nuts. "I, on the other hand, don't."

We actually had that in common.

"This is really annoying. You're treating me like a child," grumbled Sam.

"The world is filled with shysters, son. Things aren't always what they seem."

Sam's face was pinched and his mouth tight. "I hit him with my car, Dad. That really happened."

"I'm sure you did, son. But there are ways to fake an accident. Believe it or not, Dallas has a lot of con artists who throw themselves in front of cars and pretend to be hurt."

Heat flooded my swollen cheeks. Even if he thought I was some sort of scumbag, he shouldn't have had this conversation in front of me. I'd have loved to take a swing at that arrogant asshole, but I knew that would hurt me more than him. Instead I put all my energy into glaring at him.

"Jesus, Dad, just look at him. He's not faking his injuries," Sam exclaimed. He looked uncomfortable, and I got the feeling he wanted to defend me but wasn't sure how.

Mr. Foster grabbed my chart off the foot of my bed and studied it glumly. "My son's a very responsible driver. I find it hard to believe he just didn't *see* you, Harper."

"There was a ton of traffic, and it happened really fast." Sam crossed his arms. "I told you all of this on the phone."

"Still, one can't be too careful." Mr. Foster eyed me suspiciously. "Don't you agree, Harper?"

I found it annoying that he kept using my name. We weren't friends. Far from it, in fact. He was scowling at me as if I was trying to steal his wallet. Who did this blowhard think he was; accusing me of trying to scam his precious son? Every inch of my body throbbed with pain, and I had no idea what would happen to me now. Did this middle-aged bastard actually think I'd wanted to be hit by a car? He could kiss my ass. I narrowed my eyes and managed to hiss, "Fuck off. I don't want your damn money."

Sam looked shocked at what I'd said, but he didn't speak.

Mr. Foster raised his brows. "Come again?"

At that exact moment, a nurse wandered into the room wearing a pink smock with kittens on it. She stopped short when she saw Mr. Foster and Sam. "Visiting hours are long over, boys." She grabbed the clipboard from Mr. Foster and shook her head. "He'll probably be discharged tomorrow, so you can catch up on all the gossip then."

"So soon?" Sam looked surprised.

She nodded, studying my chart. "Looks like there are no broken bones. We need every bed we can get right now. Anybody who isn't on death's door gets the boot." She gave me a sympathetic glance. "Sorry."

I wasn't sure if I was relieved to be leaving the hospital so soon, or terrified. I was hopeful my wallet was somewhere nearby so I could call a cab to take me home. God, how much would a cab ride be from here to my place? I rarely had much cash on me, and my cards were maxed out. Maybe I could catch an Uber or something. That would be cheaper. But would I even be able to walk from the car to my apartment? I was still too scared of the pain and hadn't had the nerve to try and move my leg yet. Jesus, would I have to crawl up the walkway? That wouldn't be humiliating at all.

"It seems like he should stay longer." Sam bit his lip as he studied me.

Mr. Foster puffed out his chest. "Let the experts handle things, son. If the hospital thinks Harper is well enough to go home tomorrow, who are we to argue?"

Sam gave his father a surly glance, and then he addressed the nurse. "What time will he be released?"

"Oh, I'm guessing around two in the afternoon." The nurse tinkered with an IV bag hanging near my bed. She winked at me. "This is morphine. You should feel awesome in about five minutes."

It didn't even take that long before my body felt flushed and my lids heavy. The last memory I had, before my eyes slammed shut, was of Mr. Foster dragging a very disgruntled-looking Sam out of the room.

Chapter Two

Sam

"What were you thinking?" Dad growled as the elevator closed behind us.

"What do you mean?"

"Why are you in his room making nice with him?"

"I hit him with my car. Would you have preferred I just leave him in the street bleeding to death?" I crossed my arms, irritation prickling the back of my neck. Dad always treated me like I was five and had no idea how to figure shit out on my own.

"Son, I know you mean well, but that guy is no victim. I'll bet you a hundred bucks he threw himself in front of your car, hoping for a big payout."

I rolled my eyes. "You're wrong."

"You don't understand. I've seen this crap a million times. These con artist types are very convincing. I mean, I heard some of them cut themselves just so there's blood everywhere. It panics the drivers, and they're more willing to pay up."

"You saw him. Did you not notice his face was black and blue? Or do you think that's makeup?"

He chuffed. "I wouldn't put it past him." He was busy scrolling through his phone as he spoke. "He probably knows you're my son and figured why not see what we can get out of that naive kid."

"I'm not nearly as gullible as you think I am."

Dad raised one brow. "Right."

Heat crept up my neck to my cheeks. "He needs my help, and I'm not abandoning him."

Dad didn't seem to hear me. "I need to figure out if I should just let the insurance handle his hospital bills or fight him making any kind of claim at all. I don't want our premium skyrocketing. Hmmm, I better call my insurance guy."

I sucked in a calming breath. "Dad, we need to be compassionate."

"Oh, for goodness' sake. Seriously?" Dad snorted and then gave me a sharp look. "Wait. Did you admit fault to him?"

"It was kind of obvious since he was under my bumper bleeding." I scowled.

"That doesn't matter. Did you actually tell him it was your fault?"

"Yes."

He looked to the ceiling. "Jesus, Sam. Were you born yesterday?"

"I hit him with my car!" I clenched my fists. "What is wrong with you? Have you no heart?"

"He could sue us now. You know that, right?"

"He has no interest in suing."

"And you know this how?"

"He's not the type." I actually had no idea if Harper was the suing type. But my dad was getting on my nerves, so I pushed back.

"Like you would know?" He shook his head. "Believe me, he's the type. He's exactly the type."

"I think you're wrong."

My dad rubbed his chin. "I wonder if in the long run it's cheaper to just have the insurance pay his medical bills etcetera. If we fight the guy, he might sue, and that will be even more money."

"How can you only think about the financial side of this?" I grimaced.

He studied me with a resigned expression. "You're so damn soft, son."

"Caring about people doesn't make me soft."

"You'd be surprised," he grunted. "Well, luckily I can probably do some damage control by getting ahead of the problem. I spoke to one of the police officers on the scene."

"You did?" I scratched my head. "When?"

"The head cop at the scene called me. He recognized you."

"Oh." I should have known. My dad had people everywhere.

"He said there were at least two witnesses more than willing to testify that that bike kid caused the accident."

"That's a lie. If anything we both caused it."

"Yeah? Well, Sam, could you keep that to yourself please?" He put his phone to his ear. "Third-party witnesses are golden if they're on our side. They don't have a horse in the race, so to speak."

"Your lack of empathy is startling sometimes, Dad."

"I'm just trying to keep you out of trouble."

It wasn't easy to keep a straight face when he said that. "Right. That and you're trying to keep your name out of the news."

He shrugged. "Nothing wrong with doing both, son."

The elevator doors opened, and I followed Dad out of the hospital. He paused outside the sliding doors of the building, talking on his phone. I had a strong impulse to go back upstairs and be near Harper. I obviously wasn't going to tell Dad, but I'd always had a little crush on Harper. I'd seen him many times when he'd delivered things to our office, and he'd caught my eye while riding his bike on the streets. He'd always intrigued me. He was definitely sexy, and he had a kind of "fuck you" vibe that made me curious about why he'd be that way. But I'd never had the nerve to talk to him. I'd just crushed on him from afar like a coward.

Then I ran him over. Smooth move.

An ambulance pulled up with its lights flashing, and we moved to the side so we weren't in the way. I watched the attendants unload an elderly woman who was unconscious. "We need to think about Harper right now since he's the one who's been injured."

Dad frowned and put his hand over the mouthpiece of his phone. "No. We need to cover our asses as best we can and hope this Harper guy just goes away quietly."

"Harper is scared and afraid he's going to lose his job. We need to help him."

Dad rolled his eyes and went back to talking on his phone.

I squelched my impatience and leaned against a cement column while waiting for my dad to get off the damn phone. You'd never have known it by how heartless Dad seemed at that moment, but he wasn't a bad man. He could even be extremely loving and compassionate to his family. But lately, when it came to people in general, if they couldn't help him with his campaign or his plans for the country, he didn't like to waste time with them.

When he finally hung up, he immediately started talking as if I were hanging on his every word. "Herman thinks we should let the insurance pay for everything hospital related. He says it's the best way to keep the kid happy. That way maybe he won't push for more money."

I frowned. "Who's Herman?"

"My insurance guy. Herman Grumstone."

"Oh."

"I'm going to get all the details from those two witnesses. Then if this Harper kid wants to push for more money, I can threaten him with not even having his hospital bills covered."

"Jesus. Are you serious?" I bugged my eyes. "The poor guy is lying upstairs thrashed, and you're trying to figure out how to not pay for stuff he might need?"

"You don't know how the world works, Sam. It's eat or be eaten." He tucked his phone in his pocket. "Okay, I'm going back to the office. I'll talk to you later."

"Wait. You're going back to the office?" I frowned.

"Yes. Why wouldn't I?"

"Well… I thought we were going to have lunch and talk about…" I glanced around to be sure no one was near enough to hear our conversation. "You know… my situation."

"Your situation?" He pulled his silver brows together.

"Yeah… you know." Heat filled my cheeks. "You said we could talk at lunch today."

"I did?"

"Yes. Last week."

"I don't have time for lunch now."

"It wasn't really the lunch part I was looking forward to. It was the discussion I hoped we'd have about… you know."

He grimaced as he began to understand what I was hinting at. "Oh, *that*."

I winced inwardly at his dismissive tone. "You said if I was just patient… you know… I could stop pretending."

He glanced at me impatiently. "I'm kind of in a hurry, Sam."

"Oh, well… sorry…" I took a step back, feeling embarrassed. "Later, I guess."

His expression softened, and he reached out and grabbed my arm. "Sorry. I'm just really stressed out. I didn't mean to snap."

I hesitated. "It's okay."

He glanced around uneasily. "Why don't we talk about this later?"

"You always say that." I bit my lower lip, feeling demoralized.

"This isn't really a good time to do anything that might give McTarn an edge in the polls."

My heart sank even further. "It just seems like it's never a good time. Remember last year you said that I should wait to come out in the spring?" I gave a weak laugh. "Well, it's spring."

He gave a long-suffering sigh as he looked at his watch. "Why is it so important that everyone knows you're gay?"

Pinching the skin between my eyes, I said, "It's not like that. I don't need everyone to know my business. But the way it is now, I'm always afraid that I might slip up or a reporter might catch me holding a guy's hand." I shrugged. "It's a lot of pressure to watch every word I ever say. I've been doing it since I was fourteen, and I'd kind of like to stop lying."

"You can't just hold off until November?"

I slumped, feeling discouraged. "November? God, that feels like forever."

He hardened his jaw. "Sam, can we please deal with your dramas one at a time? Now we have this bike kid to worry about too."

My face warmed again. "Oh, well, yeah. But you said—"

"Look, McTarn is breathing down my neck. I don't think now would be a great time for me to announce I have a gay son. Can't we talk about this later in the week?" His phone buzzed in his pocket. "Oh, I have to get this call, it's important."

I watched him stride away across the parking lot, feeling frustrated. "Sure, *that's* important. Got it," I grumbled. I shook my head and made my way toward my car. There was a knot in the pit of my stomach that never seemed to go away these days. My dad literally didn't comprehend how horrible it was to live a lie every day of my life.

I didn't want to be the reason he lost an election, but at the same time I had a right to live my life openly. I wasn't a politician. I'd simply been born into this situation, and now because of my dad's power-hungry aspirations, I was forced to live a fake life so I didn't upset closed minded people I'd never even met.

I slid behind the wheel of my car and stared into space. Judging by my dad's inflexible demeanor moments ago, my charade needed to continue. I pushed down my depression and tried to ignore the crushing feeling of defeat that seemed to permeate every inch of my soul.

Chapter Three

Harper

I'd spent hours in the past bullshitting and getting buzzed with my coworkers after our shifts, and yet I couldn't bring myself to ask any of them for a favor. To be fair, I doubted many of them actually had a car, and they couldn't exactly give me a ride home on the handlebars of their bike.

I sat on the edge of the hospital bed psyching myself up to put weight on my leg. My shoulder was tender and sore, but I'd managed to get a shirt on this morning. My own top and pants had been shredded yesterday by the emergency technicians. But Nurse Kitty Smock, who I now knew as Nurse Patton, was kind enough to give me a Dallas County Hospital T-shirt left over from a charity event. She had also scrounged up a pair of jeans from the lost and found. They were about two sizes too big, but at least I had pants.

There was a knock on the doorframe, and when I looked up, I met familiar moss-colored eyes. Shock radiated through me as Sam smiled shyly. "I'm here to drive you home."

I hadn't thought I would see him again. I knew he'd made all sorts of promises, but I'd assumed it had been hot air. Not to mention, his dad had seemed determined to talk him out of helping me. I stared at him as if I had no manners. "You're back?"

"Of course." He came farther into the room. His eyes were bright with sincerity. "How else would you get home?"

I didn't think it was your problem.

I shrugged in place of words and immediately regretted it as my shoulder seized. "Shit," I hissed, gritting my teeth against the pain.

His face scrunched with sympathy. "Still tender?"

It felt like a lion had chewed off my arm, but I simply grimaced. "It's fine. Nothing I can't handle." I guess since I'd bothered to lie to save his feelings, I had some manners after all.

"The nurse is bringing a wheelchair."

I scowled. "What? No." My face warmed with embarrassment. "I definitely don't need that."

He smiled and little dimples were distracting. "It's hospital rules."

I guess it was my foolish pride that had me fighting the wheelchair so hard. I didn't even know if I could walk yet. Thanks to the fine staff at Dallas County Hospital, who'd given me a catheter yesterday, I hadn't had to seek out the bathroom last night.

As if on cue, Nurse Patton appeared in the doorway. "Come on, kid. I'll wheel you out in style."

"I don't need that thing." I eyed the wheelchair, feeling grumpy.

"This is not negotiable." She lifted her brows.

"Come on, Harper. Just get in the chair."

I scowled.

She laughed. "I'm not going anywhere, and neither are you, if you don't get in the damn wheelchair." She sighed and glanced at her watch. "Don't be stubborn. It'll be fine. I've never dumped anyone out of this thing yet."

I sucked in a big breath, afraid I wouldn't be able to stand without embarrassing myself. I met Sam's gaze, and he must have seen my apprehension because he immediately advanced and took my arm. The touch of his warm fingers had my skin tingling. My reaction to him had to be from residual morphine side effects because I wasn't usually the kind of person who went weak in the knees when someone put their hands on me.

"I've got you, Harper." Sam's voice was husky. "Come on. Nice and slow."

I relented. "Okay." I pushed carefully off the mattress, and my entire body protested as if I were a ninety-year-old man. It felt like my bones were about to crack from the tension my sore muscles and tendons put on them. As I allowed more pressure on my leg, a sharp, searing pain shot up my calf to my thigh. I bit my lip against the throbbing discomfort and leaned on Sam.

I caught hints of cedar from his cologne. He smelled amazing, and even though I was in pain, my body responded to his masculine scent. He was so gentle and careful with me it made me feel odd. He glanced down at me, and when our eyes met, a strange awareness flashed through his. I swallowed and straightened. I could just imagine Mr. Foster's face if he'd walked in at that moment. He'd probably accuse me of trying to seduce his darling son.

"How's it feel?" Sam asked in a velvety tone. "Can you walk?"

I gave a stiff laugh. "Not without help."

His lips curved in a smile. "That's why you have me."

"Yeah."

I gave the wheelchair a dirty look, and Nurse Patton lifted one eyebrow. "Sit," she commanded.

I hesitated and then gave in. She didn't look like someone who was easily cowed, and I figured it really wasn't fair of me to insist Sam help me hobble all the way to the car. I lowered myself carefully, wincing and groaning as I semi-bended my leg.

"Shit." I embarrassed myself when a whimper escaped my lips as the full weight of my body pressed onto the vinyl seat. I caught my breath because every inch of me throbbed and ached.

The moment my ass hit the seat, Nurse Patton grabbed the handles and started to push me. I held up my good arm in protest because even that small movement of the chair hurt. "Please wait a sec." I bit my lip, willing my throbbing limbs to relax.

"Oh." She grimaced. "Sorry."

A few seconds ticked by as Nurse Patton shifted impatiently. Sam didn't seem bothered by waiting. He stood quietly, and I got the impression he'd have waited as long as it took for me to be ready.

I let out a shaky breath. "Okay. I'm good."

Nurse Patton leaned on the chair, and with a small jolt we rolled out of the room. Sam walked beside me, his hand resting lightly on my back. I looked into the other rooms as we passed by, noticing a mixture of patients. There were kids crying while looking confused and elderly people with oxygen tubes stuck in their noses. But the one thing they had in common was visitors. They all had people standing around smiling and trying to comfort them. I glanced up at Sam as he walked quietly next to me. If not for him, I'd have been alone.

I was puzzled when the thought of that bothered me. I was used to being on my own. I'd preferred it that way much of my life. But I had to admit it felt good to have Sam beside me. I definitely felt more vulnerable at the moment, and realizing Sam was sincere about wanting to help me was comforting. The gratitude I felt for his compassion was an unfamiliar, yet pleasant, sensation.

When Sam glanced down suddenly and met my gaze, I looked away quickly. He rubbed my good shoulder, and I tried to ignore the sappy emotions his touch seemed to stir in me. It had to be the medications they'd given me. Those drugs were probably making me feel more sentimental than usual.

We rode down in the elevator to the ground floor, and Nurse Patton wheeled me through the glass doors to the sidewalk in front of the building. She knelt beside me, and her gaze was sharp. "How are you doing?"

"Fine." I glanced around, squinting against the bright fingers of sunlight that crept under the overhang.

"If your condition worsens, or you notice any unusual puffing or red streaks around the sutures on your leg, you come straight back to the hospital."

"Okay." I frowned.

"I'll make sure he does." Sam sounded gruff.

"Good." She handed me a few sheets of paper. "These are instructions on how to care for your sutures, and also a prescription for pain medicine and an antibiotic. They gave you dissolving stitches, but you'll still want to see your usual physician in about ten days from now to be sure you're healing properly." She straightened and patted my head like I was five. "Good luck to you, Harper."

"Thanks."

She left us there, and Sam sucked in a breath. "Well, that black Mercedes is me." He pointed to a slick looking vehicle parked in the front row. "I'm going to pull it around closer."

"Okay."

He trotted across the driveway and got in his car. The engine purred to life, and he circled around the parking lot and glided to a stop in front of me. He got out and wheeled me closer to the car. "I think you should ride in the back. That way you won't have to bend your leg as much."

"Sure." That sounded like a wonderful idea to me. Just bending my leg slightly for the wheelchair had been extremely painful.

He opened the back door and locked the wheels on the chair. "Ready?"

"Yep." I braced myself for the pain I knew was coming and then scrambled awkwardly from the chair onto the leather seat of the car. I groaned when I put too much weight on my sore shoulder. "Shit," I wheezed.

Sam shifted uneasily. "Is there anything I can do?"

"Not… not really." I was halfway in the car with my legs still hanging out the door.

"There must be something I can do."

For some reason the ridiculousness of the moment hit me, and I began to laugh. My shoulders shook with mirth, and it was agonizing, but I couldn't seem to stop. What the fuck had happened to my life? I purposely kept my head down and stayed out of trouble. Yet, here I was in the parking lot of a hospital, with my ass hanging out of a car, as Sam watched me like I was about to break into a million pieces.

Sam leaned into the car, his lips twitching. "What's so funny?"

That only made me laugh harder. God, he was so nice. What the hell was he doing hovering over me like I was important or something?

He gave a confused laugh. "Come on. What's so damn funny?"

I finally stopped snickering and wheezed, "Nothing. Nothing at all is funny." I took a big breath and forced myself to wiggle into the car. I let loose a string of curse words that would make a sailor blush, and Sam just grinned and closed the door once I was all the way in.

After he returned the wheelchair to the hospital, he slid behind the steering wheel and met my gaze in the rearview mirror. "Where to?"

I was feeling weak after my laughing fit, and sweat gathered on my forehead. "Go up to the main light and turn left." I gave him the remaining directions and then rested my head against the leather upholstery. I didn't mean to perspire all over his expensive car, but the pain and the drugs were making me sweat like a racehorse.

"I hope there aren't a bunch of stairs where you live."

"There aren't. Just one short flight at the entrance." I was poor enough that I rented an apartment on the bottom floor of my building. The upper stories cost a lot more because management claimed there was a view. I guess if you didn't mind staring at filthy old brick buildings obscured by smog you could say there was a view.

He cleared his throat. "Do you... uh... live alone?"

"If I didn't, you wouldn't need to drive me home."

He laughed. "Oh, yeah. I guess that's true."

I adjusted my position carefully, relaxing my head against the armrest on the door. Our eyes met in the mirror every now and again. I was still puzzled by his desire to help me out. Maybe he was one of those rich kids who liked to stick it to his old man by hanging out with people his family wouldn't approve of. And it hadn't exactly been a secret that Mr. Foster did not approve of me.

"Do you remember me?" he asked softly.

I squinted at the back of his head. "No. Should I?"

"Not necessarily. But we have met before."

"We have?"

"Yep."

"Where?" I frowned.

"At the office where I work. It's near the corner where I ... you know... hit you." He swallowed loudly. "It's my dad's firm."

"Oh." I couldn't really remember seeing him before, but then again when I was working, I was always in a rush. "Did we meet face-to-face?"

"Once. You've delivered packages to our building a few times. Usually the receptionist always signs for everything, but she was on a break, and so I signed instead." He laughed as if he was embarrassed to admit he'd noticed me. "Mostly I watched you from afar." He winced. "I don't mean that in a weird stalker way. It's just that I noticed you because you kind of stand out."

"I do?"

His cheek curved in a smile. "Uh, yeah. Most of the delivery guys we get look like they just got out of prison."

I averted my gaze. "It's a hard job. You don't get a lot of Yale graduates applying."

"Oh, yeah. I didn't mean any disrespect." He grimaced.

"Most of the guys I ride with are good people."

"I misspoke. I can see I unintentionally insulted your friends. I'm sorry."

I stared out of the window. "If you think so poorly of people like me, why are you still around?"

"I don't think poorly of… people like you. I told you I was sorry for what I said."

"And I appreciate that. But it's obvious you have a preconceived idea of me and my coworkers."

"It was a thoughtless comment."

I studied my clasped hands in silence.

He sighed. "I didn't mean to be judgmental. I simply meant you stood out because you're very clean-cut. I only said the prison thing because you make me nervous, and so I made a dumb joke."

I gave a gruff laugh. "I make you nervous?"

"Yes." His jaw clenched.

I squinted at him. "Why?"

He cleared his throat. "It doesn't matter."

"Okay."

We were silent for a while, and then he said, "I'd also seen you zipping in-between traffic many times before. You're very nimble."

"Obviously not nimble enough."

"Oh, God." He exhaled roughly. "Well, our little mishap is all on me. I was distracted watching you, and then you zigged when I thought you were gonna zag." He cringed. "And I hit you."

My aching body tensed in response to his statement.

"I couldn't believe it." He shook his head. "God. I still can't. I've never even been in an accident before or gotten a ticket." He groaned. "And then I had to go and smash you to pieces."

I grimaced. "I'm mostly still in one piece."

He grunted. "Yeah. One really sore, damaged piece."

"I'll be fine." I had no idea why I was acting like I was a superhero. Maybe because Sam's obvious guilt and vulnerability got to me. It was obvious he was torn up about hurting me, and it made me feel empathy. I wasn't usually a very empathetic person. Just ask my ex

Peter. He could tell you an earful about how cold and uncaring I could be. But Sam's innocence tugged at something deep inside that made me want to be… *kind*. Maybe it was the drugs.

"Yes, you will be fine because I'm going to see to it."

Frowning, I said, "Sam, I appreciate the ride home, but that's good enough. I already told you I don't want your money."

He snorted. "You just said that because my dad was being such a colossal prick."

I couldn't help but laugh at his disgusted tone. "You didn't hit me on purpose. Accidents happen."

"Dude, I didn't knock over your coffee. I dislocated your shoulder and injured your leg so badly you can't work. I'm going to help you."

I wasn't sure what the right response was. He had a point: I couldn't work. If I couldn't work, I didn't eat. I had hardly any savings, and definitely not enough for rent *and* food. Why was I being so nice about all of this? He actually had screwed everything up for me when he'd hit me. Still, there was something about him that made me feel soft toward him. It was weird. Very weird.

"I need to fill in for you at your job," he murmured.

I bugged my eyes. "What?" I didn't have the sort of occupation you could just step into. It was a tough, grueling job. You had to be in good condition, and most importantly, you had to know every street and side street in the city if you were going to be able to make enough deliveries in one day.

He chuckled. "Let me rephrase that: I'm going to pay someone to replace you temporarily." He pulled over in front of my apartment building. Then he shut off the car and swiveled in his seat. "I'll hire someone to help out. I haven't ridden a bike since I was six. And between you and me, I never took off my training wheels."

I studied his smooth features, dropping my gaze to his sexy mouth. I kept getting distracted by how much I enjoyed looking at him. I blinked a few times and tried to gather my thoughts. "How exactly would you go about replacing me?"

"I stayed up all night researching what you do for a living." He gave me a look filled with respect. "Your job is brutal."

"I know. How would you replace me?"

He gave an easygoing smile. "I read that some of the bigger companies have tons of riders so that they can get the jobs done fast, but each rider doesn't end up making much. Lots of those riders are hungry for jobs." He leaned toward me. "I was thinking what if we could lure one of those guys from one of the bigger firms to temporarily fill in for you?"

"I'm not sure anyone would go for that."

"Really?" He scowled. "Not even if they would be guaranteed a bigger paycheck than usual?"

"I don't know many guys who'd leave their regular gig to take something temporary."

"You don't think their old company would take them back? It can't be easy to find people who are just able to step into that job. I would think they'd want their experienced rider back. Or maybe they could ride for both companies."

"Maybe." I wasn't sure I'd risk it if I were in their shoes.

Sam rubbed his chin. "What if we were to throw a bonus at them? Make it worth their while?"

"I just don't know."

"And we'd make sure they were paid well so that they did a good job. The last thing we need is for them to dial it in and piss off your boss."

I frowned. "Let's say you can find someone. They're getting paid, but how does that help me?"

"For one thing your spot will be waiting for you when you're well. Plus, I'm going to cover all your bills for the next few months."

"What? That's crazy."

He shook his head. "No it's not. I don't want you stressed out while you're recuperating. Trust me, my dad is loaded. He won't even feel it." He grimaced. "Did you recognize him?"

I frowned. "Your dad?"

"Yeah." He looked uneasy.

"Maybe?"

"He's Senator Larry Foster."

"Seriously?" I widened my eyes. So that must have been why he'd seemed familiar.

"You've probably seen his commercials on TV. He's running them constantly." He sighed. "He's up for reelection, so he's even more uptight and paranoid than usual."

"I'm not big on politics." I didn't want to badmouth his dad to him, but the truth was Senator Foster had been such a blowhard he'd definitely never get my vote.

"Okay, well, regardless of my pain-in-the-ass dad, we have two issues to fix: we need to keep your job, and you need to eat and pay your bills while you're healing. My plan will accomplish both of those things."

I frowned as I mulled over his idea. "What's stopping my boss from just keeping that rider and getting rid of me?"

He grinned. "You have a very suspicious mind."

"Yes, I do, and for good reason. My boss, Jack, is a jerk. This replacement guy might be willing to ride for less money just to keep the job. Then I'm really screwed."

"Couldn't Jack just do that anytime he wants?"

"Sure, but in this instance I just handed him my replacement. Normally he'd have to go through a huge hassle to find a new guy. I'd be making this way too easy for him."

He pulled his dark brows together. "Good point." He brightened. "We give Jack a bonus when you return to work. That way he has incentive to keep you."

"I don't know."

"I'll call your boss this evening and set everything up."

"He can be a real dick."

"Hey, if I shied away from dicks, I'd still be a virgin." He played air drums. "This is where the rim shot should be."

I shook my head. "You're a real comedian."

"My point is: I'll handle Jack."

I gnawed my lower lip. "I'm still not comfortable with any of this. I don't want to take your money. Your dad wasn't exactly happy about helping me out."

"That's just how he is. Don't take it personally."

"It felt kind of personal."

"He has it in his head I'm as naive as Pinocchio or something." He grinned slyly. "I'm not half as innocent as he thinks I am."

My gut fluttered at the look in his eye. I was lying there bruised and swollen and I was actually getting turned on? No. I needed to rein these lusty feelings in.

"Taking your money doesn't sit right with me."

He sighed. "Really? What's your plan? You can't work." He peered out the window at my dingy apartment building. "Something tells me your finances leave something to be desired."

Heat rose in my cheeks. "That's none of your concern."

"That's where you're dead wrong." He held my gaze. "It's my fault things would get worse for you." He gave my home another wary glance. "That's not okay with me."

My desire was to be autonomous. Independent. A lone wolf. But the deep ache permeating my entire body told me I might be aiming too high at the moment.

"If you don't want my help, I guess you could sue me." He held my gaze stubbornly. "My insurance will already pay for the hospital bills, but you could always try and get more money out of them."

"I don't want to sue you. I told you it was partially my fault too." I wasn't going to lie about what had happened, and I truly did feel the accident was also my fault. Not to mention I had trouble seeing how I'd win a lawsuit against someone like Senator Larry Foster. That was a can of worms I was leery to open. I had no doubt a rich guy like him could get twenty people to say they'd seen the whole thing and that it had all been my fault. I didn't want his dad to get vindictive toward me, or he might try and get out of having his insurance even pay my hospital bills.

"Let me help you, Harper. *Please*." His gaze was brimming with sincerity. "I'll feel like the lowest human on earth if you don't."

I winced and stuffed down my pride. "Fine," I said gruffly. I hated having to accept help, but to be honest, I didn't really have much choice at the moment.

Chapter Four

Harper

I finally made it to my bed. *Thank you, Baby Jesus*. I would have curled into a fetal position if I'd thought I could manage it without making things worse.

"I'm going to go get your prescriptions filled," Sam whispered near my head, and his warm breath wafted against my ear.

I groaned in response. Whatever pain medication I'd had in my system had evaporated during my trip up the short flight of stairs to my apartment. I was surprised by how much discomfort I was in. I usually had a really high tolerance for pain. I'd fallen off my bike many a time, but I guess being slammed to the street by a car was very different.

"I'm taking the key off your key chain," he said softly. "Do you want me to help you get under the covers?"

I groaned again and managed a feeble "No."

I could picture his worried expression without even seeing it. "I'll hurry."

The front door closed with a click, and I was left in my apartment alone. The silence was soothing, and the room was dark since the sun was on the other side of the building this time of day. I was relieved Sam had been pushy and insisted on helping me. What would I have done right now if he'd listened to me and left me alone? I'd never have been able to get my prescriptions filled. I'd probably be collapsed on the front stoop. I thought about the stubborn tilt of his jaw and how his eyes darkened angrily when I'd tried to send him away.

I hated relying on other people, but I knew I had no choice. I wasn't exactly sure what he had in mind or how long he planned on staying. After he got my prescriptions, would he just leave? I braced myself for that possibility. After all, while he wanted to help financially, he'd never said he wanted to babysit me twenty-four seven.

I was probably more scared now than I'd ever been in my adult life. I remembered being terrified when I'd left home at sixteen. But at least then I'd been strong and healthy. There was nothing as frightening as not being able to fend for yourself. I was weak and vulnerable right now, and that was the worst thing I could think of. Even when my old man used to come at me when he'd been drunk, I'd felt safer than I did right now.

I was sleepy but wound up at the same time. It was an odd combination. My body needed sleep so it could heal, but my brain was on high alert. I hated to break it to Command Central, but it wouldn't really matter if I knew someone was coming to get me. There was literally nothing I could do about it.

I stared at the alarm clock and watched the little hands move around the dial. My thoughts drifted back to Sam. A tiny nudge of something shivered through me at the thought of his fingers on my forehead the other day. He'd probably make a good doctor because he had a nice bedside manner. His energy was calm and relaxing. That couldn't be said for his father. Mr. Foster had reminded me a little of my dad: a bundle of angry energy, barely contained.

Thirty minutes ticked by, and then there was the scrape of the door opening and my heart jolted.

"It's just me, Harper. Don't worry." There it was again—that natural concern for others. I heard the faucet in the kitchen and the crumpling of a paper bag. Then he entered the room and sat next to me on the bed. "You need to sit up to take these."

Oh, God. This is gonna hurt.

"Okay." I clenched my teeth and forced myself to a semi-upright position. My shoulder throbbed and ached, but because I didn't move my leg too much, I was in less pain than earlier. I took the large blue pill from Sam and washed it down carefully with water. It was a huge pill, and I worried for a second it was going to stick in my throat. But it didn't, and I breathed a sigh of relief after it was down.

"You'll need to take one of these every six hours." He frowned at the pill container. "That was the antibiotic." He grabbed another pill container out of his pocket. "This is the pain pill, and it's every six hours too."

The next pill was a slick capsule that went down easily. I slowly leaned back against the pillows. I was breathing hard considering all I'd done was take two pills. Sam got up and went into the kitchen, and I wondered if he was getting ready to leave. I bit my lip and tried to tell myself I was fine. Everything would be fine. I was used to being alone, and I'd get through this just *fine*.

I was shocked when Sam came in carrying a tray. For one thing, I didn't own a tray.

He smiled shyly, and I noticed there was even a small yellow carnation stuck in a juice glass. He set the tray over me, and then he perched on the edge of the mattress. "I picked up some wonton soup. It's from my favorite Chinese restaurant, the Gentle Lotus. It just happened to be near the pharmacy, so I figured why not grab some lunch?"

I was speechless. My chest felt tight with emotion. He'd brought me soup? I'd never had anyone take care of me when I was sick before. It was weird and unsettling. I wasn't sure how to behave. Should I tip him?

He frowned. "Are you hungry?"

"No," I whispered. I felt oddly emotional. It had to be because I didn't feel well. I wasn't myself.

"You should eat anyway."

I just stared at him.

He laughed. "Come on."

I frowned. "What about you?"

"I wasn't hungry." He grinned. "But now that I smell the soup, my mouth is watering." He adjusted the carnation in the glass. "I picked this from the front of the building."

"It's a nice touch." I laughed awkwardly.

"Do I need to feed you?" he teased.

"I feel weird eating in front of you." I grimaced. "You should get another spoon from the kitchen."

He tilted his head with a funny look on his face. "We can just share this spoon," he said softly.

I swallowed hard. "Oh. Um… I guess."

"You first." He stood and shrugged out of his jacket. His shirt rode up a little, and there was a flash of toned, tanned abs. The hunger that nipped at me was surprising—especially in my condition.

He sat back down carefully, and his hip pressed the outer thigh of my good leg. I was embarrassed when my cock warmed and hardened slightly. That was all kinds of wrong. I was thrashed, and he was just being nice. Fuck. You'd think I'd never had anyone be polite to me or something.

Irritated with myself, I took a slurp of soup. The salty broth hit my tongue, and I sighed. "Mmm."

Grinning, Sam said, "Right? Best wonton soup in town."

I was hungry, so I took another couple of spoonfuls of soup. Then I handed the utensil to him, and our fingers brushed. He dipped it into the golden broth and lifted the spoon to his lips. There was something oddly sensual about him putting his mouth on the spoon I'd just had in mine. My balls tingled, and I swallowed nervously. Maybe this was exciting to me because I knew there was no way in hell I could do anything about my feelings of arousal. I was out of commission for at least a week.

Cool your jets. He's just being nice because he feels guilty.

"God, that's good." He licked the spoon, and I looked away so I didn't get any more lusty ideas.

I tried desperately to think of something to say to him other than *Would you like to lick anything else?* I finally thought of something to ask. "Did they give you any trouble picking up my prescription?"

He shook his head. "No. I just needed your date of birth. But I saw that on your license yesterday, so it was fine." He handed me the spoon. "Finish it off."

I obeyed because he'd gone to all the trouble to buy the soup for me. As I ate, I fingered the flower, stroking the velvety petals. When I met his curious gaze, I stopped what I was doing and looked away.

He sighed and glanced around. "Do you have any spare blankets? I should grab them before you nod off. I don't want to disturb you."

Narrowing my gaze, I asked, "Why do you want blankets?"

He stood and put his hands on his hips. "So I don't freeze my ass off on the couch tonight, of course."

I dropped the spoon in the empty soup container. "You're staying?" I contained my relief and instead put on a poker face.

He scowled. "Of course I'm staying." He shook his head. "Did you think I'd leave you alone tonight? This will probably be your worst night."

"It wouldn't matter if you did go. I'm a big boy."

He lifted the tray. "Yeah, a big boy who can barely walk two inches without fainting from the pain."

I hid it from him, but I was relieved he was staying. "I could probably make it three inches with pain pills."

"You made a joke?" He gave an exaggerated look of shock. "The pain pills must be kicking in."

"I'm usually a barrel of laughs. You just haven't seen me at my best yet."

He smiled. "What about those blankets?"

"Near the bathroom, in the top cupboard there should be a blanket. Probably smells like mothballs though."

He left the room, and after a few moments I heard him rummaging through the cupboards in the hall. He came into the bedroom triumphantly. "Found it." He shook it vigorously. "You're right—it does smell like mothballs."

"I don't think I have any extra pillows." I grabbed the spare one on my bed. "Except for this one."

He held out his hands, and I tossed it to him. He clutched it. "Smells like your cologne."

"Sorry."

"No. It's nice. Much better than mothballs."

My stomach tightened at his playful remark. The look in his eye and the tone he used were borderline flirtatious. This time it wasn't my imagination.

"I guess anything is better than mothballs." I smoothed my hand over the comforter as I spoke. "But don't worry. You won't have to help me for too long. I heal fast and soon I'll be back on my feet."

"I'll stay as long as you need me, Harper," he said quietly.

I narrowed my gaze. "I still don't get why you care."

He rested his chin on the pillow he hugged. "Because I'm responsible for your injuries."

"But you could help me and not stay here."

"I want to stay here."

"Why?"

He shrugged. "It beats driving back and forth to my place."

"Your dad won't like it."

He captured his lower lip between his teeth. "I'm twenty-three. He needs to remember that."

The pain pills were beginning to take effect. I felt light-headed, and my limbs were heavy. He held my gaze, and I could see a pulse jerking at the base of his throat. "I don't get why you're being so nice. It's confusing." I hated that my voice sounded forlorn.

Frowning, he said, "I haven't done that much, Harper. Just a few gestures that barely scratch the surface of what I need to do."

My mouth was numb. I licked my lips and rested my head against my pillow. I felt safe with him here. I was used to being alone, but I'd felt freaked-out earlier when I'd thought he was going to leave me any second. I was physically weak, and I was not accustomed to it. It was terrifying. I stared into his gentle eyes, feeling foggy but pleased to have his company.

"Go to sleep and I'll think of what to make for dinner," he said softly.

"Maybe we can share a fork." I snorted.

He grinned. "I'll share whatever you want."

Chapter Five

Harper

My dad came at me with a baseball bat. I yelled and tried to move away, but he hit me hard on the back of my head. I fell on my shoulder, and it was excruciating.

"Harper. Wake up." Someone tapped my cheek gently. "Harper."

I realized I was dreaming. I opened my eyes and found Sam bent over me with his hair sticking up and his gaze worried. I had a pounding headache, and I was lying on my bad shoulder. That must have been why my head and arm hurt so much in my dream. I slowly rolled over onto my back with a loud groan.

Sam sat on the bed. "You're safe. It's okay." He trailed his fingers along my shoulder, and I shivered.

I licked my chapped lips, dying of thirst. "Shit." My leg ached like someone was stepping on it, and my armpits and back were drenched in sweat.

"What were you dreaming?" His features were hard to see because the streetlamp that shone into my room only cast shadows across his face.

I cleared my throat. "It doesn't matter." I'd had the same dream a million times, and it always felt so real. I could almost smell the whiskey on my dad's breath and see the repulsion in his eyes. I nervously searched the shadows, half-convinced he was in the room somewhere.

"Someone attacked you?" he nudged.

"It wasn't real," I grumbled. I think I was trying to convince both of us. I assumed my pain meds had worn off because every inch of me throbbed. "Can I have some more stuff?"

He turned the clock on the nightstand so he could read it. "It's too soon. You have another forty-five minutes."

"Fuck." A whimper escaped me.

"I'm sorry." He apologized as if it was his fault time moved too slowly.

I needed to take a piss, but I dreaded having to move. "I have to use the facilities." I slowly began to sit up, biting into my lip. Once I was upright, he held out his hand, and I took it. His warm skin felt nice against mine as he helped to leverage me off the bed. I was on my feet but bent over like I was looking for coins on the street. I couldn't seem to make myself straighten because it stretched the skin on my sutured leg, which was agony.

"If you try taking a leak in that position, you'll drown." He sounded amused, which was doubly irritating.

"It's not funny." I gritted my teeth and forced myself to unbend slowly. I wasn't able to completely straighten, but it was close enough if you asked me. I hobbled with his help to the bathroom. He started to follow me inside, and I stopped him. "I think I can take it from here."

"Let me know if you need a *hand*."

I gave a chuff and shut the door in his face. Flicking on the light, I shuffled over to the toilet and somehow managed to aim and hit the target. Feeling very proud of myself, I washed my hands, then made the mistake of looking in the mirror. "Shit." I took in my swollen cheek and scraped flesh. I had the beginnings of a black eye, and my blond hair was matted and poking up like one of those tiny troll dolls.

I looked like a monster. Why the hell had Sam flirted with me?

There was a soft knock at the door. "Are you okay in there?"

"You mean other than the fact that I look like a Mack truck ran me over?" I opened the door slowly, and he winced.

"Believe it or not, you look much better. The swelling has gone way down."

I just swallowed hard.

"Let's get you back to bed," he said softly. He reached past me and shut the light off. I wasn't sure if he did that to be helpful or so he didn't have to look at me anymore.

Once I was back on the bed, he stood nearby looking nervous. "Can I ask you something?" He sounded tentative.

"Sure."

He bit his lower lip and glanced toward the front room. "Do you have mice?"

He looked so freaked-out I couldn't help but smile. Big mistake. I grimaced and touched my tender face. "Ouch." I met his frazzled gaze.

"Well?" he urged.

"Yes. I think there are a few that like to eat my crackers on occasion."

He shivered and before I knew what he was doing, he'd moved around the bed to the other side and climbed on. "Oh, my God. I hate mice." He looked down at the floor like he thought they were surrounding the bed.

"What are you doing?" I asked, trying not to laugh.

"Why do you have rodents living in your place?" He wiggled his hands as if grossed out. "Don't you know they can carry the bubonic plague?"

"Um… yes. But they pay half the rent, so I let them stay."

Not even a hint of a smile appeared. "I'm serious. They're disgusting."

I sighed. "I need to buy more traps. I've been working so much I kind of forgot about them. The mice are home more than I am."

He pinned his puzzled gaze on me. "God, Harper. You shouldn't have to live like this."

I wasn't really sure why, but for some reason that comment bugged me. "Who should have to?"

He looked confused. "What?"

"Who should have to live like this?"

"Nobody." He frowned. "It seems like not having rodents running all over your face at night isn't asking too much."

I shrugged. "Mostly I leave them alone, and they do the same to me."

"Why don't you call an exterminator?"

I rolled my eyes. "Because they cost money."

He hugged himself and stared toward the living room. "We've never had mice at my house."

What a shocker.

"Rich people don't tend to," I muttered, shaking my head.

"I didn't see any signs of them in here." He leaned over the edge and examined the polished floor.

"They seem to stay in the other room where the kitchen is. I've never noticed one in here. That doesn't mean they don't hang out here when I'm at work."

He seemed a little calmer than earlier, and he relaxed against the headboard. I noticed he was still wearing the white dress shirt from earlier. He also had on silky, light-blue boxers and black socks. I had trouble ignoring that his legs were sinewy, tanned, and sprinkled with fine dark hairs.

He was sexy. Half-dressed. And he was in my bed.

Obviously sex wasn't on the table. But he was a good-looking guy, and it was hard not to notice.

"I really hate mice," he muttered.

"I understand if this is all a bit much for you. You don't have to stay the night." I stifled my nervousness at the idea of being left completely alone. "You could always just come back in the morning if you feel like you want to keep an eye on my progress."

"I'm not leaving you alone." He sounded indignant. "What if you need me in the middle of the night?"

"Well, if you're this afraid of the mice, where are you going to sleep?"

He was quiet for a moment, and then he laughed. "I could sleep in here."

I eyeballed him like I thought he was crazy. It had occurred to me that maybe he had a screw loose. Who would put their life on hold to help someone like me? He had to be mentally unbalanced. And now he was suggesting we sleep in the same bed when we'd known each other approximately a day and a half?

His smile widened. "I'm not insane."

"Prove it. Walk out the front door and don't come back."

He exhaled roughly. "Look. You need help for a while whether you want to admit it or not. I can sleep on top of the covers, and you sleep under them. I'm not gonna try anything with you."

My cheeks flushed when he added that last part. "I know that," I snapped.

"I just don't want to stay in the mouse room." He shivered. "Please don't make me."

I frowned, confused by him. "You don't think it's weird to sleep in the same bed as a total stranger?"

"I'm basically like your nurse." He shrugged and peered around me. "Speaking of which, it's almost time for your medicine."

That wonderful fact distracted me from all the other stuff. "Thank God."

"It's a little early, but I don't think ten minutes will kill you." He tapped his chin. "I made a crustless veggie quiche earlier. All you had in your fridge were eggs, wilted spinach, and cheese to work with. You'd fallen asleep, so I didn't wake you, but maybe you should have something to eat before you have your pills?"

"I'm not hungry. I'm in pain."

"You sure? Maybe just a few bites?"

I shuddered. "No. Just medicine. *Please.*"

"Okay." He scrambled off the bed and sucked in a big breath. Then he hurried into the other room and with a yelp came running back into my room like a ghoul chased him. Clutching the pill bottles, he stopped abruptly, but because he was in socks, he slid a few more feet to the bed while staring back in the direction he'd come from. "I don't think they followed me."

I laughed and then clutched my face. "Ow. Don't make me smile."

"I'm not trying to." His cheeks were flushed, and he was breathless. "Believe me, I do not find any of this funny."

"Really? Because we're strangers, and yet you're standing in your underwear in my bedroom, afraid that killer mice are going to get you." I held out my hand for my pills. "Personally I find it hysterical."

S.C. Wynne

Chapter Six

Harper

As weird as the idea seemed, I relented and let Sam sleep on the other side of the bed. Desperate times called for desperate measures.

I was only under the sheet. I didn't want all the blankets on because it rubbed against my sensitive skin too much. Sam was odd in that he faced me. I'd expected he'd turn his back on me like a normal person, but no, he was on his side staring at the side of my head. I could feel his gaze on me.

"Go to sleep," I mumbled.

"I will." His breathing was even.

We lay for a while in silence. I was having trouble sleeping, although I could sense the haze of the pain pill creeping up. His body heat radiated through the blankets, and when he ran his fingers through his hair, I smelled his shampoo. I was way more aware of him than I liked to be. I hadn't shared my bed with anyone since Peter had dumped me. I'd fucked, don't get me wrong, but usually I'd suggested we go to their place. I didn't really like letting strangers into my home.

Yes. The irony of this situation is not lost on me.

"Do you have any brothers or sisters?" he asked softly.

I gave a short, drowsy laugh. "If I answer, will you go to sleep?"

"Perhaps." He sighed. "I feel restless."

"Why?"

He didn't answer.

I could have just ignored him. But he was sleeping in my bed and had basically taken over my life at the moment. I guessed I could go ahead and talk about my background a little. "I have one younger sister who I never talk to. I haven't seen her since I was sixteen."

"Damn."

I shrugged under the shroud of darkness.

"Don't you miss her?" he asked.

"I used to. I don't really know her anymore."

"What's her name?"

"Allison."

"I have a twin sister, Kara, and if we lost touch, it would kill me. We're like the same person."

He couldn't understand not talking to a family member. I got it. But I had my reasons for keeping my distance. "It's complicated."

"It's cool. You don't have to tell me."

"Yeah. I know."

He sniggered. "But I mean, we *are* sleeping together. We shouldn't have secrets from each other."

I turned my head and looked toward him. "That would be an even bigger reason to have secrets." I couldn't see his expression.

"Oh, that's messed up." He shifted around and pulled the blanket he'd borrowed from the hall closet tighter around his neck. "Family can be annoying, but they're always there for you."

I groaned, and it wasn't because of my injuries. "You sound like a sappy greeting card."

"Rude."

"Family is just a bunch of people thrown together by chance. We're not obligated to like each other. In fact, I think the odds are quite high we probably wouldn't."

"If we were born already formed, I might agree with you. But a family grows and meshes together slowly, over time. That's why families usually like each other."

Frowning, I said, "I don't know that your data is correct there, dude."

"You think most families don't like each other?" He laughed. "*Wrong*. Don't you ever watch reality TV? People are constantly blubbering about how they miss their family. Even when they admit they've had their ups and downs, they always cry when they talk about family."

"Well, I can't stand my family." That slipped out before I realized what I'd said. It had to be the meds. Or maybe it was both the meds and the fact that Sam was easy to talk to.

"Yeah. You definitely have trust issues. Those usually stem from bad family relationships." He sounded matter-of-fact. "Is it just your sister you haven't talked to since you were sixteen?"

I was quiet for a few moments. For some reason instead of just ignoring him, I answered. "As far as I'm concerned, I'm an orphan."

He gasped. "That's sad."

"No." *It's self-preservation*.

"You don't need anyone else, Harper?" he asked softly. "You're fine on your own?"

His husky voice did something to me. I closed my eyes and changed the subject to get him off my case. "Your dad has an interesting personality."

He hesitated and for a second I thought he wasn't going to let me change the subject easily. But then he answered. "Yeah. I know. He's overbearing. I don't think he can help it."

"He doesn't want to."

"Maybe. But if he wasn't like that he wouldn't be in politics. You have to have lots of confidence and drive to be a senator."

"His whole theory about me falling in front of your car on purpose is total bullshit. You know that, right?"

I felt his gaze on me. "Of course I know that."

"Your dad didn't seem to agree with your instincts."

He grunted. "He thinks he knows best. For some reason he still sees me as a little kid."

"You do seem surprisingly innocent." The way he'd so willingly stepped in to help me was one huge indicator of that. I suspected most people would have kept going and left me bleeding in the street.

"I'm not innocent in the way your tone implies. I like to give people a chance before I judge them, but I'm not a little child."

"Your family doesn't know you're spending the night with me, do they?"

"No."

"Hiding stuff from your parents sounds like something a little kid would do." Apparently that comment pissed him off because he sat up on his elbow.

"I'm handling my responsibilities. That's something an *adult* does." He flopped back down, and I could almost feel the resentment radiating off him. "Besides, I don't tell my family every move I make."

He talked a good game, but something kept nagging at me. "What will happen if your dad puts his foot down and says you can't help me?" It was obvious he wanted to break free of his controlling dad, but I didn't know how he would do that if he lived off his dad. It didn't work that way.

"I have my own money too." He sighed. "Yes, I'm a trust-fund baby. Go ahead and make your jokes."

I turned to look at him. "I wasn't going to say anything bad."

"You know, I can't help that I was born into a wealthy family any more than you can help—" He fell silent.

"What? That I wasn't?"

"Right."

I winced as I adjusted my position. "It might surprise you to know I come from a family with some dough. Maybe not your kind of wealth, but we have money. Well, I mean they have money. Obviously I'm not sucking at that teat anymore." I thought back to elegant rooms without mice and extravagant summer vacations on white beaches. "I chose this life over that one."

"Why?" His tone was so completely mystified it was hard not to laugh.

"I have my independence."

And no one beats my ass at night if I look at them wrong.

"Oh. Well, yeah. There is that."

"Do you still live at home?" I suspected he did.

"I live on the grounds, but I have a private cottage." He sounded defensive.

Now it was crystal clear why his dad felt justified being bossy. "That's probably why your dad thinks he can tell you what to do. You're on his turf."

"I know what you're saying, but I mostly have my freedom."

I rolled my eyes. "That's like a fish saying, 'Other than the hook in my mouth, everything's awesome.'"

I was surprised when he laughed instead of getting pissed. "I know, you're right."

That good-natured quality he had made him very likeable. I respected his ability to see himself so clearly. I had no desire to examine myself closely. I imagined I'd get lost in the cracks and fissures I'd find.

"Kara's constantly telling me I need to find my own place." He sighed. "She's moving in with her boyfriend this month."

"You should do the same." My head felt woozy, and I lay back against the pillows.

"Sure. Now all I need to do is get a boyfriend." His laugh was self-conscious.

I was glad he was single. I would have died before I admitted that to him, but for whatever reason, it pleased me that he too had no one special in his life. I had no actual explanation for that. I didn't exactly have a plan to put the moves on the poor guy or anything. I was thrashed, and I looked like Frankenstein—this would not be the best time. I wondered if we'd have clicked if we'd met in a bar. Or was he only interested in me because he'd knocked me down with his car and now I was his pet project?

"A rich kid with a powerful senator for a dad shouldn't have any trouble finding takers." I had to concentrate pretty hard to speak clearly. The medicine was definitely taking effect.

"Um, yeah. I don't exactly love the idea that anyone who wants me, wants me because I'm rich and my dad is a politician."

"Are you good in bed?" Okay, yeah. The pills were definitely at the wheel right now. My cheeks felt hot as it sank in what I'd asked.

He sputtered. "I, uh, hold my own."

I gave a drug-induced giggle. "I don't think that's how it works."

His laugh was genuine. "Shut up."

I pretended to zip my lips closed.

His smile still hung on. "Anyway, my first priority is getting you back on your feet."

I frowned. "Don't put your life on hold for me."

"Hush. You're stuck with me for a while." He enunciated each word carefully.

Even though the idea of him hanging around gave me an odd twinge of pleasure, I pushed back with my inflated pride flag whipping in the bullshit breeze. "I'll survive, whether you're around or not. I always find a way with or without the kindness of rich strangers."

He was quiet for a while, and the silence was thick and uneasy. Finally he spoke. "I get that you're tough. If you hadn't been crunched by my car, I have little doubt you could take on whatever you need to. But the reality is you're a mess. You are physically incapable of fending for yourself right now. I know you'd rather stick a hot poker in your eye than admit you need a hand, but it's the truth. You don't need to be prideful. I'm here because I care about you."

I fucked up royally and laughed. God damn, I was well aware that was the exact wrong thing to do when someone was baring their soul to you. But his openness made me uncomfortable, and so I couldn't help it and I laughed. Not because he was wrong; probably more because it made me nervous that he was right.

Naturally, he misinterpreted my reaction.

He threw off his blanket and sat up. "Fuck it. I'd rather spend the night with the god damned mice than in here with a rude asshole like you."

It hadn't been my idea he should sleep in here with me to begin with. In fact, I'd been against the idea at first. But oddly enough the second he decided he wanted to abandon me, I felt strange. "Why are you mad?" I asked. I had to stop myself from reaching out to grab his wrist.

"I'm trying to help you and show you kindness. But you keep throwing it back in my face and ridiculing me." He huffed. "The easy thing to do here would have been to abandon you in the hospital. I could so easily have just washed my hands of you, Harper. No one would have blinked an eye. My father would have seen to that. If he wants someone to disappear, they disappear."

I simply stared at him in silence. I had little doubt what he said was true. If his rich and powerful father had wanted me to just shut up and go away, that could probably have been arranged. Just slip a few people some money and the witnesses to the accident would have suddenly had amnesia. I wouldn't have had the energy or the money to fight it.

He sighed and hung his head. "You know, it's not easy to do the right thing. And I'm not weak. I'm kind. I care. *It's different.*"

"All right." I cleared my fuzzy throat. "Just so you know, I wasn't laughing *at* you."

"Hmmm." He crossed his arms as if he didn't believe me.

"I'm serious. Don't be mad." It had to be the fucking pain pills that were turning me into a giant wuss. My overwhelming urge was to placate him and ask him to stay in my room with me. What the fuck was wrong with me? I was not naturally a placater.

"Don't pick on me just because I'm being nice."

"Okay."

He sighed and nestled into the covers. "Thank you."

"You're welcome." You're welcome?

Has anyone seen my spine? I seem to have misplaced it.

S.C. Wynne

Chapter Seven

Sam

Sleep was pretty much impossible. My mind raced with thoughts of how I would be able to take care of Harper without my dad knowing. It didn't take a genius to know if my dad found out I was paying for a bunch of extra stuff for Harper, he'd be upset. He saw me admitting fault for the accident as a sign of weakness and not what it was: the truth.

It was weird how my dad had changed over the years. He'd seemed to gradually lose his compassion for people less fortunate. Surprisingly, I'd actually gotten my drive to help others because of my dad. In the early years of his political career, he'd been way more moderate and community-service oriented. He'd taken us to soup kitchens, and we'd helped build houses for those less fortunate. But over the years I'd seen him morph into a more typical cliché of the power-hungry politician. He'd stopped joining me and Kara at the charity events and didn't seem to care anymore about serving the needs of the poor. All he seemed to care about now was rubbing elbows with his richest donors, which then made him beholden to serving their needs. Sometimes I didn't even recognize my dad anymore. Take yesterday for example and his callous opinion of Harper.

I studied Harper as he slept. His features were soft with sleep, and that guarded, tense expression he usually wore was gone. My fingers itched with the desire to slide along his angular jaw and sexy lower lip. My cock warmed as I stared at him, giving me a twinge of guilt. He was injured because of me. I didn't need to be lusting after the poor guy while he snoozed.

I sat up to see the clock. It was 5:00 a.m. I'd promised Kara I'd meet her at the Stewpot, a soup kitchen we often volunteered at. Since there was no way I could sleep, I got up and dressed as quietly as possible. The Stewpot began serving breakfast at 7:30 a.m., and I figured I'd just head over there now to help with prep while Harper was sound asleep. The pain pills usually knocked him out for a really long time. I figured I'd have enough time to at least put in a few hours at the kitchen before I had to rush back here. Besides, I really wanted to talk to my sister about everything that was happening.

The streets were just beginning to get busy as I arrived at the Bridge Homeless Recovery Center where the Stewpot served the meals. I made my way into the old brick building and through the group of bustling volunteers. Workers were yelling and scurrying around like crazy people in the main area of the kitchen. Kara was already there making peanut butter and jelly sandwiches for the packed lunches the center would hand out later.

She smiled when she saw me. "You're early for once."

I slipped a white apron over my head as I neared her. "I can't stay long today. I just wanted to put in a little time since I'd promised."

She frowned and stopped what she was doing. "You can't stay? Why?"

I gave a nervous laugh. "I'm helping someone out."

Her frown deepened. "What does that mean?"

"Sam! I need you to chop fruit." I jumped when one of the leads who ran the food line hurried up to me. "ASAP, kid. Just cut up some apples and oranges as fast as possible, please." Patty adjusted her hairnet. "Louisa forgot about the damn fruit this morning."

"Sure. Whatever you need, Patty."

She sighed and smiled apologetically. "Sorry. We had a church group scheduled to volunteer today, and their bus broke down," she grumbled. Her dark skin had a sheen of sweat, and her white apron was askew. "I've been scrambling ever since I got the call from the pastor that they couldn't make it after all."

I moved to the area across from Kara that had bags of fruit piled on the counter. "It's no problem. Just put me where you need me."

"I think I have most stuff covered." Patty turned and strode off in the opposite direction without another word.

Kara laughed. "Kind of ironic the church's bus broke down on the way to help the poor. Makes ya wonder if heaven is as disorganized as this kitchen."

I pulled on a pair of food-handler gloves and started chopping apples, tossing the cut pieces into a huge silver bowl. "What's that saying? God works in mysterious ways?"

"I'll say." She cleared her throat. "So you never answered me. Who is this mystery person you're helping?"

"It's kind of a long story."

"Oh, then never mind." She laughed.

I grinned and gave her an amused glance. "Dad didn't tell you about me running over a bike messenger?"

She turned toward me with her eyes wide. "He said you had a car accident but that you were fine. Didn't you get my voicemail?"

"I did. Sorry. I meant to call you back."

"Dad didn't say a word about you running anyone over. Are they okay?"

I winced. "Well… yes and no. He's alive. But his shoulder was dislocated, and his leg has a huge cut with a bazillion stitches."

"Holy hell."

"Yeah. I feel horrible." I sighed and went back to chopping fruit. "So I'm staying with him while he heals. The poor guy can barely walk."

"Oh, wow." She came over to me. "You should hire a nurse or something. Won't the insurance cover that?"

I chuffed. "I have no idea what the hell is going on with that. Dad's handling everything because the insurance is in his name. I'll tell you one thing though: Harper's well-being is the furthest thing from Dad's mind."

"For real?"

"Yes. All he cares about is trying to figure out how to not pay anything but the hospital bill. He thinks Harper is a con artist. Dad wants to use the hospital bills as leverage so Harper will just go away."

"Dad thinks the guy is a crook?"

"Yeah." I grabbed another handful of apples, and she returned to her station.

"Why?"

"Why? You know Dad. He thinks everyone in the world has an angle." I shook my head.

"True. But then again, you don't think anyone ever has any angles. You're almost too trusting."

I huffed. "I'm not being naive. I hit Harper with my car. It wasn't staged."

She held up her hands. "Okay, okay. Don't bite my head off."

"Sorry." I sighed. "Dad has me worked up. He seems more callous with every passing year. Someone needs to stand by Harper, and I seem to be the only one who cares enough."

"Well, you could still pay for a nurse out of your own pocket." Her tone was inquisitive. "You don't have to actually do the work yourself."

"I like taking care of Harper." I grimaced because I sounded so sappy. "I mean, I'm the one who hurt him, so it makes sense for me to help him out."

"Did you know this guy before you hit him?"

"No. Why?"

She snorted. "I don't know. Just something about the way you say his name. It's like you like, like him."

My face was hot, and I kept my back to her. "Well, I had noticed him in the past when he delivered things to the business." I gave a self-conscious laugh. My sister knew me so well she'd see through any smokescreen I attempted to put up anyway. Might as well be honest with her.

"I knew it."

"Thankfully, Dad doesn't know that part. But I'd have helped Harper whether I thought he was sexy or not."

"I know. You do more charity work than anyone in the family."

"You do as much as I do."

"Kind of." She lined a big box with bagged lunches as she spoke. "I did skip out on visiting that senior center last month though. I still feel guilty about that."

"I'm no saint."

"Sure. But if you hadn't have shown up today, it wouldn't have been because you wanted another hour of beauty sleep. It would be because you're already doing charity work for Harper." She laughed.

I inhaled sharply. "Do not use the word 'charity' around Harper, or he might take your head off."

"Prideful, is he?"

I thought about how he hadn't wanted me to give him a ride home from the hospital or stay the night even though he couldn't do anything for himself. "You could say that."

"So what's your plan? Are you going to hit on this Harper guy?" She grinned at me over her shoulder. "You know like… since he can't run from you?"

I chuckled. "I prefer when guys actually like me back. I don't usually force myself on them."

"I know. I'm just teasing."

I sighed and covered the bowl of fruit I'd filled with plastic wrap. "There is something about Harper though."

"You can't put your finger on what it is?"

"He's sexy as hell. He's got some serious leg muscles going on." I smirked. "But it's kind of intangible. Heck, why does anyone like anyone?"

"That's the million-dollar question."

I looked around and lowered my voice. "But it's not like I could just start dating Harper openly even if he was interested."

"I keep nagging you to tell Dad you're done hiding who you are."

"Funny you should say that. I tried talking to Dad about coming out today. Yet again."

"Let me guess: he shut you down immediately?"

"Yep."

"He's a piece of work," she growled. "How can he live with himself?"

"I want to tell him to go to hell." I frowned. "But then if I lost him the election, he'd probably never talk to me again."

"Nah. I *think* he loves you more than politics." She laughed gruffly.

"Sometimes I wonder."

"He's clueless about how hard it is on you. He figures what's the big deal? You can do what you want in private."

"Sure. No problem. Only the walls have ears, eyes, and noses. I have to be so careful about who I even show interest in."

"I know, honey. I'm so sorry he's such an insensitive clod about this." She exhaled impatiently. "I swear, Sam, you're just going to have to go against his wishes one of these days to make your point. What other choice do you have if he won't even listen to you?"

I winced. "Oh, God. I can't imagine doing that. Ideally I want his permission so that we can all get what we want."

"That won't ever work if what Dad wants is at odds with what you want. Hope you understand that."

I swallowed hard and lifted my chin. "At the moment I have no real reason to push. It's not like Harper has any interest in me, and there isn't anyone else on the horizon I want to be involved with."

"Then I guess, for now, there's no reason to rock the boat." She didn't sound convinced.

"Yep." My voice was falsely bright. "I'm sure Dad will come around soon." I ignored the little voice in my head that whispered I was fooling myself.

Chapter Eight

Harper

It took me a minute to remember why someone was in my kitchen whistling a cheery tune. Then my aching body helped me recall the full picture.

I was amazed that I'd slept fairly well during the night, especially with a stranger sharing my bed. But the heat of his body near mine had made the bed cozy, and I'd conked out the minute I closed my eyes.

Glancing at the clock, I was shocked to see it was almost noon. I clenched my jaw and slowly forced myself to sit up, grunting and groaning like a senior citizen. My body was actually achier and stiffer today than it had been last night. But nature called, so I lowered my legs to the ground and steeled myself, preparing to make my way to the bathroom.

Sam came around the corner. "You're awake." He looked well rested, and he still wore the white shirt from yesterday. The material was decidedly crumpled from having been slept in, and he had his pants on now. He sort of resembled a well-dressed hobo.

"I am." My throat sounded scratchy, and I rubbed my head briskly while yawning.

"I have an old crutch at home. Would you want me to bring it over?" He laughed. "I figure the less weight you put on your sore leg, the less pain you'll be in."

"Um… sure… I guess." I couldn't exactly say I was thrilled at the idea of hobbling around on a crutch, but my other leg was feeling tired from having to overcompensate for my injured limb.

"Then I'll do that."

"Cool."

"In other news, you have literally nothing to eat in this house." He grimaced. "I'm going to go shopping. Do you want to help me make a list?"

"A grocery list?" I laughed. "I don't think I've ever made one before. I just grab what I need while I'm there."

He frowned. "Which, judging by the empty refrigerator, is nothing?"

"I have coffee. And I think there are some Red Vines in the pantry."

He snorted. "Oh, well, what was I thinking? You have all the food groups totally covered."

"I never cook. I usually just grab a sandwich from the vending machine at work."

"Wow. That sounds super gross and unhealthy."

"I just avoid the tuna salad and it's fine." I stood in slow motion. "I need to pee. Maybe we can continue this titillating convo after." I took a step and cringed as pain shot through my leg. That crutch sounded like a better idea all at once. I bite my lip and pushed through. If I kept wimping out every time something hurt, I'd never get better.

Sam moved to help me, and I held up my hand. "Wait. I need to try and walk on my own."

"Oh. Okay." He shrugged.

"Thank you though." I wheezed out the words.

"Not a problem."

I hobbled to the bathroom and closed the door. My leg throbbed, and I took a second to let the burning pain subside. In the sunlight poking through the little window over the shower, I didn't look much better than I'd looked last night; maybe there was slightly less swelling. But the purple bruising under my eyes had spread more, so it looked worse.

When I was done, I shuffled to the kitchen and found Sam on a step stool rummaging through my pantry. "I'll tell you a couple of things that are going on the list: bleach and mouse traps." He jumped down and ran a smoothing palm over his crinkled shirt. "Do you think I could borrow something to wear? My place is all the way across town, and I'd love to get the shopping over with early."

I raised my brows as I poured myself a cup of coffee. "I might not have anything fancy enough for you."

He laughed. "These are my work clothes. I don't wear business attire all the time."

"So you will deign to wear T-shirts?"

"Of course."

"In that case, sure. You can borrow something, but you might still want to go home and get some essential stuff. I'm not loaning you underwear, dude."

He grinned. "That's fine, I wear boxers. You're a briefs guy."

"How would you know?" I sipped my coffee and winced when it burned my lip.

Turning his back on me, he folded the step stool and tucked it next to the fridge. "Because in the emergency room the doctors cut your clothes off." He laughed. "Sorry. I got an eyeful before they ushered me away."

I pressed my lips together and avoided his gaze. He'd seen me in my underwear? This just got weirder and weirder.

He cleared his throat. "Anyway, what would you like me to put on the list?"

"It feels strange with you buying me shit." I leaned against the kitchen counter and bit my lip as my leg gave an annoying twinge.

He must have noticed my discomfort. "You can take something now if you need to."

"I'm gonna try to stretch it a little. I don't want to depend on pills."

"That's very brave of you." He grabbed one of the vials. "But you still have to take the antibiotic."

I did as he said and washed it down with my coffee. Then I said, "I still feel odd about you paying for my groceries."

"Get over it." He squinted at me. "This is how it is right now. Take advantage of it."

"I don't know."

He huffed. "Look, your Red Vines aren't going to last forever. Unless you want to eat roasted mice, I need to get some food in this house."

I shuddered. "Fine, but I'll pay. They're my groceries."

"Uh, yeah. Let's break this down logically, shall we? You were already broke before I ran you over. Now, thanks to my tremendous driving skills, you can't work.

But despite that, you think the smart thing to do is buy *me* groceries *too*?"

It was hard not to smile at his wide-eyed incredulity. "I'll pay half."

"Stop. Just stop. I'm shopping on my dime, so you need to deal." He leaned toward me. "What kind of things will you eat?"

I scowled.

He snapped his fingers. "Speak. I need input. I'm buying shit either way."

"You're stubborn."

"I'm practical. Give me some ideas. Frog's legs? Escargot? Tater tots? Talk to me."

I relented. "Maybe get some fruit?"

"Okay." He typed on his phone. "Anything else?"

I shrugged.

He sighed with exasperation. "I guess I'll use my own judgment. Is there anything you're allergic to?"

"Bigots and orange M&M's."

"Ha, ha. Well, if you swell up like a tick, don't come whining to me."

He brushed past me, and my stomach warmed at his now-familiar cologne. It was weird how I hadn't even known he'd existed before yesterday, and now he made my pulse elevate just by touching my elbow.

"Should I just grab a T-shirt from your closet?" he asked.

"Go for it."

He disappeared into my bedroom and a few minutes later reappeared wearing a white T-shirt with a drawing of a bike and the word "Cycologist" emblazoned across the front.

"What do you think?" He held the hem and lifted one brow.

The thin material clung to his chest and toned biceps. He had a much better body than I'd even suspected. I nodded and played it cool. "Looks fine."

He headed to the door. "See ya shortly," he said as he left.

Once he'd gone, the apartment was quiet. I decided I was going to risk taking a shower while I had some privacy. I felt grimy and sweaty after my slip and slide on the street a few days ago. I went into the bathroom and slowly stripped off my clothes. Then I tugged gingerly at the bandage covering the stitches. The wound ran from just below my knee all the way to the top of my thigh. I had zero memory of what had carved me open. I supposed it didn't really matter since the damage was already done. The black stitches stood out against the red flesh. It was a little puffy, which I assumed the antibiotics would help with, and it was super sensitive to the touch.

I got the water warm, and I carefully stepped into the enclosure. What would usually take me fifteen minutes to accomplish took me an entire hour. By the end of my shower, I was exhausted and panting. I started to towel off but instead sat on the toilet to calm the spinning of my head. I really regretted not taking the pain pill after all. My leg and shoulder hurt like crazy, and I didn't quite have the energy to get dressed yet.

When I heard the front door open, I tensed with guilt. But I reminded myself that I was twenty-four years old. If I thought I needed a shower, I could take a damn shower. Unfortunately, despite my desire to be tough, the energy I'd expended from washing up had me drained. When I didn't come out of the bathroom for a while, Sam knocked softly on the door.

"Harper?" He sounded concerned.

"Be out in a minute." I sucked in a steadying breath and stood. I finished drying off completely and decided to leave my sutures uncovered to air out. My hands shook as I dressed in a T-shirt and shorts, and I was definitely light-headed.

When I exited the steamy bathroom, Sam was still carrying in the groceries. The minute he saw me, he paused, bugging his eyes. He had one grocery bag in his mouth and others hanging from his arms. He pulled his brows together and headed into the kitchen. He dropped the bags on the counter, and when I joined him in the kitchen, he took in my damp hair as his scowl deepened.

"You took a shower?"

My pain was off the charts now, and without answering, I hobbled to the pills. With trembling fingers, I struggled to open the damn childproof lid. "Fuck." I dropped the bottle on the counter and picked it up again.

"Let me." He took the bottle from me and snapped it open. Then with a surly expression, he handed me a pill. "What the heck were you thinking?"

Not bothering to get a glass from the cupboard, I turned on the faucet and cupped water in my palm, slurping in a mouthful of liquid. I then threw back the pain pill, and closing my eyes, I tried to ignore the wave of nausea washing over me.

"What if you'd fallen?" he asked quietly. "You could have hit your head."

"I'm fine," I whispered.

"You could have done more damage."

I didn't bother to respond because I felt like passing out. I slid down onto the floor until my ass bumped on the tile. Leaning against the bottom cupboards, perspiration trickled down my temples, and my armpits were sweaty. *So much for being clean.* It would have served me right if a disease-ridden mouse had run across my lap right about then.

Sam surprised me when he joined me on the floor. I forced myself to meet his worried gaze. After staring at me in silence for a few moments, he reached out and brushed my damp hair off my forehead. "You're so obstinate," he said gently. "You should have waited for me to help you."

"I didn't think it would be the ordeal it was." My voice was weak. "I felt dirty and gross."

"I'd have happily given you a sponge bath. All you had to do was ask." There was a smile in his voice.

I gave a feeble laugh. "We've known each other what, forty-eight hours? You sleep in my bed, do my grocery shopping, and now you want to bathe me too?"

"Do away with the grocery shopping and I could learn to love this gig."

He was flirting with me as I sat crumpled on the kitchen floor. He continually caught me off guard. I couldn't figure him out. "I'd offer to help carry groceries in, but I might puke."

"How about instead I help you back to bed?"

"Deal."

He climbed gracefully to his feet, and I held out my hand. He curled his warm fingers around mine and pulled me up. Swaying slightly, I grabbed his shoulder. He slipped his arm around my waist, and I leaned on him while favoring my bad leg. We stumbled our way into the bedroom, and with a grunt he carefully lowered me onto the bed. Lying on my back, I held his chiding gaze.

He spoke slowly. "Please don't do stupid stuff when I leave you. It makes me feel like I can't go out and do things I need to do."

I grimaced. "I just want to feel normal."

"I know. But you were hit by a car. You didn't break a fingernail or scrape your knee. You need to respect that huge wound on your leg. You'll heal quicker if you follow instructions and take it easy."

"Fine." I didn't have the energy to argue since I'd used up all my reserves getting clean.

He studied my leg. "God, that looks painful."

"It's agony." I tried to pull myself farther up the bed, but my bad shoulder wasn't having any of it. A sharp jolt of pain speared through my collarbone, and I collapsed on the soft comforter. Never mind. I decided I'd just rest with half my body hanging off the bed rather than feel whatever that was again.

"Why didn't the doctor give you a sling or a shoulder immobilizer?"

"No idea." I winced, but the pain in my collarbone was slowly ebbing. "Maybe I'll just stay like this for the rest of my life."

"Nah." Next thing I knew Sam was beside me. He wedged himself behind my back and put his arms around my waist. "Tell me if I'm hurting you."

"Hey, what—"

"Shut up. I'm helping." He placed his legs on either side of my hips and grunted while awkwardly dragging me up toward the headboard. With my upper body in his lap and my head against his chest, he was careful to keep the pressure off my injured shoulder.

"Well, this is cozy," I said dryly. I hoped my sarcasm covered the fact that my crotch had a bulge forming. Being engulfed in his arms was a little overwhelming for my neglected libido. Apparently even being run over by a car didn't squelch my sex drive.

"Yes. It's kind of nice." He laughed. "I like your shampoo. It smells like apples."

"Thank you?"

He snorted and slowly untangled himself from me. I nestled against the pillows as he rolled off the bed and stood watching me. "I hope I didn't hurt you."

I rubbed my sore shoulder. "It was minimal and well worth it. Thanks."

"Can I make you something to eat?"

I laughed weakly. "What's your compulsion with feeding me?"

Frowning, he said, "Because unless you're sneaking meals that I don't know about, you've eaten two ounces of soup the entire time I've been here."

"I'm just really tired."

He twisted his lips. "Then I guess you should sleep."

I closed my eyes, but I could tell he was still standing there staring at me. Opening one eye, I asked, "Do you need me to sign for a package or something?"

"You look so innocent when you're at rest. It's a nice change."

My cheeks warmed. "Is this your thing? Do you go around creeping on injured people?"

He smirked. "You found me out. First, I run them over, then I buy them groceries and stare at them while they sleep."

"You live a full life."

He grinned. "I'll check on you in a few hours."

"You're going to try and feed me then, aren't you?"

He sighed. "We know each other so well." He quietly left the room, and I drifted off with a smile on my lips.

S.C. Wynne

Chapter Nine

Sam

When I walked into my parents' home, I found my mom out on the back patio with a group of women. I stopped short when I realized she must be having some sort of organized function.

"Oh, sorry." I grimaced.

Mom came toward me smiling. "Sam. It's wonderful of you to drop in." She kissed my cheek and put her arm around my waist. "Ladies, do we have room for one more at our Pink Hat luncheon?"

Several of the women laughed.

I grimaced. "I'm sorry. I forgot that was today. I didn't bring my pink hat."

Mother smiled and addressed the women. "Help yourselves to more tea and cookies. I'm going to see what Sam needs to talk to me about. I won't be a minute."

We went inside the house and ended up in the kitchen. Selena, my parents' housekeeper, was in the kitchen polishing silver at the table. She looked up and gave me a warm smile.

"Sam, you came to visit your poor lonely mother?" Selena gave me a toothy grin.

"Yep. I'm being a good son."

"That you are." She cackled.

"I forgot about her women's group." I grimaced. I'd come by to pick up some clean clothes, and I'd figured I'd take my mom to lunch and talk about how overbearing Dad was being about the Harper situation.

"Did you need to see me for any particular reason, or was this just a social call?" Mom asked, running a hand over her perfectly coiffed hair.

"I was going to take you to lunch. But I guess that will have to be another day."

She pushed her lips out in a pout. "Really?" She lowered her voice and gave a weary glance toward the patio. "God, I'd so much rather spend the day with you. These women are so boring."

I grinned. "Then why do you keep having them over?"

"Because they're loaded and they give your dad a lot of money. It's the least I can do to have them over for snacks." She sighed. "They're not really that bad. I'm just frustrated I don't get to have lunch with you."

"Next week. I promise."

"Okay." She smiled and her keen gaze flickered. "You sure there wasn't anything in particular you wanted to talk about?"

I shrugged. "Nothing that can't wait."

She twisted her lips. "Let's go in the library."

"But what about your women's group?"

"They're fine on their own for a while."

She gave a surreptitious look toward Selena, and I knew she wanted to go where we could talk privately. I said my goodbyes to Selena and followed my mom. Once inside the library, my mom closed the doors and we sat on the couch, facing each other.

"Maybe you really were going to take me to lunch, but I kind of got a sense you had something you wanted to talk about." She raised her brows.

I laughed sheepishly. "You don't miss anything, do you?"

"I'm a mom. Butting into my kids' lives is what I do." Her lips twitched.

"Well, you might not want to talk to me about this subject." My stomach clenched with nerves.

"Oh, really?" She frowned.

"I'm kind of hoping I can get you on my side on a sort of sensitive subject." I laughed uneasily.

She grimaced. "Is it the subject I think it is?"

"I'm not sure."

"If this is about you coming out, dear, the timing might not be good. McTarn has gained on your dad in the polls, and he's afraid any tiny thing could cost him the race."

I hadn't dropped by to talk about coming out, and her announcement about McTarn took me by surprise. "Really? McTarn's gaining on Dad?"

"Yes. I don't know how. Nobody I talk to likes the man. Maybe it's Russian hackers or something giving him a boost." She smiled weakly. "But whatever the reason, your dad is panicked that anything that's at all negative might make him lose."

"I don't consider being gay as something that's negative. But I didn't come here to talk about coming out."

"Oh. I didn't mean it that way." She bit her lip. "I just meant the gay thing might bother his constituents. Not us. You know we don't mind."

I winced inwardly but didn't want to get sidetracked. "Either way, I didn't come here for that. I came to talk to you about Harper—the guy I was in that accident with."

She looked puzzled. "What about him?"

"Dad seems to have it in for him." I rubbed the back of my neck, trying to gather my thoughts. "Do you think maybe you could talk to Dad and get him to lay off a little? I hit the guy fair and square. Harper can't even work for probably a month. He's obviously worried about paying his bills and things anybody would worry about."

"Your dad said the insurance would pay the hospital bill."

"Yeah, but Harper has other needs. I'm glad the doctors will get paid, but Harper has to eat. He has *other* bills too."

She shrugged. "Oh, well, I'm sure your dad will take care of all that stuff."

I grunted. "I'm not sure, Mom. Dad seems really hardnosed toward Harper. He's trying to figure out how to pay the least amount of money. I don't really think that's what should be the most important factor right now. Harper needs our help."

Her expression tensed. "To be honest, your dad did imply Harper might be faking his injuries for money."

I scowled. "He's wrong."

She glanced at her watch. "I'll see if I can get him to relax a little."

"Would you? That would be great. Harper needs help, and I'm going to see to it that he gets that help."

She twisted her hands. "Now, honey, don't go getting too involved with this person. You don't really know him."

"I feel like I do."

Her expression softened. "That's because you have such a soft heart. Even as a kid you always wanted to share your lunch with every other kid in class."

"I think that's a good way to be."

"Within reason."

I frowned. "You and Dad pounded community service into me and Kara's heads. Now it seems like neither of you care about that anymore."

She stiffened her spine. "That's not true. I give to lots of charities. Your father and I give an obscene amount to be quite frank."

"I'm not saying you don't care at all. But you guys used to actually do the grunt work with Kara and me. Now it's like Dad thinks that's a big waste of time. He's changed."

She shrugged. "Politics will chew you up and spit you out if you don't grow a thick skin."

"Then I guess Dad is safe."

"Honey, that's not fair."

"You sure about that?" I sighed. "The fact that he thinks I could just hit someone with my car and then not worry about what happens next is shocking to me."

She examined her perfect french manicure. "I'll admit he's more jaded than he used to be."

"Definitely."

She glanced up. "Maybe he's not perfect, but he's a good man. He wants to help this country, and he believes being a senator is the best way."

"I know he means well."

"Do you? Sometimes I think you don't even like him."

"I love him."

She laughed gruffly. "But you don't like him?"

"Let's just say he's not always pleasant to be around when you're his son. But I still support him, and I go to almost all of his fundraising events."

"True. But often you look like you'd rather be at the dentist."

"Good dental hygiene is important." I smirked.

"Very funny. You were better about jumping through hoops when you were seeing Terry." She grimaced. "Although I lived in fear you two would somehow let on you were more than just friends."

"We were very careful." Terry was a friend of the family who worked for my dad's campaign. He was my age, and we'd had a thing for a while, but it hadn't gone anywhere serious. I sometimes wondered if I hadn't let it become more simply because of how my dad was. I hated the idea I'd have let that be a major factor in my love life. "But ultimately, we were better as friends."

"Yes. You both were discreet." She groaned and stood. "Unfortunately, I should get back to the women."

"Sure." I rose also. "I'm not at the cottage right now. I'm staying with Harper until he's well enough to go back to work. But I have my cell if you need to get hold of me."

"Wait." She pressed a hand to her chest. "You're living with a stranger?"

I laughed at her horrified expression. "Mom, he can barely hobble two feet in an hour. I can outrun him if I need to. Which I won't."

"But why are you living with him? Can't you just give him money if he needs stuff?"

"He's really banged up."

"But you don't even know him. Isn't it weird living with a person you don't know?"

It was on the tip of my tongue to say that I felt like I knew Harper better than my own parents sometimes. "We get along well."

"Hmmm, seems weird to me."

I kissed her cheek. "I'll call you about lunch next week."

"Okay." She sighed. "Be careful. If this Harper boy makes you uncomfortable, you just come on home, honey."

"I will." I forced a smile and made my way toward the front door.

As I was halfway to my car, it occurred to me I was practically running. I couldn't wait to get back to Harper. There was excitement buzzing through me at the thought of seeing him again, and while it worried me a little to feel this connected to him when we barely knew each other, it was also exhilarating.

S.C. Wynne

Chapter Ten

Harper

When I opened my eyes, the first thing I smelled was bacon. In fact, I think that's what coaxed me from my sleep.

As I carefully stretched my muscles, I had a strange sense of calm. I couldn't remember feeling this serene in years. Maybe it was a combination of narcotics and knowing Sam was handling shit for me. I didn't usually like people hovering around me, but Sam didn't bug me as much as most people.

He poked his head around the corner. "You're up?"

"Yep."

He disappeared and returned with a tray. "Dinner is served."

Squinting, I repeated, "Dinner?"

"Afraid so." He set the tray over me as I slowly wiggled upright. "It's five forty, dude."

"Are you serious?" I sounded horrified.

"You were out. I even went home and grabbed some stuff, and when I got back, you were still sound asleep."

"You went home?" Jesus, I'd been dead to the world. I hadn't heard a thing.

"Yes." His expression tensed. "I uh… had to talk to my mom and get some things."

My mouth watered as I scanned the crisp bacon and scrambled eggs on the plate in front of me. There was sliced apple on the side of the dish too. "Breakfast for dinner?"

"You know it." He took a slice of apple off my plate and nibbled it. That intimate gesture didn't seem weird at all.

I helped myself to a piece of bacon and crunched into it. The salty tang ignited my appetite, and I finished that and moved on to the eggs. The minute I started eating, I became like a hungry animal. I couldn't seem to stuff my food in fast enough.

Sam grinned at me and nodded approvingly. "I love to see a man gobbling down protein."

Once I'd filled my belly, I drank the coffee he had on the tray too and leaned back against my pillow with a satisfied sigh. "That was the bomb."

"I'm glad you enjoyed it. I'm not a very good cook, but I can get by."

"I open cans really well."

"When you remember to buy cans?"

My lips twitched. "Exactly." I smoothed my fingers over the rosewood tray. "Where did this come from?"

"They had them on sale at the pharmacy yesterday, so I grabbed one. Something told me you might not have one. You don't strike me as a breakfast-in-bed kind of guy."

"I'm usually up at the crack of dawn, so no."

"How long have you been a courier?" He sat next to me on the edge of the bed. He seemed surer of himself now. He'd definitely been more subdued around his dad, but when he was alone with me, he appeared confident and relaxed.

"Seven years."

He bugged his eyes. "Seriously?"

I dropped my gaze. "I didn't go to college or a trade school. Riding is one of the skills I have."

"That would explain your impressive thigh muscles."

I laughed. "I never need to make time in my schedule for exercise."

"Yeah, my job's pretty sedentary. I sit at my desk a lot of the day. But I do go to the gym after work most nights." He flexed his arm with a grin. "Look at my guns."

I whistled. "Pretty good for a suit type." I'd already admired his sexy body earlier, but he didn't need to know that.

He frowned as if something was bothering him.

"Everything okay?" I asked.

"I called your boss, Jack, last night." He grimaced.

"Ahhh." No wonder he was frowning.

"You were right, the guy's a dick."

"Told you." I was dying to know what had been said, but I didn't want to seem like I cared too much.

"He agreed to my proposition." He avoided looking at me.

"He did?" I was shocked. I'd assumed my jerk of an employer would have shot down Sam's idea.

"Yep. I've already called a couple of courier companies, and I think I have a guy lined up. He's been riding for three years, and he sounded like a nice guy. His name's Chris Waters." He looked at me like he thought I would recognize the name.

"I might know him if I saw him. A lot of us know each other by sight, but we rarely exchange names and Christmas cards if we work for different companies."

"Oh, well, yeah. That makes sense."

"So you're telling me Jack agreed to rehire me when I'm healed?" I watched him, feeling suspicious. My employer didn't do things out of the goodness of his heart. Anything that asshole did was because it benefited him in some way.

"Yep." More eye evading.

"Did he give you a hard time?" My stomach churned as I searched his tense face.

"Sort of. I uh… dropped my dad's name, and he became slightly more agreeable. But he wanted double the bonus amount to keep you."

"He asked for double the bonus?" My voice raised as anger flushed through me.

He held out his hands in a placating movement. "It's no biggie. I just thought it was disrespectful since I got the feeling you've been with him a long time. I didn't even realize how long until you just told me the number of years."

"That son of a bitch seriously asked for double the money?"

Gritting his teeth, he looked uncomfortable. "I shouldn't have told you."

"Of course you should have. But I can't believe the asshole would strong-arm you for more money."

Shrugging, Sam said, "He said if he was going to take you back, it had to be worth his while."

"What a jerk." I'd never heard one compliment from the guy, but I knew I was one of his best couriers. Unfortunately, I was also one of his most expensive.

"Yeah. He was definitely not nice to deal with."

"This Chris dude is probably cheaper than me. A lot of the new guys are." I felt awful that Sam now had to fork over even more money because of me. "Shit. I'm sorry."

"Don't apologize. You didn't do anything wrong."

"Still."

He sighed. "Maybe you should try riding for a nicer company."

I shook my head. "I've thought about it, but until I get fired, I'm sticking where the money is. I'd have to start at the bottom somewhere else. No, thanks."

He chewed his lower lip. "I hate the idea of you working for that douche."

I shrugged my good shoulder. "I'm used to him. I barely notice what a prick he is anymore. I'm not exactly a delicate flower."

"You shouldn't have to get used to being treated like crap," he grumbled.

"You're very big on what people shouldn't have to put up with." I mimicked his gentle tone as I continued. "You shouldn't have to live with mice. You shouldn't have to work for an asshole."

He laughed sheepishly. "Probably because I grew up around a politician. They always want to control how things are done." He met my gaze. "But I am right. You shouldn't have to be treated like shit at work."

"Maybe I should unionize?" I smirked.

"That's a good idea." He smiled. "I'll help you."

"Of course you will. You can't stop yourself, can you?"

"Nothing wrong with helping others."

I sighed. "Look, it's cool. You don't have to save me. This is my life, and I'm fine with it."

He nodded slowly. "Can I ask you something?"

"Okay."

"It's personal."

"Oh." I grimaced. "I guess."

"You said you haven't spoken to your sister since you were sixteen." He looked like he was uncertain if he should continue. "Were you a runaway?"

My stomach clenched at his question. "Does it matter?"

"No." He met my gaze. "I'm just curious."

"Why?"

"The other night when you had your nightmare, you mumbled the word 'dad' at one point. I got the definite impression you were scared of him in your dream."

I didn't respond.

"I know you haven't spoken to your sister in years. When I put that all together, it sounds like maybe you had to run for some reason."

I kept my gaze trained on my empty plate.

"If you feel like talking, I can keep a secret." His tone was encouraging.

I bit my lip and then said, "I guess I don't see why it matters."

"It doesn't. But you're cool. I like hanging out with you. I suppose I want to know you better. Who knows, maybe we can be friends eventually."

I looked at him under my brows to gauge whether or not he was making fun of me. "Like you'd need me as a friend," I said gruffly. "We don't exactly run in the same social circles."

"Yeah, I know that." He grimaced. "Maybe I'm coming off like a naive idiot again. But I like you, and I feel comfortable with you. I'd like us to be closer."

His earnest words got to me, but instead of showing it, I shook my head. "God, you're just so… *open*."

He smiled. "I guess." He stared down at his clenched fingers, and something about his forlorn expression moved me.

My throat was tight as I considered telling him a little about my past. "You really want to know this stuff?"

"Yes."

I exhaled and then forced myself to speak. "I… I bolted from home when I was a teenager."

He nodded, looking pleased that I'd trusted him enough to tell him about myself. "I had a feeling."

"I didn't have much choice."

"Were you abused?" He immediately looked embarrassed. "I mean, a lot of runaways are, so I wondered if maybe you were too. But it's not really any of my business."

My laugh was gritty. "It was a little more complicated than that."

He waited patiently for me to continue.

"My old man was a jerk when he drank. Cry me a river, right?" I felt self-conscious to be talking about this stuff after all these years. "A lot of people have alcoholics for parents."

Sam frowned. "Well, that's not the norm."

"I'm simply saying lots of people had it way worse than me."

"You don't have to be defensive." He leaned toward me. "What other people went through doesn't negate your experience."

"Yeah, and having a jerk as a dad doesn't make me special either."

"Relax, Harper. Just tell your story, and stop trying to second-guess things."

I rubbed my face tiredly. "It's hard."

"I know." His voice was soothing. "You don't have to tell me anything else if it's too difficult for you. But I won't judge you. And sometimes talking can help make things clearer."

Maybe he was right. There were moments when the memory of my past felt like a cement brick lodged in my soul. Perhaps there was nothing wrong with sharing a little of who I was with Sam. He'd been so kind and so forthcoming with me. I sucked in a big breath. "My dad was a bully," I said quietly.

"Okay."

I flicked my wary gaze to his. "He tended to take out his frustrations with his fists."

He winced. "Shit."

I shrugged. "I got used to it. I know that's probably a weird thing to say. But a part of me didn't mind too much if he was picking on me because that meant he'd leave my sister alone. I could take it. But she was so young and... fragile." I tried not to think about my sister very often because it made me sad. I'd missed watching her grow up. I had no idea who she was anymore, and I doubted she'd like this new version of me.

"Damn." His gaze was sympathetic. "Where was your mom when all this was happening?"

"My mom was always kind of distant with me, like she didn't know how to connect with me. Even when I was a little boy, I remember feeling unsure if she loved me."

"Wow. Seems like a strange thing for a little kid to worry about. It should be a given your mom loves you."

"You'd think so. I mean, to be fair to her, I was a very serious kid. I probably overthought shit even back then." I laughed stiffly. "She just didn't understand me."

"That's too bad."

"Yeah." I shrugged. "But when I got older and she realized I was gay, she basically pretended I didn't exist anymore. I guess maybe I'd been right all along and she hadn't really loved me." I gave him a searching glance, praying I wouldn't find pity in his eyes. He looked sympathetic, but not like he felt sorry for me. "She was better with Allison. Gentler. And I didn't resent that. I was just glad Allison had some positive attention since my dad was such a lost cause."

"Did you leave because they rejected your homosexuality?"

I shook my head. "No. That was hard, but I didn't leave because of that."

He bit his lip, a line between his eyes. "Something major must have happened for you to just up and leave your home."

I winced. "Yeah." A part of me was afraid to be honest with him. Maybe he'd judge me or think I wasn't worth his help anymore.

"I know we haven't known each other long. But just the few times you've mentioned your sister, I can feel how much you care about her. I know that if you left your home and your sister behind, you'd have had a good reason."

I hung my head. "I did."

He stayed quiet.

"One night… my dad went after Allison."

"Oh, God."

"Yeah. I… I uh… I beat him up pretty bad." My voice was hard, and I avoided his gaze. I wasn't ashamed at having defended my sister, but I was embarrassed that he might think I was a violent lowlife.

"Oh." I heard his swallow.

I was afraid to look at him. My gaze was pinned on a piece of apple that had a tinge of brown forming on the surface. Did I disgust him now? Was he rethinking helping me?

"Do you have anger issues?" he asked tentatively.

My laugh was stilted. "No." Meeting his light eyes, I was compelled to reassure him. I still didn't understand why his opinion mattered to me, but it seemed to. "I had to stand up for her. I had to."

He nodded. "Okay." He reached out and squeezed my chilled fingers. "If you say you had to, I believe you."

Instead of pulling away, I grabbed his hand tighter. The warmth of his fingers sent shivers of pleasure through me. He was willing to trust me based on knowing me for a few days? I didn't know why he would, but I felt gratitude to have his acceptance. I'd never told anyone my sad story before. It had been too embarrassing. It was freeing to finally say what I'd done out loud and not feel condemned.

"It doesn't bother you?" I asked softly.

He cocked his head, and he stroked his thumb lazily across my hand. "Have you ever beat up anyone before or since?"

I shook my head.

"Then I believe you when you say you had to step in. I would defend my sister if anyone tried to hurt her. I'd beat their fucking skull in."

"Okay. Good." Relief washed through me. We were still holding hands, and I didn't want to let go. What was this weird power he had over me? I didn't hold hands and stare into guys' eyes usually. That was so not me. But I couldn't seem to drop his warm gaze or pull my hand free.

"But why did you have to leave? It sounds like you were justified."

I hung my head. "My mom didn't back my story, and I got arrested."

"Shit."

"Yeah. The worst part was Allison was scared of me." I grimaced. "She was only eleven, and I guess she didn't understand I was protecting her. I don't know." I felt sick when I remembered the horror on my little sister's face that night.

"How long did they keep you?"

"Just overnight because I was a minor. My dad didn't press charges, but obviously I couldn't go back home. I couch surfed with friends for a while and slept at the bus station."

"The bus station?"

"When you're really desperate, you'd be surprised where you're willing to crash."

"Weren't you worried without you there your dad would try and hurt Allison again?"

"When I got out of jail, I had a little talk with him." I studied Sam under my brows. "We made a deal. Since I was such an embarrassment to him and my mom, I told him I'd leave town if he promised to never touch Allison again."

"Could you trust he'd keep his word?"

"My mom was ready to leave him because of Allison, so that gave me some comfort. Plus I made it clear that if I ever heard he'd laid a finger on her... I'd come back and kill him."

Sam shivered. "Jesus."

"It was mostly talk. But I needed to say something to put the fear of God into him." I was hesitant to look at Sam. He probably thought I was a disgusting, violent jerk. I expected him to pull his hand away, but he didn't. "I kept my eye on Allison for a while. But she seemed happy, so eventually I decided I needed to keep my end of the bargain."

"So you took off?"

"Yeah."

"How did you survive?" His expression tensed. "I know a lot of runaways get sucked into prostitution."

I shook my head. "Not me. I don't judge anyone who took that route, but I wasn't going to go down that path if I could do anything else. My dad gave me a grand to leave town and I tried to make that last. I stayed in shelters and did some panhandling until I saved up enough to buy an old bike. I'd always loved riding, and I started working as a courier. I took to it right away. Jack didn't give a shit if I was too young or not. I was green and he could treat me like crap cuz he knew I was so desperate for the work."

"God, Harper. I hate that."

I twisted my lips. "It's cool. That's the past."

"It's completely the opposite of cool," he grumbled.

"I make enough riding to get by on."

He looked around at my broken blinds and peeling paint. "Barely."

"At least I'm not on the streets."

"Still." His green eyes were full of concern.

He seemed so anxious it was unsettling. "Don't look like that."

"Like what?

"I don't know. You seem like you want to fix things for me. But you can't, so don't worry about it. I'm fine now." I looked down at my sutured leg. "Well, I mean, I will be."

He glanced at our clasped hands. "I don't know why, but I want to protect you." I could see his confusion clearly on his face. "It's kind of weird to be honest. I'm not usually like this."

"Me either." I frowned and then laughed. "I mean, for God's sake, I let you sleep in my bed and we aren't even having sex."

A red flush traveled up his cheeks. "Nope." He sounded breathless.

Blood pooled in my nether regions at the thought of sex with him. He had me on edge with his husky voice and the sweep of his thumb over my skin. I was usually way smoother than this with guys, and I wasn't shy about sex.

He studied me. "Thanks for telling me your story."

I cleared my throat. "Thanks for not judging me."

"It wouldn't occur to me."

I believed him. "You're the only soul I've ever told."

"Really?" He smiled. "Wow. I feel special."

I didn't respond. Instead I pulled my hand away, feeling uncharacteristically rattled.

"Your story is safe with me." He sighed. "And even though I hit you with my car—" He winced. "I want you to know I'd never *willingly* do anything to hurt you."

A smart-ass reply hung on my lips. I didn't do affection well. I had a tendency to say something flippant just to make people back away. But instead of being rude, I bit back my sharp comment, and I met his gaze feeling vulnerable. "I don't want to hurt you either, Sam." I swallowed and forced myself to continue. "And I appreciate your help."

He stood and grabbed the tray. His wide grin sent a warm rush through me. "From the look on your face, Harper, I'll bet that hurt to say."

I held back a smile. "You have *no* idea, Sam."

He just chuckled happily and carried the tray out of the room.

S.C. Wynne

Chapter Eleven

Harper

Sam had said he couldn't cook, but after eating his food for four days, I had to disagree. He'd never made anything that wasn't delicious. Or maybe I was just in the habit of eating cold soup from a can, so anything fresh was amazing. Whatever the reason, I loved his cooking.

I'd just finished wolfing down a killer ham-and-cheese omelet he'd made us, and I must have scraped my plate with my fork one too many times because it got Sam's attention.

"Do you want half of mine?"

"No." I put my utensil down carefully, feeling self-conscious about how I'd been attacking my empty dish.

"You sure? You're one step from actually licking the plate."

"Shut up." I laughed.

He looked pleased that he'd made me smile. "I'm serious. I don't need to finish this."

"Why are you trying to give me your food? Of course you need it." He truly was the most selfless person I'd ever spent time with.

"I don't want you to go hungry."

"I just ate a three-egg omelet stuffed with ham. I should be fine in a minute. My mouth just doesn't realize I'm full yet."

He ignored me and scooped his omelet onto my plate.

I tried to wave him off. "No. What are you doing? That's yours."

He had a stubborn set to his mouth. "Shhh. Just shut up and eat." He stood and took his empty plate into the kitchen.

I stared after him, but then with a shrug I finished off his omelet too. I was getting to know him well enough to realize when he had that ornery look on his face, there was no convincing him of anything.

He wandered back into the room, chomping on an apple. He sat down and swallowed his mouthful of fruit. "Do you like movies?"

I pressed my napkin to my mouth. "Kind of depends on the movie, but yeah."

"I brought *Titanic* from home, and I thought we could watch that tonight. Boy, that Leonardo DiCaprio sure can act."

I froze.

A wide grin split his face. "I'm kidding."

My lips twitched. "Very funny."

"I had you going for like a second there." He took another bite of apple while looking very smug.

"I guess I figure anyone willing to babysit a complete stranger might be a softie. It makes sense you'd love romance flicks."

He scowled. "I'm not a softie, and I don't love romance flicks."

I snorted a laugh and leaned back on the legs of my chair.

"You're joking too, aren't you?"

"Yep."

He watched me with a funny look as he finished off his apple. Then he twirled the core by the little stem as he spoke. "I noticed you don't seem to have a DVD player or a Roku or anything movie related, so I brought my laptop from home. We can stream a movie."

I grimaced. "My internet is shit."

He laughed. "Dude, I have an AirCard. We're going strictly satellite."

"That works."

"Hopefully you can stay awake. I know your pain pills knock you out."

I moved my arm, and my shoulder gave a twinge. "The pain is manageable at the moment. I think I want to skip the pain pills if I can. I don't like how they make me so groggy."

He nodded. "Okay. But don't be a hero."

I forced myself to get up from the table to take my plate into the kitchen. Sam made an impatient noise, but I ignored him. I needed to be as independent as possible. What if he got sick of playing nursemaid to me? This might seem fun to him at first, but I couldn't trust that hanging around all day with me wouldn't get old real fast.

Pathetic as it was, hobbling to the kitchen and rinsing my plate made me tired. It was embarrassing to be so weak, but it was what it was. My body was using a lot of energy to heal the big slash down my leg. I needed to be patient.

I made my way to the couch and slowly lowered myself with a groan. Sam joined me with his computer, and he booted it up. He sat closer to me than a stranger usually would. We'd seemed to have formed an instant intimacy without us even really trying. And the really weird part was, I didn't even mind. I actually enjoyed his company.

He put a pillow on my lap, and then he set his laptop on that. "I'll be right back." He jumped up, and I frowned after him. He disappeared into the kitchen, and after about five minutes, I heard a loud whirring sound and then the distinctive noise and scent of popcorn popping.

I laughed and shook my head. I didn't own a popcorn maker. I sighed and stared at his computer's desktop. There was a picture of him, his mom, his dad, and a girl who looked just like Sam. I assumed that must be his sister. There was also a dark-haired guy I didn't recognize. They all stood in front of a huge American flag. Sam's mom looked nice. She was plump, blonde, and didn't seem to share the intense stare of her husband. The dark-haired guy had his arm around Sam. I knew Sam only had one sibling, so I was curious who that guy was.

My stomach clenched oddly when I stared at Sam and that other guy. They seemed close. It was obvious in the ease with which they held each other. I wanted to move the laptop, so I could stop staring at Sam and that mystery man, but it was too awkward of an angle with my shoulder injury. Sam had said he was single, so the guy wasn't his boyfriend. But they definitely had a couple look in that photo. Maybe he was an ex. Yeah, the ex theory was definitely possible. The guy looked like the type of man Sam would date; he had a rich-boy vibe with his expensive suit and designer eyewear.

Something about the guy's self-assured smirk annoyed me.

Sam came into the room humming a cheery tune. If he noticed my surly expression, he didn't acknowledge it. He set a big bowl of popcorn on the coffee table, along with some napkins.

"I don't have a popcorn popper," I grumbled. My earlier good mood seemed to have evaporated.

"I brought mine from home." He flicked his gaze to mine. "Is that okay?"

I grunted.

He sat down and grabbed his computer from me, putting it on his thighs. "Do you like comedies?"

"I guess."

He glanced over and frowned. "Hmmm. You don't look like you're in a laughing mood."

"We can see any movie you want. I'm not picky." I attempted to hang a more pleasant expression on my face. He'd definitely now picked up on my disgruntled disposition, and that was embarrassing. I had no right to have an opinion on his personal life. So what if that guy looked like an ass? It had nothing to do with me. Sam could date whoever he wanted. He was only here until I healed, and then he'd go back to his perfect life and I'd go back to riding until I dropped every day.

He flicked through some screens. "There's a ton of new releases on this site." He narrowed his gaze as he peered at his laptop. "Do you have a preference?"

"Like I said, anything's fine." I wondered if Sam was still friends with that guy on his laptop. I'd never been able to remain friends with any of my exes. Sam probably would though. He'd most likely be the kind of ex who would always be there for you no matter what.

He glanced at me. "We don't have to watch a movie if you're too tired?"

"I'm not."

He narrowed his eyes. "Is everything okay?"

"Yes." I moved gingerly, grabbing the bowl of popcorn and the napkins just so I could distract myself.

"Am I bugging you by being here?"

"What?" I grimaced. "No." He should have been bugging me, but he wasn't. He'd fit into my life quite easily.

"Promise you'd tell me if I was?"

I laughed. "Like it would do any good?"

He grinned. "True."

I took a handful of the popcorn and stared straight ahead as I chewed. I hadn't had a movie night with another person in ages. Even when I'd been in a relationship, Peter and I had gone out a lot. Staying in hadn't been our style. Clubs, drinking, and sex had been our thing. He hadn't really been into sitting around at home. Or maybe I hadn't been. Either way, we'd rarely hung out at home just doing movie nights.

"How about an action flick? That way if you go in and out because you're sleepy it won't matter." He studied me.

"Sure."

He leaned back and started the movie. It wasn't a great film by a long shot, so we ended up making jokes through most of it and laughing at how bad it was. It felt great to just let loose and have fun. I'd gotten into a really unhealthy routine of work, work, and more work. The one social thing I did was sometimes hang out with my fellow riders after work and have some beers, but it wasn't intimate like a night at home.

As we continued to watch the flick, I definitely liked the hard push of Sam's shoulder and the heat of this thigh next to mine. Something about hanging out with Sam reminded me of when I'd been a carefree kid. To be honest, his presence in my home was more like we were having a sleepover than that he was helping me convalesce. Maybe this summer-vacation vibe was because I didn't have to worry about going to work. I'd been scrambling to survive for so long, not having that obligation was strange.

When the movie ended, he moved to set his laptop on the coffee table and to clear the popcorn bowl away. "Wow."

"Well, that was a shitty-ass movie," I said, grimacing.

He was smiling when he returned from the kitchen. "But it was fun ripping it to shreds."

"True."

His gaze fell to my mouth, and he licked his lips but then looked away quickly. "Um... I think it's time for your medicine."

"Okay." I could sense he was fighting being attracted to me. We'd had a connection from the first moment we'd met, which was bizarre considering the circumstances of our first meeting. But I felt cautious because getting closer and closer might lead to problems. Mostly because Sam seemed like relationship material, and I was more about casual hookups. Those two didn't usually mix very well, and someone always got their feelings hurt. Of course, realistically, I wasn't in any condition to be having sex, casual or otherwise.

He went into the kitchen again and returned with my meds and a glass of water. I took the pills and handed him the empty cup. "Thanks."

His phone buzzed in his pocket. When he glanced at who it was, he pulled his brows together, looking annoyed. He slipped it back in his pants and went into the kitchen. He was in there a while, and I thought I heard him talking on his phone. His voice was slightly raised, and he sounded frustrated. After a while he came back and sat beside me, his jaw tense.

"Who was on the phone?" I asked quietly.

"My dad."

I didn't say anything, I figured if he had something to tell me, he would. Sam shared his feelings easily, unlike me.

Sure enough, after a few minutes he exhaled roughly and said, "He seems to think I'm an idiot or something."

"Why do you say that?"

He slid his gaze to mine. "You saw how he was in the hospital. He's overbearing and arrogant. He's worried about his reputation."

"Is he always like this?"

"Yeah. But he's worse when he's running for reelection because his supporters are super conservative. He's terrified of anything turning them off of voting for him."

I frowned. "How's that work when he has a gay son?"

His expression shuttered. "It's complicated."

"I'll bet."

He shrugged.

"Are you... out?"

"Like I said—it's complicated."

I held up my hands. "It's none of my business."

His internal struggle was obvious on his tense features. Finally he said quietly, "He doesn't order me to hide that I'm gay, but let's just say he also doesn't go out of his way to share my sexuality with people. He makes it clear to me that he would rather I don't let it be known that I'm gay."

"I see. Couldn't one of his rivals just announce that he has a gay son?"

He smirked. "If they know, they don't for some reason. I think it's because if they try and use my sexuality as a weapon, it makes them look like they think something is wrong with being gay. Maybe they're afraid that might turn off the independent voters. It's not like I know. But so far there are only rumors, and my dad just doesn't address them."

"He's not one of those conservatives who believes in conversion therapy... is he?"

He shook his head. "No. He's not that bad. But part of why he hates me staying here is he's terrified someone will think you and I are shacking up, as he'd call it."

"Well, that and he thinks I'm a con artist."

He gestured to my leg. "He won't listen to me when I tell him this whole thing isn't an act. He's stubborn."

I looked down at the long, jagged wound on my leg. "Maybe you should send him a selfie with your head between my legs to show him the scar."

He grinned. "Hey, I'm fine with anything that gets me between your legs."

Oddly enough my face warmed. I certainly wasn't the kind of man who blushed at the mention of sex, but I blushed all the same.

He took in my uneasy demeanor and smirked. "I'm kidding."

"I know." I cleared my throat. "So what are you going to do about your dad?"

"I'm not sure."

"Does he want you to come home?"

He chuffed. "Well, duh. He didn't want me here to begin with."

"Oh, right, cuz I'm a scam artist. I purposely threw myself in front of your car because I magically know when someone is rich."

"He said you could tell because I drive a Mercedes."

"Jesus, I was just minding my own business, and next thing I knew I was on the asphalt."

"I know." He grinned and shifted toward me. "Of course, you didn't exactly endear yourself to him when you two met. I thought his head was going to blow off that day in the hospital when you told him to fuck off." He chuckled. "That was awesome. No one ever talks to him that way."

I grimaced. "I was pretty out of it."

"Nah." His eyes were filled with admiration. "You speak your mind."

"Well, I'm not a con artist, so his attitude was pretty infuriating." I studied him, wondering if one reason he was hanging out with me was to annoy his dad. I didn't love the idea of him using me just to get back at his father. "So did you tell your dad to mind his own business?"

He bit his lip and nodded. "Basically."

"And what did he say?"

"He gave me two weeks to come to my senses."

I frowned. "What does that mean?"

He shrugged. "He said either I stop staying with you, or he's kicking me out of my cottage."

My mouth dropped open. "Sam, you need to listen to him. That's your home. You should do what he wants." I lifted my chin. "I'll be fine on my own."

He scowled and his eyes darkened with anger. "Bullshit. I'm not five, and he doesn't get to boss me around as if I am. I hit you with my car. You're my responsibility, and I'm not abandoning you because my father is worried about his political career."

I surprised myself when I laughed. He was so passionate it was almost funny. I couldn't understand why he was taking a stand against his dad because of me. But it was obvious he'd dug his expensive heels in and wasn't going to bail on me just yet.

"I hope you don't live to regret this."

He leaned closer, and I caught a whiff of his spicy cologne. "I like it here with you. You've kind of reminded me there's another way to live. That it's okay to stand up for shit. This is my choice to be here. I feel awesome, like I'm finally living my life."

"Yeah, but… this is just temporary, Sam. You still have to face your dad. You work for him, right?"

"Yes. But like I said, I have my own money too."

"Look, I appreciate all that you've done for me. But I'm not worth some big family feud. You've been great, and I'm better now. You should go home."

"You're better now? It's been four days." He scrunched his face in a frown. "You're still a wreck. It takes you twenty minutes to pee. You're breathless just walking from the kitchen to your bed. You're not even close to healed."

I grimaced. "I'm getting there." Slowly.

"You certainly can't ride yet." He pinned me with his sincere gaze.

"Well, I should be able to in a few weeks or so. Just don't push your dad too far. Okay?"

"When you can walk without limping, and I feel comfortable that you can take care of yourself, then I'll leave you alone. But not until then."

I was surprised by the relief that flooded me. He wasn't going to leave me just yet. Without thinking, I grabbed his hand, wanting to convey my gratitude but not knowing how to put it into words.

He nodded and squeezed my fingers. "I get that nobody ever had your back before, Harper. But I do." His voice was husky and firm. "I one-hundred-percent will not leave you until you tell me to go."

"I've been telling you to go the whole time."

"You know what I mean. I'm sticking close until you're safe and ready to work again."

I didn't answer because of the huge lump in my throat, but I managed to nod.

"My dad is probably just bluffing anyway."

I hoped he was right. If he managed to piss off his dad and get kicked out, it wasn't like I was in a position to help him. But I decided not to worry about it. He wasn't going anywhere just yet. I'd just go with the flow and see where that took us.

S.C. Wynne

Chapter Twelve

Sam

"Hello, I'm Sam Foster, Senator Larry Foster's son." I forced my most charming smile, and the woman who'd opened the door hesitantly took the brochure from me.

"Oh, you're his son?" She frowned at the full-color flyer. "That's nice."

She glanced at Terry, my ex, who still worked for my dad and had accompanied me on this canvassing trip. "Are you related too?"

Terry smiled. "No. I just believe in Senator Foster's message."

"I see." She glanced at me again.

"We were wondering if we could count on your vote in the upcoming primary." I hoped I looked friendly and nonthreatening. There was a fine line between seeming confident and badgering.

"I'm a registered Independent," she said firmly.

"Is that right?" I was glad to hear her party affiliation actually. We had way more of a chance of swaying her to vote with my dad than if she'd been a staunch Democrat like his opponent.

"Your dad is a Republican, isn't he?" She fingered the flyer.

"Yes. He's a moderate though." I didn't bother to add that I'd never have been able to support him otherwise myself. "He hates having to be labeled by either party, but that's how the game is played."

"Yeah, I hate labels too," she said softly. "Neither party is perfect."

"That's it exactly." Terry leaned toward her, giving her a warm smile. "I'm a registered Independent myself." His voice was smooth as velvet, and she seemed to relax a little as she studied him.

"Is that so?"

"Yes." Terry nodded. "I hate labels as well."

"What made you become an Independent?" she asked.

"Well... I've always been interested in politics, and I wanted to do something to help my country." He gave another charismatic smile. "But I'm too chicken to be a Marine."

She laughed and leaned on the doorjamb, allowing the door to open more. That was a good sign. Anytime they didn't slam the door in my face I was happy.

"It seemed to me the best way to shape the narrative of this country was to be a part of a campaign," Terry said. "I wanted to work for one of the candidates, but that person needed to be someone who was everything he or she said they were. I didn't want political-speak."

"That seems reasonable." She smiled.

"I'm a reasonable guy." He laughed. "I visited John McTarn's field offices, and they were okay people. But then I went to Senator Larry Foster's field office, and believe it or not, the senator was actually in the office when I got there."

She raised her eyebrows. "You don't say?"

"Yep. He talked to me for a long time and by the end of the day, I was so impressed, I signed up as a volunteer for his campaign."

"Wow."

"I know." Terry grinned. "He truly loves this country, and I know he only wants the best for everybody no matter what race, gender, religion." He grimaced. "McTarn... I'm sure he's a nice guy but.... did you see that story on CNN about how he was arrested for domestic abuse in college?"

I had to admire how deftly Terry slid that little nugget in there.

The woman gasped. "I didn't hear about that."

Terry nodded. "It was about five years ago, before he was married to his third wife."

His third wife? Damn. You're a sly dog, Terry.

"Oh, gosh. That domestic abuse thing is awful." She held our brochure close to her chest. "I guess it's hard to really know these candidates."

"Talking with them helps," I said.

Terry turned to me. "Hey, isn't Senator Foster going to hold a community meeting soon?"

Why, yes he is.

"Oh, that's right. My dad is having a town hall in a few weeks. You should come." I smiled at her encouragingly. "All the info is on that brochure we gave you."

"Maybe I will." She narrowed her eyes. "I'm glad you boys dropped by today. You've definitely given me some things to think about."

Terry winked at her. "I'm glad we could be of help."

She gave another warm smile to Terry. "Will… um… will you be at this meeting?"

"Kind of depends on whether the senator has other things for me to do." Terry held out his hand. "It was wonderful to meet you."

She took his hand. "You too." She waved and closed the door.

We headed down the walkway and out onto the sidewalk. Once we were far enough away, I elbowed him. "Nice work. She'd be very disappointed though to know you're gay."

He laughed. "I did what I had to do for the cause. Besides, once we get her to that meeting, I think there is a much better chance she'll like what your dad has to say."

"So then you're doing her a favor?"

"You know it."

I shook my head and shuffled my armful of brochures. "My feet hurt. What do you say we grab a quick lunch?"

"Sure."

"I should get back to Harper soon anyway."

Terry was conspicuously quiet.

I glanced over, observing his blank face. "Everything okay?" I asked.

"Sure."

I squinted. "Liar."

He laughed gruffly. "I'm trying to be diplomatic." He put on his sunglasses and smiled at me. "How am I doing?"

"I have no idea what you're thinking with those on. Is that the point?"

"Maybe." He sighed.

As we neared the car, he held out his key fob and the alarm beeped. He opened the trunk, and I put the flyers in. Then we walked to one of our favorite bistros just down the way. The hostess seated us promptly, and we both ordered iced tea and Southwestern chicken salads. It was funny how alike Terry and I were in many ways. He was more confident than me and he was slicker-looking, but we liked all the same movies, food, and music. In fact, sometimes I thought the problem we'd had dating each other was we were too similar. There hadn't been enough surprises to keep things interesting.

I leaned back in my chair and pinned him with my curious gaze. "Why do you think you have to be diplomatic just because I mention Harper's name?"

His mouth tensed. "Do you really even have to ask?"

"You mean because of my dad?"

He lowered his head. "Obviously. I'm between the two of you, and it's fucking awkward."

"I'm not sure why he's dragging you into this." I huffed.

"He wanted me to talk some sense into you." His lips twitched. "As if I have that superpower."

We paused our conversation when the waitress set our drinks down. Once she'd gone, I leaned toward

S.C. Wynne

him. "I won't be bullied because I'm doing the right thing. Please tell me you're not on his side on this subject?"

He shrugged. "I don't know this guy, Harper. But I know you well enough to see you must really like the guy, or I don't think you'd be bucking your dad so hard." He rubbed his chin thoughtfully. "I've never seen you this obstinate to be honest."

"I'm doing the right thing. Someone has to fight for those who can't do that for themselves."

"And you're sure the guy's not just scamming you?"

I took the lemon out of my tea and set it on the little bread plate. "If you could have seen how scared Harper was when he realized he couldn't work for weeks." I swallowed. "He tried to hide that he was afraid, but it was pretty obvious. He wasn't faking. Heck, he didn't even want my help at first. But he had to trust someone, or he was completely screwed."

"So he trusted you."

"As much as Harper trusts anyone I guess." I grimaced.

"Your dad says you're basically living with him."

My face warmed. "Terry, he couldn't even shower or go to the bathroom by himself he was so thrashed. I felt he'd be safer if I just stayed with him and helped nurse him back to health."

"So you're really just playing nursemaid to the guy?"

"You don't believe me?"

"I never said that." He sipped his drink, but I noticed his hand shook ever so slightly.

"You shouldn't let Dad put you in the middle like this."

He shrugged. "I'm glad he's keeping me in the loop. If this guy is a shyster, I'd like to know that."

"Why?"

"I don't want you to get used by this guy if he's an asshole who's manipulating you."

I couldn't tell if he didn't like Harper because my dad didn't like him, or if he was maybe a little jealous. "My dad misjudged Harper, and that's the truth."

"He seems pretty convinced he's right."

"When has my dad ever not thought he was right?"

"Touché."

"You don't need to protect me from Harper. Seriously."

He gave me a stiff smile. "I'm just going by what your dad says since I don't know Harper."

"Nope. But you know me."

His expression softened. "True enough."

"You can trust me on this. My dad is letting money rule his thinking."

"And what are you letting rule yours?" He arched one brow.

"Compassion."

He pressed his lips together and studied me for a few moments. "I believe you truly think this guy is worth your time. It's obvious. And I'd be a liar if I didn't admit that a part of me is envious that this guy gets so much of your undivided attention."

I frowned. "Really?"

"Hell, when we were together, we had trouble making dinner plans without them being canceled more often than not."

"You canceled as much as me."

"True." He smiled politely at the waitress when she set the salads down. Once she'd walked away he added, "That doesn't mean I'm not still envious."

"Where is this coming from?" I squinted at him. "Since when do you feel territorial about me?"

He laughed. "I guess I'm just surprised at how taken you seem with this guy."

"I'm not *taken* with him." I picked up my fork. "I'm simply nursing him back to health."

"Right." He nodded and took a bite of his salad.

I knew Terry well enough to know he didn't believe me. "Why are you letting Dad get to you? You don't have to take sides."

He glanced up. "Your dad always has a way of making me feel like I do."

"But you don't. This isn't your battle."

"I still care about you." He cleared his throat. "You know… as a friend. I don't want anyone to take advantage of you."

I clamped my teeth to control my irritation. "It would be nice if people would treat me like an adult instead of some clueless toddler."

"Oh, come on, Sam." He looked like he was squelching a laugh. "You walk way too well to be a toddler. You're at least a preschooler."

I gave a grudging laugh. "Shut up."

He kept his gaze on his food. "Just be careful."

"Would have been nice if you told me that before I ran poor Harper over."

His smile was forced. "Yeah."

"It will all work out." I stuffed a big bite of chicken and lettuce into my mouth.

He gave me an affectionate look. "Slow down. I don't want to have to do the Heimlich on you."

I shrugged and kept chewing.

We ate in silence for a while, and then he set his fork down carefully. "I know you say you're just taking care of Harper... but do you have actual feelings for him?"

I was so surprised by his question I almost choked. I patted my chest, and then with my eyes watering, I asked, "What?"

"You heard me."

"Yes. I did."

"Well?"

I exhaled roughly. "This is a weird conversation to have with you."

"I know. But I feel like there's more to this than you're telling me. I believe you want to protect this guy because of your natural desire to help people. But I can't shake the feeling there is more to it."

My face felt hot. "You really want to go there?"

"Yep."

I grimaced. "Fine. I have a tiny crush on him."

A muscle in his cheek clenched. "That seems pretty fast to catch feelings."

"I knew him from before. From afar. I've had a thing for him for a while."

His gaze flickered. "Does he reciprocate?"

"Harper doesn't trust people. I don't get the feeling he does relationships."

"And that's cool with you?"

I winced. "It's not like we've discussed this stuff. It's just kind of unspoken that there's a mutual attraction between us."

"I see."

"I doubt he'd want someone like me." I laughed uneasily.

He looked at me like I was nuts. "Why not?"

"We're really different people."

He gave a gruff laugh. "Maybe that's exactly what you need."

"Meaning what?"

"I think you and I were too much alike. When we were together, we were both so afraid of offending your dad we danced around the relationship thing." He shrugged. "Now I see you putting it all on the line for this Harper guy. Maybe he's what you've needed all along: someone worth fighting for."

I wrinkled my brow. "When you say stuff like that it makes me feel bad. Like you think I didn't think you were good enough or worth fighting for."

He scowled and gave me a cocky smile. "Oh, hell no. I know I'm fucking awesome."

I laughed, relieved he wasn't upset. "Yes you are."

His mouth had a melancholy tilt to it. "Thanks." He picked his fork up again, and he poked at the lettuce. "I can admit it bugs me that I wasn't the guy who motivated you to stand up to your dad. But I'm glad you're finally doing it. I mean that."

A lump formed in my throat as I held his sincere gaze. "Thanks, Terry."

"Sure." He sighed. "Now I just hope this Harper character is worth the trouble."

S.C. Wynne

Chapter Thirteen

Harper

At the end of the first week after my accident, I drummed up the courage to take another shower. This time I was prepared for how exhausting it would be, and it went much smoother. When I came out of the bathroom with a towel around my hips, Sam was in my bedroom, stripping the sheets from the mattress.

"What are you doing?" I frowned, leaning against the doorframe.

"I'm changing the sheets. We've been sleeping in the same ones all week."

There was a stack of new linens on the dresser. "Where did those come from?"

He laughed. "I had them delivered here instead of my place. Amazon.com, baby." He held up his thumb.

It didn't take a genius to see they were a thousand times nicer than the cheap sheets I'd had. There was also another big package that looked like a comforter and pillows. "You didn't just get sheets? This is a little overboard, don't you think?"

He shook his head. "Hell, no. You needed more pillows for when guests stay over, and your bedspread has holes in it." He shivered. "Probably from the mice."

"No. More like because it's a hundred years old." I'd had that raggedy navy blue bedspread as long as I could remember. It wasn't like I was going to miss it, but once again, it felt weird having him buy me stuff. "And I don't have guests very often."

"Well, now if you do you're all set." He snapped the flat sheet, and it floated down onto the bed. He tucked the corners and paused when he noticed me staring. His gaze ran over my bare chest, and he cleared his throat. "You just gonna stand there half-naked all day?"

I looked down at my towel. "Is it hard to ignore my amazing sexiness?"

He sighed. "It actually kind of is. Sleeping next to you every night without trying to make a move takes enormous willpower. I hope you appreciate that."

I laughed at his candor. "You must have better options than me."

"I have options. But I'm more interested in you."

I moved to the closet to grab a shirt, feigning nonchalance. "You'd probably hyperventilate if I took you up on your offer." I pulled the top over my head, and because it was long enough to cover my private parts, I dropped the towel and headed to the dresser for some clean briefs. I caught his reflection in the mirror as he watched me, and the heat in his eyes made my stomach clench.

"I wouldn't be so sure about that."

His husky voice had my pulse spiking. I slowly pulled on my underwear and a pair of shorts, being careful not to scrape my stitches. "You don't strike me as the kind of guy who fucks around."

"Why would you say that?" He plumped a pillow after slipping on the new cover.

"You seem... innocent." I ran my fingers through my damp hair.

He snorted. "No I'm not." Without warning, he tossed a pillow at me, along with a cover. I managed to grab the pillow without hurting my shoulder, but the cover fell on the floor.

I scowled at him. "It's going to be a while before I can play catch."

"You treat me like I'm a little kid sometimes. I don't like it." His mouth was a straight line.

I laughed uneasily. "I do?"

"Yep. I don't like it when Dad does it, and I don't care for it when you do either." He pulled a brown blanket from a bag on the floor and spread it over the bed. "I've been in several relationships. I can read the signals of when a guy thinks I'm attractive, and I can see you do."

I shrugged. "So?"

He looked like he was surprised at my response. "What?"

"You're a good-looking guy. I'm not blind."

He seemed pleased. "Let me ask you this: if you weren't injured, would you do shit with me?"

"You mean sex?"

"Yeah." His cheeks were pink.

Running my gaze over his lean body, I nodded slowly. "If I thought you could handle fucking without falling in love, sure."

He bugged his eyes. "Wow. You have an ego on you."

I grinned. "No. I don't mean it like that."

"Right." He shook his head.

"I'm not saying I'm irresistible. I'm saying you're probably the kind of guy who likes a relationship." I managed to grab the pillow cover off the floor with a grunt, and then, because my arm was still stiff, I struggled with actually getting the fabric on the pillow.

"And you're not?"

"Not really." I thought about the guy on his laptop, and curiosity got the best of me. I glanced up. "That guy on your laptop, he was a relationship, right?"

"Guy on my laptop?" He pulled his brows together, and then he seemed to realize what photo I meant. "Oh, yeah." His cheeks flushed a little. "That was my last boyfriend, Terry."

"Since he's on your laptop, I'm going to assume he's still in your life?"

"Yeah. He helps with my dad's campaign. We started out as friends, and then it turned sexual for a while." He shrugged. "But we're better as buddies. He's a great guy, but there wasn't really that thing you need to keep a relationship going, you know?"

"Don't look at me."

"You're telling me you've never been in love?" He looked like he didn't believe me.

"I've been in lust." I shrugged my good shoulder. "But I've never felt that spark everyone talks about, where you just have to be around that person or you're lost without them."

"That's too bad." He sounded sincere. "Because it's awesome being in love."

"I'll take your word for it." I finally managed to get the cover on the pillow. I was sweaty and had little doubt a child could have put it on faster, but at least I'd succeeded.

He bent over and grabbed the comforter from the ground. He turned his head suddenly and caught me checking out his ass. "Ha. I knew you were attracted to me."

"Didn't we already establish that?"

"Maybe when you're better, we can test my theory."

I frowned. "Which one?"

"The one where we fuck and I don't instantly fall in love with you." He curled his lip.

"Probably not a good idea."

He chuffed as he tossed the comforter in a heap onto the bed. "I know how to separate my feelings from my dick."

I propped myself against the dresser, feeling chilled and tired. "Sam, you're getting offended over nothing. You should be flattered. I like you enough that I don't want to sleep with you and screw things up."

He smoothed his hand over the down comforter and gave a half-smile. "You're kind of a wreck emotionally, you know that, right?"

"That's what I'm trying to tell you. You can do better." I felt more relaxed now that I could see he wasn't actually pissed at me.

"You shouldn't sell yourself short."

"I'm not. But if I haven't fallen in love with anyone by now, it probably isn't in my nature."

"You don't know that. You're only in your twenties."

I avoided his earnest gaze. "Maybe." I didn't bother pointing out that people younger than me, including him, seemed to have no trouble falling in love. My problem stemmed from being untrusting and wasn't age related.

He sat on the edge of the bed facing me. "You look tired."

"I feel beat. I guess I used a lot of energy showering." I winced. "Which is pathetic to admit."

"Maybe we should get you one of those tubs for old people."

"Very funny."

"Think about it: you just open the little door and walk in to your bubble bath. I'll even buy you a rubber ducky." He grinned.

"You sure do amuse yourself, don't you?"

"Yep."

I rolled my eyes.

His smile faded and he cleared his throat. "I have something to ask you."

"Okay." I hugged myself, wondering if I should have dressed in long pants instead of shorts since I couldn't seem to warm up.

He grimaced. "Would you be willing—" He laughed gruffly. "Um… my… my sister wants to meet you."

"What? Why?" I widened my eyes in surprise.

"I told you we're close, and she's protective of me."

I studied him with my eyes narrowed. "I still don't see why I should meet her."

His cheeks were slightly flushed "She knows I think you're cool, and I guess she wants to make up her own mind about you."

"So another family member who probably thinks I'm scamming you." I sighed. "I'd rather not, Sam."

"You're just scared because you think she'll judge you. She's not like Dad. Not at all." He sounded sincere. "Neither is my mom. My dad's the only one that seems to think the world is out to get him." He twisted his lips. "Maybe I could invite her over here one of these days."

I grimaced. "Really?" Just because I was doing better didn't mean I wanted visitors. I glanced around at my dingy apartment. "I don't love the idea of anyone coming here."

"It would just be a super casual meeting. I promise you she's cool."

"I'm not sure I'm ready to meet any more of your family."

He sighed. "You sure are stubborn."

I shrugged.

"Well, if you won't meet my sister, maybe we could reach out to yours. She'd probably love to hear from you."

I bugged my eyes. "What?"

"Why not contact her?"

"Are you kidding?" I hugged myself, feeling chilled and uneasy. "She doesn't even know who I am anymore. I'm sure she has no desire to talk to me."

"You'll never know if you don't try."

I shook my head. "No. I don't have the guts right now." What if Allison rejected me? I didn't think I could handle that.

"You must know she would want to see you, right?"

"You don't know that," I snapped. "You… you should just worry about your own family life."

He held up his hands. "Fine. Don't get mad."

"I'm not mad… but I'm also not ready to reach out to Allison. I can't even believe you would think that was a good idea."

"Okay." His gaze softened. "I didn't mean to upset you."

"It's fine. I… I didn't mean to snap at you. I'm just tired." Shivering, I glanced longingly at the bed. No doubt the apartment's piece-of-crap heater wasn't working again. It didn't seem to matter how many times I complained to maintenance, nothing was ever fixed.

He must have noticed me shivering because he said, "It's like an icebox in here."

I gave a weak laugh. "I thought maybe it was just me."

"It's probably affecting you more because you're already rundown." He moved closer to me, and he pulled back the covers. "Get in the bed."

"Really?" I dropped my gaze to the fluffy new comforter.

"Why not?"

"I feel like all I do is sleep," I muttered.

He chuffed. "You're shaking and white as a ghost. Get in the damn bed, Harper."

I relented with a groan, and I dropped my shorts. I crawled in the bed, sinking into the velvety covers. Until my accident, I hadn't been a person who napped, but lately I could barely go four hours without needing to rest. The sheets were soft against my bare skin, and the feather pillow cradled my head. "These sheets are so amazing." My body trembled, still feeling chilled. "They're really nice."

"Thanks." He laughed softly. "Are you still cold?"

"It'll pass." My teeth chattered slightly. "I'm... I'm fine."

"Why did you put on shorts if you were freezing after your shower?" He scowled.

"I was airing out the sutures." I tugged the blankets up to my chin.

He rolled his eyes and surprised me by stripping off his jeans.

"What are you doing?" My voice wobbled when I realized he was about to climb under the covers with me.

"Trying to warm you up."

"But..." We'd slept in the same bed every night for a week because of his skittishness about the mice. But he was usually on top of the covers.

"Don't be a prude." His leg brushed mine as he scooted closer.

"I'll be fine. You don't need to do this."

He ignored me. "You're shivering. My body heat will warm you up quicker."

"Sam—"

"Shhhh." He pressed closer and my body tensed, arousal making my gut clench.

The heat of his body felt good against mine, and it was impossible not to feel turned on. I clenched my jaw, willing my cock to stay down. "This is a bad idea."

His eyes were bright, but he kept his hands to himself. "I'm just trying to warm you up."

"You sure about that?"

"Yep." He smirked. "But I mean… if you want to fool around, I'm game."

I laughed gruffly. "If only your dad could see us now."

Irritation flashed through his eyes, but then he pinned his gaze on my mouth. "I'm an adult. He doesn't rule my personal life."

I felt breathless as he scooted even closer. "Are you trying to coerce me into letting your sister come over?"

"No." The pulse in the base of his throat beat swiftly as he put his arms around my waist.

"What are you up to?" A soft groan escaped my lips.

"I told you. I'm warming you up."

"Sam." My voice held a gentle warning. "You keep touching me like this and I'm going to get turned on."

"Would that really be so bad?" he asked quietly, his eyes heated.

I swallowed hard. I was definitely feeling warmer with his body pressed to mine. Even though we both still had our underwear on, it was impossible not to notice we had erections. As the heat of his flesh sank into mine, it was difficult to remember why I thought sex with him wasn't a good idea. But even as excitement and lust coursed through my veins, I knew I needed to control myself. It didn't matter how much I *wanted* to fuck him, I couldn't risk popping open my sutures.

I forced myself to speak. "I'm not quite ready for sex. You know that, right?"

"I know." He watched me intently, his hand fluttering lightly over my lower back. "There are other things we could do."

"Come on, Sam. Stop." My concern over my leg was gradually being overshadowed by the aching needs of my cock. It was a delicious agony to want him so bad and know there was no way I could have him.

"Why?"

"This is torture," I whispered.

He gave a little smile. "Is it?"

I nodded. "Yeah. And you know it too." My balls were swollen and warm, and my cock was constricted in the soft cotton of my underwear. I just wanted to peel off his briefs, climb on top of him, and fuck him hard. I wanted to pound into his tight ass until his self-satisfied smile disappeared as he begged me to let him come.

His eyes were bright. "Let me please you."

I licked my lips, a little whimper escaping me. "No."

"I want to. I want to taste you."

Lust stabbed through me. "You're killing me."

"I want to please you so bad, Harper."

"Sam—"

Without another word, he ducked his head under the covers and tugged at my underwear. I should have told him to stop, but I didn't. In fact I lifted my hips to help him peel my briefs off me. Once he had them removed, he pushed my shirt up and kissed a trail down over my beaded nipples, abdomen, and groin. I hissed with pleasure when his mouth engulfed my cock, and I arched my back with a loud groan.

"Oh, *fuck*." I panted as he sucked and teased my cock. I kept my injured leg as still as possible but couldn't stop myself from thrusting into his mouth. My bad leg ached, but still I pushed between his lips. His throat was tight on my dick, and I pushed my hands farther under the blankets and tangled my fingers in his hair.

He gave muffled groans, his mouth still stuffed full with my cock. My body tingled and throbbed with the need to come. I hadn't expected this moment, but it was so beautifully pleasurable, I was weak with gratitude. "Oh, God yeah," I whimpered when he suckled the head of my cock, licking and nibbling the tender flesh. "Oh, fuck, Sam, yeah."

Maybe he came off as naive sometimes, but there was nothing innocent about the way he swallowed my cock and worked my balls and hole with his fingers. I was so turned on I felt like a rubber band about to snap. The warmth of his mouth and the suction was perfect. Fucking perfect. I pumped my hips, the slide of his mouth causing hair-raising friction. I gripped his soft strands as I thrust deeper and deeper into his throat.

I couldn't see his expression because of the blankets, but the sounds he made were pleasurable. I suspected he was jerking himself off as he sucked me because of the frantic movement of his arm beneath the sheets.

The tingling sensation at the base of my cock alerted me I was close. I let go of his head and growled, "I'm gonna come."

I expected him to pull off, but he didn't. He sucked harder and doubled down, taking me even deeper. The fact that he wanted to swallow my cum just made me even more turned on. I gripped his hair again and thrust harder, panting loudly. "Oh, shit, Sam. Oh, fuck."

He mumbled something and shuddered, and a spurt of his cum swirled over my thigh. His hot release dribbled between my legs, and I lost it. I came hard, my muscles jerking and shaking as I shot down his tight throat. He didn't pull away; instead he swallowed every drop like a good soldier. Once my cock was spent, he let go, kissing the quivering flesh of my dick like it was the most precious thing in the world.

What the fuck just happened?

Still trembling with pleasure, my brain was a fuzzy, jumbled mess. Sam popped up from under the covers with a huge grin. His hair stood up and his cheeks were flushed, but he looked happy.

"Why did you do that?" I asked breathlessly, still enjoying the warm afterglow of my climax.

"Why?" He looked at me like I was crazy. "Because I wanted to, obviously."

I gave a weak laugh. "Jesus. That was unexpected as hell."

He inched up higher and rested his head next to mine on the pillow. "Yeah." He smirked and said softly, "But I'll bet you aren't cold anymore."

Chapter Fourteen

Harper

Once we'd crossed that intimate line with each other, it was hard not to want more. But as another two weeks passed, Sam didn't push for more and I didn't either. We spent time together, laughing and enjoying each other's company, but we were both careful to keep our hands to ourselves. A part of me wondered if Sam had given me a blow job just to prove to me he could remain friends after being intimate with each other.

The perplexing part was, I seemed to be the one struggling with needing more. I'd talked a good line about worrying he'd get attached to me if we fooled around. But he seemed fine. It was me who couldn't stop thinking about taking this sex thing to the next level. I couldn't understand what was going on with me, but I found myself watching Sam as he cooked or brought in groceries. I wanted to kiss him and know what he tasted like. I wanted to be inside him so bad it was embarrassing. Instead of taking the edge off my lust, that day we'd fooled around seemed to have made me twice as hungry for him.

There was also the added complication that I liked him as a person. It made him harder to dismiss. I hadn't met a lot of truly kind people in my life. Often people who pretended to be kind had ulterior motives. But Sam seemed like the real deal, and one indication of that was that his promises of taking care of me while I healed had remained in place. He'd gathered all my bills and paid them, and he'd also paid my rent ahead of time.

That last part probably had my landlord reeling with shock since I'd never paid on time before, let alone early.

I was definitely regaining my stamina and feeling much better. My shoulder seemed to have healed up well, although my leg wasn't ready for the grueling job I had yet, but I was getting there. I figured another week of babying my body might do the trick. I'd have to work a bit to get back in shape, but I felt mostly like myself again. I forced myself to take long walks each day to strengthen my leg. Often Sam would join me, and that made the time more enjoyable. I was excited to be getting better because nothing freaked me out more than feeling weak and vulnerable, but there was a weird melancholy with the knowledge that also meant soon Sam would leave me. Once I was strong enough to ride, everything would go back to the way it had been before Sam had hit me with his car. It would be just me against the world again.

Why does that seem so depressing?

One night after eating dinner, I hobbled into the living room preparing to watch a movie like we often did. I'd just settled onto the couch when Sam hurried into the room, his keys jangling as he pulled them from his pocket.

"Sorry. I won't be able to watch a movie tonight." He sounded breathless as he slipped into his hoodie.

"Oh, really?" I frowned. Sam didn't usually go out at night. Once he'd cooked dinner, we'd eat and watch movies or just hang out and talk. That nightly ritual was one reason I was growing attached to Sam. I'd rarely had friends, and I liked being around Sam. I enjoyed our cozy nights together. "You're going out?"

"Yeah." He didn't meet my gaze, which seemed odd.

I really wanted to ask him where, but I bit my tongue. That wasn't my place.

He glanced toward the kitchen with a grimace. "I'll do the dishes when I get home tonight."

"Don't worry about that. I'll do them." I didn't really care about the dirty dishes. I was more surprised with the fact that he was leaving me alone for the evening. I couldn't tell if he was glad to be getting out, or annoyed.

He raked a hand over his hair. "You're going to be okay alone?"

I wrinkled my brow. "Of course."

"Sorry to bail on you like this." He sighed. "My dad called me last minute. He wants to have a serious talk." He used a mocking tone, but from the little wobble in his voice, I was able to tell he was nervous.

"Oh."

He gave a gruff laugh. "I even guilted Terry into joining us."

I frowned. "Really?"

"Dad likes him, and he's a good mediator."

Dad likes him.

Those three words annoyed the hell out of me, but I was mindful not to show that. "Well, good luck I guess?" I didn't care for the idea of him and Terry as a team, but I wasn't really sure why it bothered me.

He moved to the door. "Don't worry. I'm not going to give in to my dad."

I crossed my arms. "Please don't do anything stupid, Sam. I don't like being the reason you're at odds with your father."

"You're not the only reason. We had plenty of issues before you ever came along."

"He gave you two weeks to move back home. Time's more than up, right?"

"Yes, but so what?"

I sighed. "Maybe it's time you gave in to him where I'm concerned, and instead focus on how callous he is about your sexuality."

His face flushed. "You still need me."

I shrugged. "Well, not to be too blunt, but I need your money not your company."

He winced. "Ouch."

I smiled grudgingly. "I like your company. But that's not really the point, is it?"

He bugged his eyes. "I'm in shock you'd admit you like my company."

"I doubt that's a secret."

"It was to me until just now."

I couldn't help but laugh. "I don't let guys I don't like suck me off. That should have been your first clue."

He licked his lips, a smirk hovering. "Maybe I should just stay here and make you like me even more."

My body flushed at the lurid look in his eyes. "You're getting off track. We're talking about how you need to give in to your dad's request and move home."

His jaw hardened. "I'm not doing that. Not yet."

I felt guilt that he'd already let me cause so much trouble for him. "Sam, this is nuts. You can't take a stand like this for me. I'll be ready to ride soon. The last thing you need is to get kicked out of your place."

He dropped his chin to his chest. "Look, like I said, my dad and I have many issues. It's not just about whether or not I move home." He rubbed the back of his neck. "These last few weeks with you have been freeing."

I frowned. "How so?"

"I don't know... I like how you don't let people push you around. You stand up for yourself, and I respect that." He sighed. "Meeting you has woken me up to what a doormat I've been with my dad."

"Don't fool yourself about me, Sam." I gave him a stern look. "I don't stand up for myself all the time."

"You stood up for Allison. You stood up to my dad."

I squinted at him. "And I let my boss treat me like shit."

"Okay. I'll give you that. He's the one guy you don't stand up to. But that's because you need your job, not because you're weak."

He looked at me with such admiration it made my gut ache. "Sam, you have me all wrong." I waved my hands. "My place is infested with mice. Even before the accident I was dirt-poor. I have no real future. I have no friends. I've never been able to have a healthy relationship. I'm not a man you should look up to. Jesus, you have ten thousand times the potential and future if you just move back home and throw your dad a bone."

"And keep pretending I'm straight?"

I hesitated. "You could come out. You said your dad doesn't force you to lie about being gay."

His mouth drooped. "I've been thinking about that a lot lately."

"Meaning what?"

He sat on the arm of the couch, looking frustrated. "If I'm honest, of course my dad is forcing me to hide my sexuality. He doesn't come right out and demand I hide stuff, but he says just enough that I've always instinctively done that. I'm kind of shocked I've been so pliable. I need to examine why I've let him control me like that."

"Well…" I frowned. "Okay. That's legit. Talk to him about that, but leave me out of this. I'm going to be back on my feet soon and out of the equation. If you want to get into it with your dad, do it for yourself. Not me."

He frowned. "You probably can't wait for me to go away and leave you in peace."

"That's not true." I spoke a little too quickly, and my face warmed.

He smiled as if pleased at my swift response. "Really?"

I lifted one shoulder. "You saved my ass, Sam."

Wincing, he said, "Sure. After I broke it first."

"Yeah, but you could have bailed, and you didn't. I won't ever forget that."

He studied me with an enigmatic expression. "I always wondered what you'd be like as a person."

His gaze was so intense I felt self-conscious. "Well… now you know."

"Yep." He stood slowly, glancing at his watch. "Shit. I'd really better go or my dad will be mad that I kept him waiting." He headed toward the door.

"Have fun." I smirked.

"Yeah. Very funny." He left, closing the door behind him.

I sat where I was, listening to the deep silence. Had it really only been around three weeks ago that Sam barged his way into my life? I flicked on the TV, staring at the screen with my thoughts a million miles away. I hoped things went smoothly for him tonight, and I hoped he heeded my warning and didn't bother using me to stand up to his dad. He definitely needed to live his life as an openly gay man, if that was what he wanted. That was the real battle he should have with his father. Maybe he found it easier to defend me rather than himself. I could understand that. I'd done that with Allison.

I closed my eyes and tried to imagine Sam gone for good. My heart felt heavy at the thought, but that made no logical sense. Not when you considered I'd spent most of my adult life distancing myself from people on purpose. Although, to be honest, I hadn't met many people who interested me that much. But I really did enjoy Sam. He was smart and funny, and I was embarrassingly attracted to him. I felt good when he was around. His positive energy made me happy. Me. Happy. Those two things together in relation to me seemed strange.

Sam and I don't make sense.

That was certainly true. He had a bright future, and I'd settled long ago for mediocrity. Since leaving home, my only goal had been survival. Maybe somewhere along the line I should have adjusted my aspirations and tried to do something with my life, but I'd never bothered. A guy like Sam could definitely do better than me.

My thoughts drifted to Terry, and my stomach tensed. Sam had wanted him there tonight as backup. Why did that annoy me so much? If Sam was going to approach his dad about coming out of the closet, he needed someone there with him. He certainly couldn't have invited me to this little meeting. I'd have only made things worse. His dad wasn't exactly a fan of mine.

I tried to push thoughts of Sam from my mind and spent the remainder of the evening pretending to watch TV. However, I found myself glancing at my watch every few minutes. When midnight hit and Sam still wasn't back, I went to bed. I tried to sleep, but it felt odd not having him in the bed next to me. I'd grown accustomed to his body heat and drowsily talking with him until we fell asleep. I was surprised he was taking so long coming home, and I had to push away unpleasant visions of him sleeping with Terry. He'd said they were just friends now, but sometimes it was easy to sleep with friends and satiate lusty needs. My face warmed remembering how he'd sucked me off a few weeks ago, and my cock twitched with interest.

I scowled and rolled over onto my stomach, trying to find a comfortable position. But I couldn't fall asleep, and my insomnia had nothing to do with comfort. There was a nagging ache in my gut that I worried might be jealousy. But that couldn't be true because I wasn't a jealous type of guy. Sam wasn't mine, and I had no right to feel possessive of him.

It was 2:30 a.m. when I finally heard the sound of Sam unlocking the front door. I lay still, pretending to be asleep as he entered my bedroom. He stumbled a little and let out a soft laugh. I kept my breathing even as he undressed and went into the bathroom to wash up. When he returned, he stumbled again and plopped ungracefully on the bed.

I frowned and lifted my head. "How'd it go?"

He jumped, and in the dim light I could see him turn to face me. The streetlight cast shadows across his features. "You're awake?"

"Obviously." I sounded way snippier than I'd have liked as I wrestled with my feelings of jealousy. It was none of my business where he'd been, who he'd been with, or how late he'd stayed out.

"I'm sorry I woke you."

"It's fine." I cleared my throat and repeated my earlier question. "So, how did it go?"

"Not great." He gave a gruff laugh, and I caught a whiff of alcohol and toothpaste on his breath. When he slipped under the covers, I stiffened. He usually slept on top of the comforter with a blanket over him. He didn't seem to notice that he was doing anything different than usual—maybe because he was inebriated. He turned on his side to face me, exhaling roughly. "God, I'm exhausted."

I had a million questions I wanted to ask, but I didn't want to seem too interested. I waited a few moments, and then I casually asked, "Did you guys have a fight?"

He ran his hand through his hair. "Oh, yeah."

I frowned. "Damn. So having Terry there didn't help?"

"It helped. But my dad was still a jerk." He fell silent.

I sat up on my elbow, needing answers more than I needed to be cool. "Tell me what happened."

He fingered the edge of the blanket, keeping his eyes down. "I told him I wasn't ready to come home yet because you still needed me." He swallowed hard. "And he said he didn't care whether you were shipshape or not. I needed to get my ass home."

I hesitated. "Did you really expect different?"

He glanced up, his expression hard to read in the shadows. "How can he just not care about you? Why did he even get into politics if he just doesn't give a shit about people?"

"He might be afraid I'm a bad influence on you."

He chuffed. "You mean because you're gay too?"

"Does he know I'm gay?"

"I got the feeling he did."

I shrugged. "Well, maybe it's that, and maybe it's because he thinks I'm a con artist."

"Well, if it is partly the gay thing, then why isn't he worried about me hanging around Terry?"

I tried not to frown at the use of his ex-lover's name. "I don't know."

He was quiet for a while, and when he finally spoke, he sounded breathless. "I'll tell you why… because he can tell how much I like you. Terry is the past, and he knows how to control him. But you're a wild card."

"You should have told him I was on his side."

He scowled. "Excuse me?"

"I mean about you moving home. You should have told him I said you should listen to him."

He laughed. "I doubt he'd have believed me."

I lay down again, rolling onto my back. "So where did you leave it?"

"He demanded I come home, and I told him no. He yelled. I yelled back." Rubbing his eyes, he continued. "Then Terry suggested we take a break and talk another time."

"How very reasonable."

His white smile was visible in the dark. "If I didn't know better, I'd say you're jealous of Terry."

"Pfft." I scrunched my face in distaste. "Hardly."

He inched closer, leaning in to get a better look at my face. "Maybe my special brand of charm is finally getting through to you."

The heat of his body had my cock warming and my pulse spiking. "Aren't you supposed to be on top of the covers?" I hoped he didn't pick up on the wobble in my voice.

"Oops." He made no move to get on top of the covers. "I've thought about that day a lot. Have you?" he asked softly.

"What day?" I knew what day he meant. The memory of his lips around my cock was forever burned in my mind. But I never knew how to handle him when he tried to put moves on me. Probably because I had to fight my own wish to give in to him. My attraction to him was unsettling. Plus, a part of me still suspected he was using me as a way to get back at his dad.

"Don't play dumb." He didn't seem discouraged by my standoffish attitude; in fact he moved even closer. "You know I'm talking about the day I took your beautiful cock in my mouth and sucked you dry."

My stomach somersaulted with excitement, but I clenched my jaw. "Sam, you're drunk."

He laughed. "Yeah. I am. So what?"

"So you're probably thinking with the wrong head."

I could feel his impatience. "I know you want me too."

"So?"

"So do something about it." He moved to stroke my cloth-covered cock. "We both want it. You don't have to worry about your leg. I'll do all the work."

I grabbed his wrist, digging my fingers into his skin. "Stop."

"Why?"

"Because you're just mad at your dad, and I don't want to be used."

"Could we please stop talking about my dad?"

"No. I suspect he's the catalyst for this behavior."

"You're crazy. I want to have sex because you turn me on. That's the catalyst."

I swallowed hard, fighting my lust. "Well, I don't want to be the reason you get kicked out of your home. You've grown up with your family's wealth and protection. You have no idea what it's really like out there in the real world without them shielding you."

"Uh… if we fuck, I'm not going to send a video of it to my dad. He wouldn't even know. I'm not sure why you keep intertwining us fucking with my relationship with my dad."

"I told you, I think you're using me to get at your dad."

"That's stupid."

"That's probably why you stuck it out with me this whole time."

"What?" He sounded exasperated.

"You were trying to prove something to your dad."

"No, Harper, I was proving to *you* that there are still good people in the world."

I shrugged. "Well, fine. You made your point, then. You're a good guy." I sighed. "I'm just saying that if you want to go head-to-head with your dad, don't do it because of me. Do it for yourself."

"Is there some reason I can't do both?"

"You should worry about you. Not me."

"Maybe I like worrying about you."

"Well, I won't be in the equation much longer because it's probably about time you moved back home."

He stiffened and yanked his hand out of my grasp. "I can't believe you're trying to get rid of me."

My heart tugged at the plaintive tone. "Come on, Sam. I'm thinking of what's best for you."

"Yeah, right."

I ignored how hurt he sounded. "I can get around okay now. You don't have to watch me every second like before. There's no real reason you need to babysit me."

"You still can't work."

"No. But in about a week I'll be back on my bike. I'm sure of it." I hoped I sounded confident. As much as I liked Sam, I really wanted to be self-sufficient again.

"Whatever." He rolled onto his back.

"I know you don't believe me, but I'm really trying to think of you." He had no idea how rarely I did that.

He huffed and fell silent.

"I mean it, Sam."

He exhaled roughly. "Why does life have to be so fucking confusing?"

I stared up at the dark ceiling. "It's not confusing at all. Just keep your head down and take care of yourself. That simplifies things plenty."

"You're so full of shit."

I lifted my head in surprise. "Excuse me?"

"You heard me."

I smiled. "Yeah. I did."

He turned toward me. "You act all tough and aloof, but I know you care about me."

"So what if I do?"

He laughed gruffly. "That's a fucked-up response."

"It's realistic though. It's been fun hanging out with you, but I'm not good long-term. I have plenty of exes to prove it too."

"That's because you're afraid of getting hurt. You don't want to trust or depend on anyone."

"It's not that simple. This isn't a movie where I'll suddenly turn into a saint because I meet a nice guy." My voice was gruff as I struggled to keep him at arm's length. I knew a relationship with him wouldn't work. No way. We'd crash and burn as soon as he figured out how little I had to offer anyone.

"I'm not the naive idiot you think I am. I feel something real for you—something that drives me toward you, even when you try and shove me off. There's a connection between us, and pretending it's not there doesn't make it go away."

"Sam, I'm not worth your time. I don't know why you won't believe me."

"Bullshit." He scooted closer, and his warm body pressed to mine. He balanced on his elbow, looking down at me. "Don't be afraid of me, Harper. I won't hurt you."

My chest squeezed and I stayed still, trying not to hyperventilate. There was something about him that always seemed to slip past my defenses. I hated the idea of hurting him, and it paralyzed me at moments like these. I wanted him physically, and a part of me wanted him emotionally too. But I didn't know the first thing about dating a guy like Sam. I was afraid I couldn't give him what he wanted beyond physical pleasure. I knew he'd want more. A guy like Sam deserved more too.

He trailed the tip of his finger down my cheek, and then he cupped my jaw. "The first time I saw you, something happened inside of me. I can't explain it. And I know you don't feel like that toward me, but I think you do care about me. I can feel that much."

"Sam," I whispered, feeling uneasy. "Don't."

"Maybe you'll send me away soon. But don't deny me this, Harper. Give yourself to me even if it's just this once." His voice trembled and his thumb swept over my lower lip. "Let me have you tonight."

I was embarrassed when a whimper escaped me.

He sighed and lowered his head, taking my lips softly, tenderly. I opened my mouth, swallowed his groan as I pulled him closer. Once I touched him, it was like a floodgate opened. He started kissing me as if he couldn't get enough, and he only paused to slip out of his underwear and shirt. Then he was back, practically lying on top of me, his hands roaming my body eagerly.

I managed to wiggle out of my underwear and pulled his lean body against mine. Our cocks rubbed together as I flexed my hips, wanting to be inside him desperately. "Sam," I moaned. "Oh, God, Sam."

The moonlight caught his face as he sat up, straddling me carefully. His lips were curved in a warm smile, and his face was a canvas of happiness. I wanted to please him. I wanted him to know how much I cared, even as I fought to hide it. I rested my hands on his narrow hips, and he stroked my cock.

"You can trust me, Harper." His voice was husky and his eyes glittery. "I'll keep your heart safe."

My eyes stung and I couldn't speak because of the lump in my throat. He leaned over and grabbed the lube and a condom from my nightstand. Then he slowly tore the packet open as he held my gaze. The lump in my throat kept me from telling him to stop—that and my intense hunger for him.

He rolled the condom over my rigid cock, and when I hissed at his touch, he smiled. "I've wanted this since my first night here. Lying next to you and having you so close, but not touching you like I wanted has been torture."

I knew I should probably push him away, but I didn't. Instead I tried to make sure he knew the score.

"This is just sex. Don't make it anything else in your head," I warned.

"Oh, Harper." He slathered his fingers with lube and stroked my cock. "I know you better than you think I do."

I arched my back and moaned, "I mean it."

He leaned in and kissed me again, and I cupped his cheeks, groaning because it felt so nice to give in to my need. My hands traveled to the bottle of lube he still held, and I managed to lube my fingers even though I couldn't see what I was doing. I slipped my hand between his thighs and found that sensitive spot behind his swollen balls.

He shivered at my touch. "Yeah, get me ready. I want you inside me so bad."

Excitement coursed through my veins. "I'm gonna fuck you, Sam." My voice shook with pent-up emotions, even as I tried to tell myself this was no big deal; it was simply sex between two horny guys. But still, my heart hurt when our eyes met because I liked him so much.

He frowned. "Don't look so worried. I'm a big boy, Harper. I know what I'm doing." He leaned down again, his full lips inches from mine. A whimper left me as he pushed up against me, his hard body molding into my body like we were made for each other. God, how was I supposed to ignore him when his body felt so fucking good next to mine?

He pressed his mouth to mine and a snap of electricity seemed to arc through my body, pushing a groan from me. I pushed my tongue into his mouth and he opened willingly, our tongues tangling and probing. I couldn't hold back from the need he drummed up in me, and I put my hand on his hip, sliding around to cup his firm ass. Our erections crushed together, and I thrust against him, wanting to fuck him so bad I was shaking with need.

My leg throbbed, and I knew I'd pay for this behavior later, but I didn't really care at the moment because all I could think about was his scent and sweet taste. He lifted his head, and his eyes were drenched with lust. "I'll do all the work. Just lie back and go with it," he whispered.

I shouldn't have let it go this far. I should have pushed him away and told him to leave. But I didn't. Instead I nodded. I just wanted to push his cheeks apart and sink in so deep he could taste me.

"Sam," I whispered. This didn't just feel like sex. It felt way scarier. My heart ached with the need to belong to him, and that thought scared the shit out of me.

"I've wanted this every day since I got here," he murmured. "Every night I fantasize about climbing on top of you while you sleep." I moaned and rolled my hips, and he squeezed me tighter. "Yeah, that's right. Thrust against my hand."

I obliged him, bucking my hips and loving the friction of his touch on my aching cock. "Feels good," I moaned.

He moved so that he hovered over my dick, and he lowered himself onto my cock. The tight muscles of his ass clenched against the head of my dick as I pressed that tender spot. He bit his lip, and my cock slipped into him as he gave a chest-deep groan.

"Oh, *fuck*," he whimpered, clamping his ass on my shaft. He panted and moaned as he adjusted to me entering him.

The squeeze of his ass made me groan as he lifted himself and sank back down. He did that a couple more times, and the slick, tight glide had my eyes rolling up in my head it felt so fucking good. Instinct took over, and I started slowly rocking into him, thrusting up and holding his hips to keep him in place.

"Yeah, fuck me. Fuck me," he panted.

I smoothed my hands up over his rippled abs and flat nipples, loving what a beautiful, muscular body he had. I pumped into him, ignoring the ache of my leg. Sweat beaded on my face, and I just kept sliding in and out of his beautiful ass. "Oh, God, Sam."

He held my gaze with every thrust, making the moment feel even more intimate. A lock of raven hair fell over his forehead, and his lips parted as he fucked himself on my cock. He met every thrust into his body with an eagerness that ramped up my excitement. "Yeah, just like that. Fuck me hard. Fuck me as hard as you want." His voice was hoarse.

I obliged, ramming into him and wanting to satisfy him. If we were together just this once, I wanted him happy and satiated when I finally came inside him. Buried in the heat of his body, all I could think about was watching him come. I wanted to see the look on his face at that most intimate and vulnerable moment. My chest hurt when I thought of how much I liked him. I thrust deeper and deeper, chasing my release and loving every second I got to spend inside him.

He threw his head back and arched his back, stroking himself. "Oh, fuck, I'm gonna come."

"Yeah," I panted. "Come for me, Sam." I thrust harder and pounded into him, and he exploded, cum spurting from his cock and streaming down his fingers.

He cried out, squeezing his ruddy cock as his release splattered onto my heaving stomach. "Harper," he whispered, holding my gaze as his face shivered with pleasure.

Two more uneven thrusts and I came too. "Oh, fuck," I groaned, the delicious explosion radiating up my shaft and into the rubber buried in his body. My entire body quaked, and I rolled my hips, chasing earth-shattering pleasure.

He collapsed on me, and I wound my arms around him, my twitching cock still buried inside him. Our sweaty skin pressed together as we allowed our breathing to return to normal. My chest ached with all the strange emotions rolling around inside. I felt so close to him at that moment my eyes stung. I wanted to pretend it had just been sex, but it had been so much more.

He stirred, and he pulled off my softened cock. He cleaned off with tissues from the nightstand, and then he lay beside me, facing me. I turned my head, meeting his open gaze and my heart squeezed with affection. "You scare me," I whispered.

He frowned. "Why?" He kissed my shoulder. "Why, Harper?"

I didn't know how to articulate my feelings. How could I explain I was afraid of losing him when I didn't even have him? Realistically we barely knew each other, and yet the first moment I'd locked eyes with him something had happened inside of me. I didn't like caring about him. I didn't want to get used to him being in my life. But since I didn't have the words to explain my confused emotions, I just held his warm gaze.

Maybe he could read my dilemma on my face because he smiled and pushed closer. "I won't let you down." He wound his arm around my waist and sighed. "Soon you'll see that I'm the best thing that ever happened to you, Harper."

I swallowed hard and said softly, "That's what I'm afraid of."

S.C. Wynne

Chapter Fifteen

Harper

I smelled smoke. It dawned on me gradually what that acrid scent was, and I opened my eyes and sat up in panic. I shook Sam, who snored softly next to me. "Wake up." I moved to get out of bed, wincing as my stiff leg protested.

"What?" He sat up abruptly, looking confused. He sniffed the air. "Shit. Is there a fire?" He jumped out of bed with a swiftness I envied. He quickly pulled on his pants and raced out of the bedroom.

I followed him slowly, favoring my leg. The living room looked fine as did the kitchen, but the apartment was hazy and my smoke alarm was buzzing loudly. Someone pounded on our door, and a deep voice growled something unintelligible through the wood. Sam ran to the door, and he threw it open. A fireman in full gear stood there with an axe lifted, as if he'd been about to break my door down.

"Get out. Now," he growled through his mask.

I stared at him as if frozen. "What?"

"Get out of the building," the fireman barked.

Sam strode over to me and grabbed my hand. "Come on, Harper." He tugged me past the fireman and down the short smoke-filled hallway to the front stoop of the building. Once outside, we found three fire engines rumbling in front of the building and the place crawling with firefighters hauling hoses into the apartment structure.

I coughed roughly. "What the hell happened?" I muttered, stumbling sideways as a firefighter pushed past me.

Sam pulled me toward the street and away from the workers. When I turned to look back at the building, I could see the top six floors were fully engulfed in flames. My heart pounded as I watched the orange flames lick hungrily up the side of the building. Black smoke billowed from the windows, and nearby one of my neighbors was sobbing as she clutched her cat.

"I didn't grab anything." I shivered and Sam put his arm around my shoulders. "What about my stuff?" My voice was hushed as I stared in horror at the burning building.

"Maybe the fire won't get to your apartment." Sam's voice wobbled with uncertainty.

My eyes and nose burned from the smoke, and I covered my mouth as I stared at the flames consuming the old structure.

An elderly man stood near us, and I recognized him as my immediate neighbor. He slumped as he met my gaze. "It's probably a lost cause. I think the best they can do at this point is to try and stop it from spreading to the buildings next door." He shook his head. "What a damn shame."

My heart sank at his solemn words. I hadn't had any time to grab anything from inside my apartment. I didn't have much of value, but there were a few pictures of my sister I'd have taken if I'd been thinking straight. "I didn't have time to save anything."

Sam rubbed my back. "Shit. I'm sorry, Harper."

I stared in horror as the fire continued to engulf the building I'd called home for many years. Maybe my little apartment had been rundown, but it had been mine. Now I had nowhere to live. My worst nightmare had come true, and I truly was homeless.

"Does God hate me or something?" I growled.

"It'll be okay," Sam said softly.

I wasn't sure how he figured that was true, but I didn't have the energy to argue. We stood for what felt like hours, watching the firemen struggle to contain the fire. Eventually it became obvious the building was a lost cause, but they did manage to keep the fire from spreading to the nearby structures.

"I'm so fucked," I whispered, feeling hopeless.

Sam put his arm around my shoulders. "No. I'm here, Harper. You'll be okay."

My gut churned. "How? How the hell will I be okay *now*?"

"Because you're coming home with me."

I shook off his arm and gaped at him like he was nuts. "What?"

He narrowed his eyes. "What did you think I was going to do? Leave you here?"

"No way. Your dad won't stand for you bringing me home with you."

"He's just going to have to. I'm not leaving you on the streets." He chuffed. "My cottage is plenty big for both of us."

"I can't go home with you."

"You can and you will."

"Sam, he was ready to kick you out for merely helping me. He's not going to be cool with me moving in with you." My stomach ached with stress as I stared at the charred remains of my home.

"What he doesn't know won't hurt him."

"Right. And when he finds me there, you'll get your ass tossed out. That's not cool with me."

"It's not like he drops by for tea. He never even comes to my house."

"It's too risky."

"And do you have a better plan?" he asked, his brows arched.

"A hotel might be more practical."

He grimaced. "Why? I have clothes and everything you'd need at my place."

"If your dad finds me living in your house, we might both end up homeless."

"That's not going to happen. Besides, he's mostly bluffing. I know my dad way better than you." Sam sounded confident as he tugged me toward his car.

I dug my bare feet into the grass. "Wait. I can't just leave." I gestured toward the shell of a building. "Everything I own is in there."

"You can't go in. They won't let you in there."

"But—"

"It's like a bazillion degrees in there. You can't just waltz in and grab stuff." He cleared his throat. "If there's even anything left to grab."

"Oh, God." I slumped.

"I know." He shivered and hugged himself, his cheeks ruddy from the cold. We were both only wearing thin T-shirts, and I was in shorts. "We can come back tomorrow when the fire is good and quenched."

I eyed the burned building, struggling against my frustration.

"Harper, you know you can't go inside there right now."

"Then I'll just wait."

He scowled. "No. That's crazy."

"I don't feel right leaving."

"I'm telling you, there's no way they're going to give you access to that building tonight. You must know I'm right." A tremor went through me, and he sighed. "Come on. Come home with me, Harper." He rubbed my back softly. "Let me take care of you."

I clenched my jaw. "You mean as usual?"

"I like taking care of you."

"And I like taking care of myself," I grumbled.

"I know." He glanced around and lowered his voice. "Let's not argue out here. Come home with me, and tomorrow we'll come back here and see what's up."

I gave him a suspicious look. "Promise?"

"Of course."

I rubbed my face roughly. "I can't fucking believe my bad luck."

"Things will turn around. You just watch."

"Right." I sighed and followed him to his car, giving one more glance back over my shoulder toward the charred building.

He unlocked the car, and we slid in. He started the engine, and I huddled down in my seat, feeling lost. He pulled out onto the street, carefully weaving in and out of the police cars and fire engines. "I know this feels like a setback, but it'll be fine."

I gave a hard laugh. "I can't work and I have no home. This is more than just a setback."

"Your job is safe right now because of Chris Waters covering for you, and as for having no home, my house is way nicer than your apartment."

I scowled at him. "That isn't really the point, is it?"

Grimacing, he said, "I just mean you'll be comfortable."

"I'm not worried about that so much as everything I own just went up in flames. Everything." I squeezed my eyes closed, trying not to panic.

"I know. But it's not like you had much, and anything you need I can buy you."

I snapped my head toward him. "I already had stuff, Sam."

"Well, not much."

Irritation welled in my chest. "The only pictures I had of Allison were in that building."

He sucked in a quick breath. "Oh, shit. I'm sorry. I… I wasn't thinking about things like photos. Damn."

"Whether my stuff was high-end or not, all of it's gone. Everything is just gone."

"I'll buy you anything you need."

"It's not that simple, Sam. Jesus, I already hate you paying for shit all the time. Now you have to shell out even more money?"

"It's fine."

"It's not even close to fine," I said curtly. "Stop being such a Pollyanna."

"I'm trying to comfort you. There's no need to bite my head off," he grumbled.

"You're trying to pretend it's no big deal that everything I own just went up in smoke, literally." My voice was hard. "It's a big fucking deal to me. You think money can solve all my problems, but you're wrong."

"I'm trying to make it better."

"Yeah, Sam. But you can't. You need to let me vent a little. I have a right to be upset. I mean, maybe most of my stuff was junk to you, but it was mine. I've lost all my photos, books, clothes. Everything. Even my wallet. It's all just gone."

Sam frowned. "Okay," he said quietly. "Maybe I did just brush over that."

"Ya think?"

He sighed. "Only because I don't want you upset."

"Of course I'm upset. Buying new stuff isn't going to make it all better. Not to mention, I already hate taking your money."

"But, Harper, you need my help."

Again.

I gritted my teeth. "I was looking forward to being independent soon."

His scowl was evident in the orange glow of his dashboard. "You need to accept help without feeling like it makes you less of a man."

"This has nothing to do with my masculinity."

"Okay, maybe it isn't about your manhood exactly, but I have no doubt you think it makes you look weak because you need assistance right now."

"Anyone would feel this way."

"They shouldn't."

"You wouldn't understand."

"Oh, really? Why not?"

"Because you're used to living off your dad."

He stiffened. "Excuse me?"

"Am I wrong?"

"Yes, you're wrong. I've told you many times I have my own money."

"You live rent-free on your dad's property."

"Okay. But I pay all the utilities."

"I think you're out of touch with the real world."

"Why? Because I don't pay rent?"

"That and you work for your dad's company. Everything is set up for you to succeed."

"Why is that bad?"

"I didn't say it was bad. I'm saying it makes you sheltered. Most people don't have a guaranteed job at their dad's business."

"You do realize that while I work for my dad's company, I actually do work, right?" His voice was hard. "I earn my paycheck."

I sighed. "Fine."

"You don't believe me?"

"It doesn't matter what I think. I'm annoyed because I've just lost everything I own, and you're acting like it's no big deal because *you* have money. Your money isn't mine, Sam. It's going to take me a lot to get back on my feet, and the last thing I wanted was to have to lean on you, or anybody, even longer."

"Okay… I understand you hate depending on anyone. But this is just how it is right now."

"Well, I don't like it," I snapped.

He shot me an impatient look. "I guess you need to get over that."

I snorted. "Sure. I'll get right on that."

"You're too prideful."

I bristled. "I wouldn't expect somebody who has everything handed to them on a silver platter to understand."

"Why are you being such a dick to me? I'm not your enemy. I didn't start the fire."

"Hey, I'm just keeping it real."

"No, you're being an asshole."

"You're just touchy because you resent me pointing out that your rich daddy supports you."

"For the last time, I don't live off of him," he growled. "I work. I have my own money too."

"That first day in the hospital, you said your dad would pay for everything."

"That was because the insurance on the car is through his company. That's what I meant."

"Wait… so your dad owns your car?"

"This is a company car." He gripped the steering wheel tighter.

I snorted. "How can you think you don't live off of him?"

"This vehicle is part of my salary compensation. He didn't just give it to me." His words were clipped. "My dad's company provides cars for lots of the executives."

"Just keep telling yourself that."

"You think I'm lying?"

"Mostly to yourself."

He shook his head. "You know what? Fuck you, Harper."

I shrugged. "Whatever."

He clamped his mouth shut and just drove in silence. I could feel his resentment coming off him in waves, but he didn't say a word. Now that I'd let off some steam, I actually did feel bad for being so hard on him. I was depressed and frustrated about the situation, and he'd been the easiest target.

After a while we pulled up to a huge black iron gate, and he clicked a remote on his visor to open it. The headlights illuminated thick trees and flowers lining the long driveway that led to the main house. When we finally reached the big house, even in the dark the sheer size of it took my breath away. It was definitely more of a sprawling mansion than a house. The architecture was colonial with ornate columns and fancy dormers that jutted from the roof.

He drove past the big house about a half mile and parked in front of a white cottage that looked like something out of a fairy tale. He got out quickly, and I followed more slowly, trailing behind him up the uneven brick walkway. When we reached the door, he slipped his key into the lock and stood back to let me go in first.

I hesitated and then moved to brush past him. "Thanks," I said gruffly, and he gave me a curt nod.

Once inside, he flicked on a lamp near the door and the small room was illuminated in golden light. The décor was exactly what I'd have imagined Sam's house to be. There were comfy brown couches and dark wooden bookshelves. A small fireplace with a brick façade was the focal point of the charming room. He still hadn't said a word to me, and he left me there to head into a side room.

I followed him, cautiously poking my head into the room he'd entered. He was busy pulling back the covers on a twin-sized bed. "The sheets are clean, and the mattress is good," he said stiffly. He turned his back on me to pull a pair of pajamas from the chest of drawers near the bed, and then he tossed them onto the mattress. "These should fit."

I was nonplussed when I realized he wasn't planning on sleeping in the same room as me. I don't know why I'd expected he would. I guess I'd forgotten that the real reason he'd first shared my bed was because of his disgust at the mice in my apartment. Looking around at the immaculate room, it was a safe bet there were no rodents living here. While I'd never have admitted it to Sam, I was disappointed he wasn't sharing the same room as me. I'd gotten used to him being beside me at night.

He faced me, his mouth pinched. "If you need anything, I'm in the room across the hall."

"Thanks."

"No problem," he said coolly.

He left the room without another word, and I sat on the mattress, feeling lost. I'd managed to piss off the one person in the world who'd seemed to actually care about me. I felt bad about what I'd said to him. He had been a little obtuse about my things, but I knew he'd been coming from a good place. If I weren't so prideful, I'd have gone into his room and said I was sorry for losing my temper. But instead, I changed into the clean clothes he'd given me, and climbed into the bed, curling into a semifetal position.

I closed my eyes, wanting to sleep, but my mind buzzed with thoughts of the fire. The cottage was so quiet compared to my apartment it was difficult to drift off. I was used to the *swoosh* of traffic outside on the street at all times of the day.

I squeezed my eyes shut, trying to keep my fear of the future at bay. I hadn't felt this hopeless in a long time, and it wasn't just because of the fire either. There was a dull ache in the pit of my stomach that I might have fucked everything up between me and Sam for good.

Chapter Sixteen

Sam

I felt sick. Harper had seemed like he almost hated me earlier in the car. During the last few hours, my emotions for him had gone through the blender. When we'd had sex tonight, I'd never felt closer to him. I'd been positive he was falling for me just like I was him. He'd been vulnerable and warm. When he'd held me after, his feelings had been so raw and recognizable. Usually he hid every single emotion from me, but he hadn't in that moment. I'd been over-the-moon happy. I'd felt like maybe, just maybe, Harper could really want me like I wanted him.

But then the fire had torn us apart.

I winced when my words from earlier echoed in my head. God, I'd been trying to comfort him, and in the process I'd made him feel like nothing he'd lost had mattered. That hadn't been my intention, but in my clumsy attempt to keep him from feeling scared, I'd managed to piss him off. I'd made him feel like everything he'd lost was nothing important.

It's not like you had much, and anything you need I can buy you.

I punched my pillow and groaned. Jesus, I'd been so insensitive. He'd lost all his photos of Allison and who knew what else? And my solution had been to tell him I could solve all of his problems with my money. I'd wanted him to feel protected, but he'd been right about me dismissing his feelings, and I felt like an asshole.

Maybe I would have apologized too, but before I could do that, he'd attacked me. He'd made me feel like shit by saying I lived off my dad. Yes, I had undeniable privileges because my dad had money and power. But I really did work hard for my dad, and he didn't give me many breaks. If anything he was harder on me because he thought I needed that or I'd be soft. Harper didn't know any of that obviously. But his attitude had stung and definitely hit a nerve, and I'd then lost my temper too.

My heart hurt at the idea that I'd lose him forever. I wanted to go to him. I wanted to crawl in his bed and hold him. I knew he was terrified right now, and of all the nights not to be there with him, surely this was one of the worst. But I still had the memory of his angry stare and words burned in my brain. I was too unsure of his feelings toward me to creep into his room. If he rejected me I would be crushed, and I didn't have the strength to deal with that right now.

Instead of going to Harper, I gave in to my cowardice and pulled the covers over my head with a groan. I prayed maybe sleep would find me eventually and I'd have some relief from my jumbled emotions. But as agitated as I felt, I had a feeling it was far more likely I was in for a long, sleepless night.

Chapter Seventeen

Harper

The next morning I sat alone at the large kitchen table, eating a vanilla yogurt, when there was a knock on the back door. I immediately froze, concerned that it might be Sam's father. Sam had barely said two words to me this morning, and he'd gone to take a shower, so I wasn't sure what to do about the unwelcome visitor.

"Sam?" a female voice called. "It's Kara."

Relief that it wasn't his dad washed through me, even as anxiety attacked me because it was his sister. I stood slowly and moved to the living room, listening if the shower was still running. It was, so I returned to the kitchen just in time to see a dark-haired girl peeking in the window over the sink. She looked confused when she saw me, and we stared at each other for a few awkward moments.

She waved. "Hi!"

I wasn't sure what to do, but since she was Sam's sister, she probably belonged here more than me. I moved to the kitchen entrance and cautiously opened the door. She came around the corner of the house with a warm smile.

I took a step back and stared awkwardly.

She stuck out her hand, smiling hesitantly. "I'm Kara." She looked so much like Sam it was unsettling. They had the same light green eyes and dark hair, although her features were more feminine.

"Um…" I glanced back into the house. "Sam's in the shower."

"I hope I'm not interrupting anything?"

My face warmed. "No." If she only knew how pissed her brother was at me, she'd never have asked that.

She came up the short flight of steps with a curious expression. "I'm Sam's sister."

"I know." I cleared my throat. "I'm Harper."

Her eyes widened. "You're *the* Harper?"

I wasn't sure how to respond, so I just stared at her some more.

"Sorry. It's just… I've really wanted to meet you, but Sam was being all secretive." She looked past me. "Do you mind if I come in?"

"Oh." I stepped aside. "Of course not."

She brushed past me and stood near the sink. Her gaze was inquisitive as she crossed her arms. "My brother can't say enough good things about you."

"Oh, well…" I had a feeling he might have a few choice words for me after last night. He'd been very frosty to me this morning, although, in true Sam fashion, he'd still been polite enough to tell me to eat and drink whatever I'd wanted. Even when he was snubbing me he was nicer than most people. "He's been very kind."

"I would hope so." She laughed. "When you smash into someone with your car, you do need to step up and be a man about it."

"He's been gr… great," I stammered because her stare was so intense it made me feel like a bug under a microscope.

She glanced around. "I thought you two were staying at your place?"

"We were. There was a fire."

Her mouth dropped open. "What?"

I winced. "At my apartment building. There was a big fire last night, and the building burned down."

"Oh, my God." She bugged her eyes. "That's horrible. Was anyone hurt?"

"I don't know. I don't think so, but I don't really know." I felt a twinge of guilt that all I'd mostly been concerned about was my stuff burning.

"That's awful. I'm so sorry."

"Thanks."

"Were you able to save any of your things?" She stepped closer, her eyes warm and concerned.

I shook my head. "No."

"Oh, wow." She bit her bottom lip. "That's horrible."

"Yeah."

"So you're going to be staying here now." She seemed to take that for granted.

"I'm not sure." After last night, I wasn't a hundred percent sure Sam still wanted me here.

"Really?" A line appeared between her smooth brows. "Where else would you go?"

"I'll be fine."

"Of course." She nodded, hanging a polite expression on her face. "But where will you live if you don't stay with Sam?"

I skirted her direct question. "I hope to be back at work by the end of next week." I rubbed my thigh absentmindedly. "I think Sam's spent enough time and money taking care of me."

"Oh, I don't think that's how he feels." She laughed. "Now my dad might think that because he's a jaded individual."

"Yeah. He's convinced I'm a con artist."

She rolled her eyes. "He thinks everyone wants something. It's a wonder Sam and I turned out so trusting."

I gave a grudging laugh. "Sam doesn't seem to have a suspicious bone in his body."

Her gaze was keen. "He trusts people until they give him a reason not to."

"Sounds like a good way to be." I turned my back on her and tossed my now-warm yogurt into the trash.

"Sam told me you didn't want his help at first."

I faced her, studying her under my brow and wondering what she thought of me. Did she see me as a user like her dad? Sam had said she was protective, so it wouldn't be that weird if she didn't trust me. "I'm used to taking care of myself."

"I can respect that. Although from what I've heard, my brother injured you pretty severely when he hit you."

"If I had a desk job, it probably wouldn't have been that big of a deal."

"Not sure I agree with you, but either way, you don't have a desk job."

I shrugged. "I'm better now."

"Sure." She gave a gruff laugh. "Sam said you were hard to read, and he wasn't kidding. I can't get anything much from your expressions."

Heat crept up my cheeks. "He said that?"

"Yeah." She laughed. "My brother tells me everything."

Everything? Please, God, not everything.

I must have looked horrified because she grinned and said, "Don't let it freak you out. I do the same with him." She shrugged. "We're twins. We can't help it. My boyfriend, Ken, doesn't like it any more than you do, but he's used to it now because we've been together two years."

I watched her with my face still hot.

She laughed. "You'll get used to it too."

"I probably won't need to."

She wrinkled her forehead. "You don't plan on hanging around?"

"I'm not sure." I thought about how pissed Sam was at me and figured the decision wasn't really all mine. "Sam and I don't exactly run in the same social circle."

She crossed her arms, and her jaw tensed. "Sam really likes you."

Excitement warred with anxiety in my gut. "Sam probably likes a lot of people."

"Not like he likes you." She sighed. "God, he'd murder me if he heard me saying this stuff to you."

It was odd to have such a direct conversation with a person I'd only met moments ago. But I could see and feel her concern for her brother, and I figured she'd appreciate my honesty. "I really like Sam too, but I've never promised your brother anything."

"Okay."

"I've even tried to discourage his feelings for me."

"It hasn't worked."

I grimaced. "So, like your dad, you'd probably be happy if I disappeared?"

"Not exactly. I'm not sure what to think. I want my brother to be happy."

"Believe it or not, so do I."

"You seem to make him happy."

"Not always." I grimaced, remembering how mad he'd been at me last night.

"Well, nobody is perfect. But he's more confident since meeting you. My dad would say obstinate, but I see it differently. He's becoming his own person. Naturally my dad hates that."

"Your dad has me all wrong. I didn't fake the accident."

"I'm inclined to believe you, but there are a lot of users out there."

"True. But I'm not one of them." I rubbed my jaw. "I'm sure a lot of guys would milk this situation and try to get their claws in Sam. I'm not like that. It might even surprise you to know that only yesterday I told Sam to move back home."

She narrowed her eyes. "You did?"

"I did."

"Huh."

"It was never my idea that he should stay with me to begin with."

"Now that, he did tell me." She smirked. "He said you were a stubborn fucker."

"He's equally obstinate, since he didn't listen to me."

She laughed. "Obviously."

I figured since we were speaking so openly, I should be completely honest with her. "I know he has feelings for me, and I like Sam too. A lot. But I'm not really a relationship kind of guy."

"He told me you'd said that."

I chuffed. "Of course he did."

"He also told me you've encouraged him to come out."

I lifted my chin. "Yeah. I have."

Her sharp gaze softened. "That's one mark in your favor, Harper. I've been telling him that for years."

"I'm glad we agree on something."

"He's considering it, thanks to you." She twisted her lips. "This is the first time I can really remember him defying our dad. On the one hand, I'm glad to see him making his own choices, and on the other hand I'm afraid for him."

"Why?"

"Because I don't want my dad to kick him out. Because people are assholes, and I don't want them to say bad things about him in the media."

"I can't speak to what your dad will do, but unfortunately there are a lot of homophobic jerks out there. You can't protect him from that completely."

She hung her head. "I know."

We were interrupted when Sam walked in the room. The second he saw his sister his entire face lit up, and they hugged warmly. After that he leaned against the counter, giving me a guarded glance. "I see you've met Harper."

"Yep." She smiled at me. "I'm afraid I was in full-on protective sister mode too."

Sam blanched. "Oh, God. What does that mean?"

I shrugged. "Kara was charming. Nothing to worry about."

"I see." Sam frowned and turned to his sister. "I thought you were in Paris."

"Got back last night."

"But you were only there two days." He frowned.

"I forgot about Dad's big fundraising dinner tonight, and I had to fly back early." She laughed. "That's why I came by to see you. Dad's adamant the whole fam has to be there."

"I'm not going." Sam's tone was hard. "I already told him."

"I was afraid you'd say that." She sighed. "Please, Sam. Don't make me go without you. Ken has to work, and Dad's been a pill lately."

Sam's gaze flitted to me briefly and then away. "I'm not in a party mood."

"It's not fair I'm stuck going." She scowled.

"You should have said no."

"Yeah. Right. And have him pissed at me the rest of the month? No, thank you." She sighed and glanced at me. "You could bring Harper. Then it would be more fun for you."

I bugged my eyes. "What? No way. I'm not going anywhere near your dad. He hates me."

"Hate is way too strong of a word." Kara avoided my gaze.

"Kara, Dad would lose his shit if I brought Harper." Sam looked almost more horrified at the idea of bringing me than I did.

"You've brought guy friends before." Kara shrugged.

"Yeah, but... Harper is different." Sam rubbed the back of his neck and gave me a wary glance. "You know that."

My pulse sped up at the emotions buried in his eyes.

"I'm not saying bring him as your date. I mean, I would in a heartbeat if I thought you'd actually do it, but I know you won't." She sounded resigned.

"I'm not coming out at Dad's fund-raiser," he grumbled. "That would be disrespectful."

"Like he hasn't been disrespectful all these years pressuring you to hide who you really are?"

"Kara, there's no way I'm announcing I'm gay tonight."

"I thought you were tired of being Dad's dirty little secret?" Kara pinned her brother with her stony gaze.

"I am, but there's a time and a place for something like that, and tonight is neither."

"You're out, right, Harper?" Kara asked.

"I've never been in the closet."

She pursed her lips and turned her attention back to her brother. "Doesn't that sound freeing, Sam? Can you even imagine not having to hide who you really are?"

"I'll come out when the time is right."

She studied him. "When will that be? When you're eighty? You must know as far as Dad is concerned there is no right time."

"I'll probably talk to him about coming out after the election."

"That's like six months away." She bugged her eyes.

He scowled. "Kara, I'm not going to lose him the election. He'd never forgive me."

She sighed. "He's got a lead over McTarn. Yes, he'd lose some votes if it came out he has a gay son, but I think he'd still win. McTarn is so smarmy. Dad is a blowhard, but he's a mostly honest blowhard."

"Mostly?" I arched on brow.

She shrugged. "There have been whispers about him accepting money from dubious groups."

"Huh." I studied her. "How dubious?"

She winced. "Possibly some Russian oligarch. Regardless, he's in the lead."

"Mom says the gap between him and McTarn is tightening."

"Really?"

"Yes."

She frowned. "Oh, well... you still gotta live your life, Sam."

"I'm not coming out until after the election, and that's final." Sam's jaw had a stubborn jut.

"Okay, fine." She slumped. "Shit. You're really going to make me go to this damn function alone tonight?"

Sam sighed. "Don't try and guilt me."

"Oh, yeah, I will. It's unfair I'm stuck going. Jesus, I flew in from Paris to support Dad, and you can't even drive an hour to do that?"

"I go to almost every single event. Why the hell can't I miss one?"

She laughed sheepishly. "Because I want you there."

He gave me an uneasy glance. "I don't want to leave Harper here alone."

I pulled my brows together. "Why?"

Kara looked puzzled. "Yeah, why? He's a big boy."

"I don't want him to be uncomfortable."

"I won't be." I was surprised he didn't want to leave me. I'd have thought he'd be only too happy to have a break from me after last night.

He scowled. "I have too many things to do. I promised to take Harper over to his apartment to see if there is anything there that can be salvaged."

She looked at her watch. "We wouldn't have to go to Dad's thing until later tonight. It's only 11:00 a.m."

Sam shoved his hands in his pocket, looking conflicted. "God, I really don't want to go tonight." He stared at his shoes. "I hate those things. Everybody is so fake."

"Exactly, which is why I'd rather have you there."

"You should go," I nudged. "Maybe it would be nice to go out and do something besides babysit me."

"I like hanging out with you," he said quietly, and then he cleared his throat and added, "I mean, anything beats going to one of Dad's fund-raisers."

Kara watched our exchange with a funny look on her face. But then she straightened and said cheerfully, "Come on, bro. Keep your poor sister company tonight."

He gave me one last enigmatic look, and then he slowly nodded. "Okay, fine."

"Really?" Kara squeaked, clapping her hands. "You'll come?"

"Yes."

"Oh, thank God!" She jumped up and down and then stopped and grabbed her cell out of her pocket. "Do you have your tux ready to wear, or do you need it cleaned?"

"That black Dior one I wore to Margo's wedding is in my closet," Sam said.

"Good. I have a bomb dress I brought back from Paris. It's Chanel and it is just stunning from bodice to hem."

Sam gave me an uneasy glance. "You sure you're okay alone tonight?"

"I'm positive." I hoped I sounded disinterested. "I need to get used to being alone again anyway."

He wrinkled his brow. "Yeah, you probably can't wait."

I didn't respond and instead kept my expression blank. My time with Sam was coming to an end. I just needed to get back to work and I'd begin to feel more like my old self. Once I had enough money saved for a deposit on a new apartment, I'd get out of Sam's life for good. I prayed I could save up quickly. Seeing Kara and Sam together, discussing their designer evening wear, was a good reminder of how much I didn't belong. Chanel gowns and fitted tuxedos couldn't be further from who I was. No way would a guy like Sam end up with someone like me.

I'd been stupid to sleep with him because all it had done was complicate things between us. But ultimately, we didn't belong together, and there was no way Sam couldn't see that truth, just like I did.

S.C. Wynne

Chapter Eighteen

Harper

I made sure I was nowhere around when Sam left for the fund-raiser. I was in my room with the door closed, and I didn't respond when he knocked and said he was leaving.

I had a good excuse for wanting to hide away in my room to lick my wounds. We'd gone by my apartment earlier in the day, and just as I'd feared, none of my things had been spared in the fire. Sam had tried to comfort me, but it had been awkward between us. Our natural comradery seemed to have evaporated in smoke, like all of my possessions.

Once Sam left the cottage, the silence felt oppressive. It was bothersome that I now found being alone depressing. I'd been so good at being alone before Sam had literally crashed his way into my quiet life. I'd had myself convinced I didn't need people and that I didn't even enjoy them that much. While that might have been true about most people, I really had developed feelings toward Sam. It was a terrifying thought because I knew we had no future.

Meeting Kara had reawakened memories of my sister, Allison. I'd thought about her all day and was heartbroken that I'd lost my photos of her. While I hadn't looked at the pictures very often, I'd known they were there if I needed to see them. I'd been comforted to study them on occasion when my sister's face had been hard for me to recall. Now they were nothing but charred pieces of carbon in a burned desk drawer.

Sam got home late from the fund-raiser, and I was in my room with the door closed, pretending to sleep. When he passed my room, he paused, and I heard the floorboards creak as he hesitated. My heart rate ramped as I waited to see if he'd knock or try and come in. But then his heavy footsteps continued on to his own room. I was shocked at how disappointed I was that he didn't come in. I should have been relieved, but I wasn't.

I lay there another half hour, staring at the ceiling. Eventually I got up to go to the couch in the living room. I flicked on a table lamp and grabbed a book from his shelves. I didn't really even look at the title, I just needed something to occupy my overactive mind. I settled on the sofa and tried to focus on the book, but my mind thoughts kept drifting to Sam. I couldn't help but wonder if Terry had been at that function tonight. It was a safe bet he had been. Jealousy spiked through me, but I shoved it down.

Don't be an idiot.

I was rereading the same page for the millionth time when Sam's door opened. I stiffened and glanced up warily. He stopped when he saw me, and he looked like he started to go back in his room, but then he lifted his chin and approached.

"I guess you can't sleep either?" His voice was gruff.

"Nope." I ignored how my cock twitched with interest as I took in his tanned legs beneath his boxers. "How was the shindig?"

He shrugged. "Boring. Long. The usual."

Was your boyfriend Terry there?

I clamped my teeth so that pathetic question didn't escape my lips. What was wrong with me? I had zero claims on Sam. Zero. Nada. None.

"At least you made the effort to go."

"Yeah." He sighed and came closer. "My dad barely said two words to me. I don't know why he insists I go to those things."

"He probably wants you all to look like one big happy family. That idea plays well with soccer moms."

He perched on the far end of the couch. "I get tired of keeping up appearances all because of his political career."

"I'll bet."

He cleared his throat. "So how did you amuse yourself this evening?"

"Watched TV. Stared into space a lot."

His lips twitched. "Sounds titillating."

"It was." I was surprised how happy I was he was actually talking to me again without that pinched expression he'd had since the night of the fire.

"Even staring into space was probably better than my night."

I smiled tensely. "No doubt."

He shifted uneasily. "I… uh… was thinking… your license and all of your credit cards were in your wallet, and they burned in the fire."

I winced. "Yeah."

"I have a half day at work tomorrow. How about I take you to the DMV after?"

I hesitated. "Oh… I can just take an Uber."

He pulled his brows tight. "Really?"

"I don't want to impose."

His gaze flickered. "I don't mind taking you."

I'd made him feel like shit the other night, and here he was offering to drive me to get my license on his half day off. I'd never met anyone so selfless. His unending kindness was puzzling to me. "No, that's okay."

"Why?" He frowned.

"Like I said, I'll just take an Uber."

"Yeah, but why?"

I lifted one shoulder. "You shouldn't have to spend your afternoon carting me around. You must have better things to do."

He exhaled. "Harper, your cell was destroyed in the fire. How are you going to book this Uber ride?"

Shit.

"I'll just call from here."

"The DMV has long wait times. There's no way for you to know when to schedule a return pickup ahead of time, and how do you figure you'll schedule a ride back without a phone?"

"Maybe I can borrow someone's phone at the DMV."

His face twisted with irritation. "Or you could just let me drive you to the DMV like I suggested in the first place."

"I don't want to be a bother."

He chuffed. "Jesus, Harper. Driving you there would take less time than this conversation has."

"I'm trying to be considerate."

"There's no need for that. You need a new license, and I have tomorrow afternoon off. Let's get this done."

I hesitated, not sure what to do. I needed to get my license replaced as soon as possible. I couldn't rent an apartment or even a hotel room without some form of ID.

He sighed. "Come on, Harper. Just let me drive you. It's seriously not a big deal."

I grimaced and swallowed my pride. "Fine."

He looked relieved. "That's better. What time do you want to go tomorrow? I'm free anytime after one."

"Whatever is convenient for you?" We were being so polite with each other. I couldn't help but think about all the times he'd driven me places like the doctor's office in the past, and on those trips we'd talked and laughed the whole time, feeling so comfortable with each other. Now we were like courteous acquaintances.

"I'll pick you up here at 2:00 p.m. Does that sound good? I have a few errands to run for my... fake job... but then I have the rest of the afternoon free."

I winced, clenching my teeth at his sarcastic reference to his job. I deserved that snide comment. He had every right to still be stinging from the shit I'd hurled at him the evening of the fire.

Apologize. Just apologize for being a dick to him the other night.

I truly wanted to tell him I was sorry. I'd said a lot of stupid, hurtful things, and he deserved an apology. But I had trouble forcing the words from my tight throat. My fucking pride was getting in the way as usual.

Just say the words: I'm sorry I was an asshole to you.

Before I could speak up, he cleared his throat and said, "How about while we're out tomorrow, we buy you some clothes?"

I gaped at him like a trout. "What?"

"Let me take you clothes shopping."

I practically recoiled as if he were a rattlesnake. "No way. I am *not* letting you buy me clothes on top of all you've done for me." Was he literally a saint? What the hell was wrong with him?

"Harper, you need stuff."

"No I don't. I never go anywhere." I pointed my finger at him. "You have issues. No one should be this nice."

His lips twitched. "What are you talking about?"

"Sam, I don't deserve how sweet you are to me. You must know that?"

He sighed. "Look, I know things are a little awkward between us, but come on. All your stuff burned. Unless you want me to just go buy stuff for you, you need to go with me so we can get those essentials."

I stood. "No."

"Why are you so stubborn?"

"I'm stubborn?" I widened my eyes. "You're the stubborn one. How many times do I have to tell you to stop buying me shit?"

He laughed, and his cheeks were pink. "I can't help it. I like taking care of you."

"Sam," I whispered. "Don't be so good to me."

He got to his feet too. "Why not?"

My chest ached taking in his sincere expression. "Because."

"That's not a reason."

"I have to stand on my own two feet. I have to."

"Fine. But you don't have to do it all alone. You don't have to go through life so fucking scared of someone caring about you, Harper."

"Believe me… that's not usually a problem for me."

"Well, I care about you."

"Sam… don't."

"Too late."

"What are you doing?" I squinted at him. "What do you get out of this?"

"That's a stupid question." His eyes glittered in the glow of the lamp.

"There's no logical reason for you to be so kind to me all the time."

He scrunched his features. "Why would I need a reason?"

"Everybody has a reason for why they do shit," I muttered.

"I already told you my motivation: I care about you."

I moved toward him, my heart banging against my ribs. "Stop saying stupid stuff like that."

"No. I mean it."

"Stop it."

"No."

My chest burned from holding back a flood of emotions that wanted out. I studied him as confusion clutched me. The familiar sweep of his angular jaw and beautiful green eyes made my gut clench with feelings I didn't know how to handle. "I don't want you," I growled, stuffing down my need for him. "I'm fine on my own."

"Liar." He lifted his chin.

His stubborn response threw me. "Sam—"

"Is this the part where you warn me off? Tell me you could never love anyone? That you're a lone wolf or some other bullshit?" He stepped up to me, and our faces were only inches apart. "You're so full of shit, Harper. You had me fooled for a long time, but I know you feel the same as me. I *know* you do. You think you're so good at hiding your emotions, but you're not. I see through you, and I'm tired of waiting for you to stop being afraid."

I didn't speak. I just held his gaze, frozen with fear.

"You're not gonna be able to chase me off. It won't work. I want you. All of you. I need you. Fuck, I don't really even have a choice. You can be mad at me if you want, but it won't stop my feelings for you. I'm falling in love with you, Harper. That's just a fact."

My eyes stung and I shook my head.

"*Trust me.*" His voice rasped.

"Yeah, right." I tensed my jaw.

"You must know I only want to protect you. Surely you see that?"

"Stop this," I whispered. "Just stop being so stupid."

"You think it's stupid to care about someone? To want to be a part of their life?"

"When it comes to me? Damn straight I think it's ridiculous."

"Well, luckily, I don't need your permission."

"What do you want from me?"

"Nothing."

I narrowed my gaze. "Oh, really? You're just gonna tell me something fucked-up like you're falling in love with me? And I'm supposed to just go on about my day?"

"I guess you could punch me. You look like you'd like to."

I stared at him, feeling bewildered. "What the hell is there to love about me, Sam?" I shook my head. "I've been a jerk to you. I was a jerk to you just the other night."

His jaw tensed. "You were upset."

My anger seemed to drain from me suddenly. "Yeah. I was. But I still shouldn't have said the stuff I said."

He shrugged. "I won't lie and pretend it didn't hurt. But I have enough negativity in my life because of my dad. I'd rather not be angry with you too. You were upset and you lashed out. I decided to let it go."

I gave a hard, confused laugh. "You just let it go? Just like that?"

"Yeah." His mouth drooped. "I don't want to fight with you. I told myself you didn't mean what you said. That... that you were just scared and lost and so you said some hurtful things to me. So what? I'm a big boy. I can take it. Our relationship is more important to me than some angry words."

"We don't have a relationship."

"Hey, it's dysfunctional, but it's a relationship of sorts."

A hard laugh escaped my tight throat. I was completely confused by him.

He sighed. "Look, I want us to go back to how it was. I miss you. I miss hanging around you. I don't want to be at war."

I missed him too. As shocking as that was, I truly did regret the distance that had developed between us. I didn't want to want him. Didn't relish the idea he had wormed his way into my affections regardless of my defenses. But he had. The little bastard had somehow made me care about him.

"Stop fighting me so hard." He scowled.

I stared at him speechless, as odd feelings rolled through me. I think I surprised both of us when I reached out and pulled him against me. I just needed to touch him. I couldn't explain why exactly.

"I hope this means you like me too," he muttered, his voice muffled by my shoulder.

I lifted my head, studying his tense face. "You're so fucking relentless."

He smiled weakly. "I really like you."

"Yeah?"

He nodded. "Let's move past all the drama. Okay?"

I squinted at him suspiciously. "Water under the bridge?"

"Why not?"

Why not indeed? I wanted him and he wanted me. I was beginning to feel stupid for resisting. I kissed him tentatively, and he gave a soft groan and kissed me back. His hands roamed my back, and he opened his mouth and let my tongue sweep his mouth hungrily.

His cock was hard against my inner thigh, as he whispered, "Harper."

"I'm sorry I was mean to you." I kissed a delicate trail along his stubbly jaw.

"It... it's okay."

"No it's not."

"It is. I promise." He was breathless as he captured my mouth and kissed me passionately, his lips trembling against mine with need.

The warm feel of his mouth on mine made my knees almost buckle. I lifted my head. "I don't want to be like that. I don't. I want to be nice to you. I was upset and I took it out on you."

"I understand."

I stroked his cheek. "I didn't mean any of it."

"You sure?" A line appeared between his smooth brows.

I grimaced. "Yes."

"I know I have opportunities because of my dad. But I do work hard."

"I know. You kind of put a hundred percent into everything you do. It's obvious." I sighed. "I was scared. I'm still scared."

"Don't be. I won't hurt you." He pressed his soft lips to mine and then whispered, "You have my word." He took my hand in his and turned toward his room.

I balked, even though my cock was tenting my boxers. "Where are we going?"

He laughed. "Take a guess."

"I don't know." I wanted him. I wanted to show him how much I felt for him because words seemed to always fail me. But I felt overwhelmed with how much I needed him. Could I trust his feelings for me? Was that even something I was capable of? If I gave him my too much of myself, he would have so much power over me. That was a terrifying thought. I hadn't known many people in my life that had done what they'd promised.

"Don't turn me down." He kissed me again and rubbed his hand over my obvious erection. "You want this too."

"Sam." I shivered with pleasure. "Of course I want you."

"I missed you. I miss touching you." Our kisses became more desperate and needy, and he moaned, "Come in my bed, Harper."

Lusty hunger shot through me at his pleading tone, and I let him lead me to his room. He pushed open his bedroom door, and it squeaked a little as it swung wide. There was a large bed in the middle of the room, and he let go of my hand and crawled on the bed first. "Come on," he whispered.

I couldn't speak because of the lump in my throat, but I moved toward his bed and climbed slowly onto the mattress. Our eyes were locked as I hesitated. "Sam, are you sure?"

He watched me, his face in shadows. He held his arms out to me. "Yes. Come closer."

I couldn't deny my desire any longer, and I reclined next to him. Smoothing my hands over his body, he sighed and arched into my touch. I pushed his shorts down, and he lifted his hips to help me. He kicked them off, and he pushed at mine too, helping me slide them off. We faced each other, our naked cocks nestled together, heavy and heated. He twisted and reached into his nightstand and grabbed lube and a condom.

I took the bottle from him and slathered my fingers. I stroked his cock first, squeezing the thick length and coaxing groans from him. I wanted him turned on and ready when I finally entered his beautiful body. I fingered his hole, smoothing the gel over his anus and teasing his opening until he was trembling against me.

"Fuck me," he begged.

"Yeah. I will." My selfish side just wanted to give into his pleading and slip into his warm, tight body whether he was ready or not. But I held myself in check, wanting to make this moment pleasurable for both of us. His need was palpable, but still I rubbed and fingered his hole until I knew he was good and ready for my cock.

He moaned and tugged at my hips, begging me to fuck him. "Please."

I slipped on the condom and crouched between his muscular thighs. "You sure you still want me?" I asked softly, still ashamed at how mean I'd been to him.

"More than anything," he said softly.

Relief that he'd forgiven me made me so grateful, I wanted to please him. I didn't understand why he was falling for me, but I could feel that he was in his words and touch. I pushed my cock to his entrance. I could feel his desperate hunger as I pressed the head of my dick against his clenched muscles. "I was afraid I'd ruined everything." My voice trembled as I let him see my vulnerability.

He pulled at my hips. "No way."

"Yeah?"

"Swear." He kissed me and then said, "Fuck me, Harper. I need to feel you inside me again."

"Need you too."

"Really?" His voice was so hesitant and vulnerable it crushed me.

"Fuck yeah." I pushed in and he groaned and shuddered as I slid inch by delicious inch into his body. His tight channel clutched and squeezed my cock so tight I almost came the second I slipped in. But I forced myself to hold off, wanting to fuck him until he cried out my name.

He gripped my shoulders and arched his back, panting and groaning as I rocked into him. I drove into him hard, loving the sounds he made with each thrust deep into his ass. I'd been terrified I'd screwed up what we had, but somehow I hadn't. I rolled my hips, and he cried out, his fingers digging deep into my skin.

"I'm not gonna last," he hissed, clenching his muscles on my cock.

I groaned because he was so tight I could barely stand it. We shared hot, ragged breaths as I pounded into him, holding each other desperately. Our bodies moved and contorted as one, curling around each other, seeking our release. He thrust his hips up to meet mine, the friction driving us both crazy with need.

"Want you all the time." My voice wobbled as I slammed into him. "Need to sleep next to you."

He nodded and his eyes were pools of lust. "You'll stay in my room from now on."

I sucked his full lips and jacked my cock into him over and over. "Yeah?" I panted, thrusting slow and deep. "I want to be in here, Sam, so I can roll over and take you anytime I want. Just spread your thighs and push inside your body when I need this."

His eyes burned into me. "Oh, God. Yeah. You'd just fuck me cuz you need me?"

"Yeah. Anytime I want."

"Oh, fuck," he whimpered. His body stiffened and a wave of warm release flooded between us. His body jerked and shuddered as pleasure washed over his beautiful features.

I thrust hard and deep until I knew he was finished, and then I came, groaning his name and pushing against him desperately as my cock jerked inside him. Intense pleasure radiated through every inch of my body until I collapsed on him, breathing hard and basking in the glow of my orgasm. Eventually I rolled off him, and we lay there without moving for a while. Then I tossed the rubber in the trash, and he wiped off and curled up next to me.

I stroked his back and kissed his soft hair, overcome by emotions I'd never felt before. I knew he wanted to take care of me, and a part of me ached for that. But I needed to be my own man too. If Sam really was falling in love with me, he'd understand that I had to be independent to a big degree. Not depending on anyone for too much was how I stayed sane.

My heart ached with all the feelings I had for Sam. I'd tried so hard to ignore those emotions. I felt foolish for even having them. But Sam had wiggled in deep. He'd become a part of my life and I'd barely realized it was happening. Maybe I'd complained a lot about him barging into my life, but now I had trouble picturing my world without him in it. And that terrified me. Sam had fit into my life, but I couldn't see me doing the same with his. His dad would never accept me as anything permanent in Sam's life.

God, what am I even thinking?

Did I actually want a relationship with Sam? For real? Had I completely lost my mind? Yes, Sam was probably the most amazing person I'd ever been involved with. But I wasn't amazing. I wasn't even close to being in Sam's league. But my feelings for him were real. I didn't have it in me to just push him away. All he had to do was look at me with his beautiful green eyes and I wanted to give him whatever he wanted. I knew this would probably end badly for me. But as I held him in my arms, I knew there was nothing in the world I wouldn't do for him. Even if that was just to stay by his side until he tired of me. Because he would eventually; I was certain of that fact. And even though the thought of that broke my heart, the idea of sending Sam away was harder still.

"So you want to move into my room for real?" His sleepy voice cut into my depressing thoughts. "That wasn't just something you said in the heat of the moment?"

"I want to be in here with you."

"You missed me, didn't you?" He sounded amused.

"I've grown accustomed to your snoring."

He laughed softly. "I missed you too."

I pulled him closer and squeezed my eyes shut, letting myself enjoy having him in my arms for now. "Whatever this is between us, Sam, it won't be an easy road. You know that, right?"

And it will probably have a bad ending.

"I know being together will have its challenges. But things don't have to be as hard as you make them either, Harper."

The lump in my throat ached at his optimistic tone. I hated the pain that lay ahead more than ever. Because I knew Sam didn't even see the heartbreak coming. He didn't know enough to be prepared for it. But I'd be ready. I'd be braced for impact when it all fell apart. If there was one thing I was good at, it was taking a punch.

S.C. Wynne

Chapter Nineteen

Harper

"Of course this Specialized Sirrus Comp is the top-of-the-line." The bike salesman patted a sturdy-looking silver model. "Retails for $1200. However, if you buy today I'll knock $200 off, and that will save you some money."

I winced at the price. "Seems a bit high for my needs." My bikes took a thrashing with as much as I rode, and I'd never owned such an expensive ride before. I didn't want to have to worry about somebody trying to steal it all the time.

"I want you to get the best." Sam rubbed his chin as he studied the bike.

"I don't need the best. I just need a sturdy ride." I fingered the sleek handlebars. "Besides, one of my coworkers said the steering was a little twitchy on these and that it was hard to hold a line in a crosswind."

Sam frowned. "Do you get a lot of crosswind in downtown Dallas?"

I laughed. "I think something less flashy would suit me better."

The salesman studied me with an amiable expression. He was an older man, and he seemed savvy enough to know better than to push the more expensive bike on us. He moved on to the next bike on display. "If you're looking for sturdy, this baby is a great choice."

I nodded and ran my hand over the seat. "I've heard good things about the Trek."

"Yep. It has disc brakes, an aluminum frame, and Shimano components, which makes zipping through traffic easier."

I knelt down and studied the wheels. "I like the Bontrager rims."

"You know your bikes." The salesman smiled.

I straightened. "What does this one run?"

"I think it's around $880, but I'll have to see if we have them in stock."

"If you had to order, how long would that be?" I chewed my lower lip, scanning the bike carefully.

"Couple of weeks at most."

I grimaced. "Hmm. I kind of need it by next week."

"Let me go see what our stock situation looks like." The salesman headed toward the back of the store.

"There's no big hurry," Sam said softly, giving me an impatient glance. "What's the big deal if you start working in a few weeks or next week?"

"I've put it off long enough."

"You're so stubborn."

I ignored him. He didn't seem to understand how much I needed to get back to work. I craved my independence. Sam and I had grown closer and closer ever since the night he'd said he was falling in love with me. But his feelings for me just made me even more determined to get back on my own two feet. If we were going to have an actual relationship, I couldn't rely on him like before. We needed to be more equals. Not that we could be financial equals, but I wanted to get back on my bike and earn my keep. Especially if I was going to stay with Sam longer. I wanted to do things like pay my own cell phone bill and contribute to groceries.

The salesman approached. "You're in luck. I have three of these models in stock."

"Excellent." I nodded and turned to Sam. "I think this one works."

"Okay." Sam pulled his wallet from his back pocket. "We'll take it."

I shoved down my frustration that he had to pay for the bike. I told myself it was no big deal, but it still bugged me.

Sam must have seen something on my face because he frowned. "The insurance paid for this."

I gave him a wary glance. "You'd probably say that whether it was true or not just to spare my feelings."

"Maybe. But the insurance settlement actually did pay for this, so I don't need to lie."

Some tension left my shoulders. "Okay."

The salesman rang us up, and then he set a time for us to pick up the bike the next day after it was assembled. We left the shop, and Sam suggested we grab lunch. We settled on an Italian cafe Sam loved and frequented, and we sat out on the front patio because it was a beautiful day.

Once the waitress had taken our order, Sam leaned over and took my hand. I sighed at the comforting feel of his hand around mine. "Thanks for the bike," I said quietly. "It's ten times nicer than the one I had."

"You don't have to thank me. I told you the insurance handled that. Besides, it's because of me that you'd need a new bike." He rubbed his thumb over my skin, sending tingles through my hand.

"You always say that, but I played a part. I rode in front of your car."

"If I'd been paying attention, I wouldn't have bumped into you. I was distracted watching you."

I shrugged.

"But I can't say I regret what happened that day that much." He laughed when I looked at him like he was crazy. "I mean, I regret hurting you, of course, but I don't regret the fact that I got to know you better."

I grimaced. "It would have been easier on my body if you'd just asked me out to dinner one day."

He chuckled. "True." He cleared his throat. "Would you have said yes?"

I cocked my head and studied him. "Probably not."

His mouth turned down in a pout. "Really?"

I squeezed his fingers. "Not because I wouldn't have been attracted to you. But I'm sure I'd have felt like the two of us made an odd couple." I laughed. "Because we do."

"No we don't."

I raised my brows. "You're in denial." I glanced around. "Ask anyone on the street here if they think a broke bike messenger and Senator Larry Fosters' son belong together. Odds are you're going to get a lot of people who agree with me."

"Maybe from closed-minded stupid people who only see things in a financial way," he grumbled.

"Yeah, but that's just the way the world is. We have social circles that most people stick to. Rich people marry other rich people."

"Wealthy people sometimes marry people with less money."

I snorted. "Yeah, and everyone around them whispers that the person without money is a gold digger."

He pulled his brows together. "God, you have such a jaded view of the world."

"No. You're wearing rose-colored glasses, my friend."

He exhaled and let go of my hand. "If you say so."

My lips twitched as I took in his tense face. I loved the little glower he got when he was annoyed, and the way his green eyes darkened to the color of the deep sea. "I can't help what I see."

"It doesn't matter." He folded the edge of his napkin. "All I know is I'm happy to have you in my life."

With just those few words, he managed to make me feel loved and valued. My eyes stung as I stared across the busy street. My life was so different now that I had Sam in it. Even though on the surface I probably still seemed like the same jaded character he'd first met. I did feel a little more optimistic than before. I still didn't trust that what Sam and I had could last. But that wasn't because I didn't want it to. It was because I was smart enough to know there were people like his father who would work hard to split us apart.

The waitress delivered our pasta and iced teas, and we ate in silence for a while just enjoying the beautiful spring day. Once I was full, I pushed my plate away and sighed. It was weird to slow down and actually enjoy life. I'd never taken the time to have pleasant lunches at street-side cafes in the past. It had always been work, work, work, and there had always been another delivery to be made.

"Do you plan on staying with me still?" Sam's gentle voice broke into my thoughts.

I met his uncertain gaze. "You mean when I start work again?"

He nodded. "I want you to stay."

I winced inwardly because I knew he wouldn't like my answer. "I'll stay until I can afford my own place. But then I think I should move out."

"Oh." His face fell, and he set his fork down with a clatter. "Why?"

"Well, for one thing your place is farther out of the city. I'm going to need a car ride into work every morning, or I'll blow my legs out before I get to the job."

He frowned. "Oh. I hadn't thought about that."

"I know." I sighed. "But I have. It makes way more sense for me to live down where I work."

"If it's just a matter of a ride, hell, I'm happy to drive you to work every morning. My dad would be thrilled if I started work earlier than I usually do." He gave a lopsided grin.

His warm smile made my chest hurt. I took his hand again, needing to feel his warm skin on mine. "I don't think it's that simple."

"There you go again, making shit complicated."

"Sam, I don't make it complicated, it just is." I scowled. "The longer I stay with you, the more chance there is your dad will discover I'm living with you. Did that never occur to you? You don't think he might eventually notice you're driving me around everywhere?"

His didn't speak; he just frowned.

"Does he know my apartment burned down?" I asked.

"I'm not sure."

"Well, he was already nagging you to move home. He knows you're living at the cottage again, I assume?"

"Yes."

"And he's never asked you what happened to me?"

"To be honest, I've been dodging his calls the last week." He let go of my hand when the waitress came to refill our iced tea. Once she'd left he said, "I want to tell my dad about you, but I have to handle it very carefully."

My gut clenched. "Sam, you can't tell your dad about us."

His expression hardened. "Harper, of course I'm going to tell him."

"Jesus, Sam. How's that work? Your dad already dislikes me intensely. You must know he won't be cool with us being a couple, right?"

"I know he won't be thrilled, but I've done a lot of thinking about this. I have a right to be happy. I have a right to live my life openly, just like anyone else."

"Obviously I agree with that. But I thought you were adamant about not coming out until after the election?"

"I've rethought that because of you."

"Me?"

He avoided my gaze. "Something tells me you won't be in a relationship with me if I'm in the closet."

While it was true I didn't usually date closeted guys, I'd been willing to do that with Sam because his circumstances were rather unusual. "Shit, Sam. I'd never force you to come out."

"I know. But I want to have a real relationship with you. I don't want to sneak around and pretend you're my platonic buddy."

I leaned back in my chair with a groan. "Your dad will have enough on his plate if you come out publicly. You don't need to rub salt in his wounds by also telling him you're living with someone he detests."

"But I want to be with you. Are you saying you're cool with me being in the closet?"

"I guess I assumed that was how it had to be for now because of your dad's political career. I never thought much past that. You were so firm about not coming out till after the election."

And I didn't think we'd last that long.

"That was when it only concerned me and my dad. But now you're in the mix. I want you, Harper. I'm willing to do whatever it takes to be with you."

I was shocked at how determined he sounded. I'd never even admitted out loud that I loved him, and yet he was willing to lay everything on the line for me? "Sam, I don't know what to say."

He swallowed hard and his gaze flickered. "Say you want me back."

Heat swept my cheeks. "I think you know I want you."

"I mean for real. Not just in bed. Are you willing to go through some tough shit with me so we can be together for real?" His voice wobbled. "Or is this just fun and games for you?"

I held his gaze with a million responses swirling around in my head. Some of them were to save his feelings, some to make it easier on me, but none of them were the truth. Because the truth was I loved Sam, but I saw no happy ending for us. I didn't know if the smart thing to do would be to cut this off now or keep getting deeper and deeper into a relationship with him. Did I even have the strength to let him go if he wanted me this much?

"I don't know what to do about you," I said quietly.

His mouth tensed. "I want honesty right now. I don't need you to be careful of my feelings. I need to know if you're in this for real or not. Because if you aren't… then maybe I don't need to bother upsetting the status quo yet." He swallowed hard and his Adam's apple bobbed in his throat. "But if you're in this with me? Well, I'd do just about anything to make it happen. And that's the God's honest truth."

My eyes stung. "You have a lot to lose. I don't."

"I'm only concerned about losing one thing right now, and that's you."

I licked my dry lips, feeling confused. "You want honesty?"

"Yes."

"I don't see how this ends with us together."

He visibly winced.

"Not… not because I don't want that, Sam. But because I just don't think people will make this easy on us. And life is hard enough when you don't have people actively working against you, right?"

"I'm not nearly as fragile as you seem to think I am."

"Are you prepared to lose your family for me?" I scrunched my face. "Because if you upset your dad enough, that could be a real possibility."

He shook his head. "No. You don't understand family very well because yours was so fucked-up. There will definitely be some drama. But my family isn't going to toss me out because I'm in a relationship with you. My dad won't stop loving me because I come out and upset his constituents."

"Then why didn't you do it long ago?"

"Because I was afraid of backlash. And since I had no real reason to rock the boat, I didn't."

"And now you think you do because of me?" Even I could hear the doubt in my voice.

He looked at me like he thought I was insane. "What part of 'I love you' are you not getting, Harper? I'd take a fucking bullet for you. Do you seriously think I wouldn't put up with people being rude to me if it means I get to have you?"

"Jesus, Sam." I felt breathless. "You definitely don't have trouble sharing your feelings."

His gaze was intent. "I need you to know where I stand."

I rubbed the back of my neck. "I think I get the picture."

He squared his shoulders. "So be frank with me. Do you want me or not? Are you willing to put up with all the bullshit that will come with being with me? My dad *will* be an asshole, that's a given. I'm either worth it to you, or I'm not."

Studying his rigid features, my heart ached. Could I even begin to think about sending him away? The thought of that made me sick. There was no way I was ready to stop seeing Sam. I didn't even want to contemplate never hearing his husky laugh or seeing his face every day. I couldn't remember a time when the thought of breaking up with someone had me willing to do just about anything to avoid splitting. The idea of putting up with his stupid-ass dad and the nosy press seemed so much easier than saying goodbye to Sam.

I exhaled and met his gaze. "I haven't even said I love you."

He smirked, a glimmer in his eyes. "Oh, please."

I narrowed my gaze.

"I know you love me. Jesus, Harper. If you didn't, you'd have gotten rid of me a long time ago."

"I tried. You wouldn't leave."

"Pfft. Seriously? That's how you want to play it?"

I couldn't help it, and I grinned. He was right. I'd have figured out a way to get him out of my place long ago if I didn't crave his company. "You're pretty sure of yourself," I said softly.

His smile faded. "No. Not even a little. I know you might tell me this is too much trouble."

"I should." I gave him a stern look. "I should just wash my hands of you the second I have my bike. I'd find somewhere to sleep until I saved enough for a deposit on an apartment."

"You could certainly do that," he said. When I reached over and covered his hand, a slow smile spread across his face. "You won't regret this."

My stomach churned as I held his optimistic gaze. "Yeah, but you might."

Chapter Twenty

Harper

My first shift back at work was stressful. It was amazing how just not riding for a month or so had my legs like jelly and my lungs burning by the end of day. When I rode back to the main building afterward, my boss, Jack, smirked as he took in my bedraggled state.

"You sure you're ready to come back to work?" He shook his head and tossed a crumpled paper into the trash. "You look like shit."

"Thanks," I muttered as I headed to my locker.

"Don't mention it," he called after me.

I put my helmet in the locker and bullshitted a bit with the other riders who wanted to know how I was doing. I didn't mention the fire or Sam because I didn't want to get into anything too personal. For all they knew, life was as it had always been. But the truth was life was so much better. Sometimes I had to pinch myself that someone like Sam would give me the time of day. I loved every minute I spent with him, and I savored them too because I never knew when it would all come crashing down.

I walked toward the exit, and Jack stopped me. "Hey, Jones, hang on a second."

I stopped and faced him.

He stood and moved closer. "So how the hell do you know Senator Foster's kid?"

I froze. "I'm sorry?"

"I recognized him from TV. When he dropped off the bonus check, I knew I'd seen his face before somewhere. Then it clicked." He narrowed his eyes. "You been holding out on me? You secretly rich and famous?"

I snorted. "Yeah. I'm actually fabulously wealthy. I've just been filming a documentary on douchebag bosses of Dallas for the last seven years."

He grinned. "There's my favorite asshole. I've missed you too. Chris was a good rider, but he was too nice. With you I know I can treat you like crap and you just come back for more."

I clenched my jaw. "Yep."

He chuffed. "So how the fuck do you know Sam Foster?"

"Does it matter? You got your money."

He shrugged. "I'm just curious. He was very protective of you. Seemed weird since I wouldn't think you two would run in the same crowd."

"We don't."

"And yet he was negotiating for you and willing to pay me a shitload of money to take your sorry ass back."

I held his surly gaze. "Who knows why people do stuff?" I hoped he couldn't tell how flustered I felt at his questioning.

He put up his hands. "Forgive me for caring about my riders."

I scowled. "Fuck off, Jack. You and I both know that isn't why you're sticking your nose in my business. Knowing you, you're just trying to figure out some angle where you can make more money off the deal."

He didn't respond, just sat back down at his desk, chuckling.

I left the building with a gnawing in the pit of my stomach. I didn't like the fact that he had recognized Sam. Jack wasn't a nice guy, and he could easily cause problems if he wanted to. I didn't know how much Sam had told him about my accident. Did he know Sam was the one who'd hit me on my bike? Would he use that knowledge to cause Sam problems?

I leaned against the outside of the building, waiting for Sam to come pick me up. He'd dropped me off this morning bright and early. When his Mercedes pulled up, my pulse fluttered. I hurried toward his car, thankful he had tinted windows. If Jack was spying on us, he probably couldn't see who was driving. At least, I hoped not.

Sam popped the trunk, and I loaded my bike in quickly. Then I got in the car as swiftly as I could. "You shouldn't park right in front when you pick me up."

Sam frowned at my gruff tone. "Hello to you too."

I grimaced. "Sorry." I glanced around nervously. "Let's get going."

He laughed and pulled out into traffic. "Are you on the run from the law or something?"

I sighed and sank down in the seat. "My boss was asking a lot of questions about you. Apparently he recognized you from TV."

"Oh." He pulled his brows together. "Does that matter?"

"If it were anyone but Jack, I would say no. But he's such a greedy fucker. Who knows what he'll try and pull?"

"God, I really wish you didn't have to work for him."

"Yeah, me too. But like I said, I don't want to start over at the bottom at some other company."

"I know." He sighed. "There are other options."

"Such as?"

"You could start your own messenger service."

I snorted. "Sure. Why not?"

"I mean it."

I gave him a confused glance. "Sam, believe it or not, the bankers of the world are not lining up to give me a business loan."

"I could loan you the money."

"No way."

"Why?"

"Jesus, Sam. You've done enough for me. Please don't say crazy things like me starting my own company. You're giving me a stomachache."

He laughed. "Okay. I'll drop it for now." We rode in silence for a while, and then he said, "We shouldn't have to worry about Jack outing us."

"Yeah. But for now we do."

"It's so exasperating."

"I know."

"I tried talking to my dad again about coming out. Surprise, surprise, he cut me off and changed the subject." The frustration in his voice was obvious.

"I'm sorry." I studied his rigid profile.

"Does he seriously not see how wrong it is to ignore my feelings like this?"

"He's probably only thinking of himself."

"I want to go places with you without being worried about holding your hand." He clenched the steering wheel. "I want to date you for real, not hide you away."

"Your dad doesn't even know we're seeing each other, right?"

"I don't think so." He sighed. "Who can tell though? For all I know he's got a PI on our tail at all times."

I didn't say anything because I didn't know what to say. I didn't know how to fix this for him. I knew hiding his true self was eating at him more and more with every passing day, and I hated hiding too. If we were openly dating, then things like my asshole boss wouldn't give me an ulcer. If the truth were out, Jack wouldn't have anything to hold over our heads. He couldn't expose us because we'd be happily out and living our lives together.

"Kara says I need to force the issue," he said softly.

I gave him a startled look. "Really?"

"Yes."

"What does that mean exactly?" My heart thumped against my ribs.

"She thinks we should go to a public function together."

"You and me?"

"Yes."

"What… what kind of function?"

"A political one."

I bit my lip, but I didn't speak. The idea of facing Sam's dad in a public setting made me feel like puking. I knew he didn't like me, and I had no idea what he was capable of.

"She says Dad will never be okay with me coming out. There will always be another election or race to run. I'm beginning to think she's right."

I rubbed my face roughly. "Wow. That would be a terrifying ordeal. I don't know if I have the stomach for it."

"Really?" He sounded disappointed.

I scowled at him. "You do?"

He grimaced. "I don't know. I'm just sick of hiding. It's demoralizing."

"I… I know." His sad expression made my heart hurt. "Maybe in the future. I'm not sure I have the balls to face the wrath of your dad just yet."

"Sure." His jaw tensed. "I understand."

I could feel his frustration, but he was too polite to try to make me feel guilty. "I'm not saying I'll never do it. I'm just saying not right now."

"Right." He cleared his throat. "Well, I have to go to yet another dinner party tonight, so I guess you'll have to feed and amuse yourself this evening."

I stared out the window at the passing scenery, feeling guilty that I was making him go alone tonight. "How many of these things does your dad have at year?"

"A lot. They need to constantly refill the coffers. There's this one tonight, which is a smaller affair, and then a huge one Friday where a bunch of Dad's most loyal donors will be there." He turned into his driveway, and we waited for the iron gates to swing open. "But I understand why you don't want to be there."

I had to admire his ability to hide his true feelings on the subject. I knew he was discouraged that I wasn't ready to jump into the fray with him just yet. "To be honest my legs are killing me after today. I probably couldn't have stood all night at a party anyway."

He glanced over at me, and his expression softened. "Oh, yeah. How was it today?"

"A struggle. But I'll get back where I was soon, I'm sure. It was hard on the old legs, but it's just a matter of reconditioning myself. You can't lie around doing nothing for a month and expect to maintain your same level of fitness."

"True." He sighed. "I need to get back to the gym. I've been lazy."

"Not lazy. Just consumed with taking care of me."

He shrugged.

Once we reached his cottage, I showered first because I was the grungiest. Then he had to go get ready for his big night out. When he came out into the living room in his tux, my heart skipped a beat. He was so damn handsome, and his suit clung to his thighs and shoulders perfectly.

I whistled. "You look good, dude."

He smiled, and puffed out his chest. "Thanks."

I stood and approached him slowly. "I can't wait until you get home."

"Oh, yeah? You want to do a little James Bond role play or something?"

"Sure. Sounds fun."

He grinned when I took hold of his lapels. "You've got a horny look in your eyes," he said.

"Can you blame me? You look good enough to eat." I pulled him in for a long, tongue-filled kiss.

When our mouths finally broke apart, he was breathless. "Shit. I wished I could stay here and finish this."

"Later. I'll remind you." I smirked.

He adjusted his cock through his pants. "Like I'll need reminding?"

I laughed and swatted his ass as he walked toward the door. "Behave."

"Always." He waved and left the house.

After he'd gone, I sat back down on the couch and tried to think of what to do with my evening. I didn't want to eat dinner, but I knew if I was going to get back into shape I needed to build muscle. I couldn't do that if I starved myself. I made myself an omelet, and its lackluster qualities made me think of Sam and how much better a cook he was. Without him around to force me to eat healthy meals, I'd most likely fall back into the habit of eating canned goods and Red Vines.

Around dusk I decided to take a walk. I knew there was no danger of running into Mr. Foster since the whole family was at the fund-raiser. The air was sticky and warm, and off in the distance dark clouds threatened rain. I walked past the neatly trimmed evening primrose, fingering the little yellow blossoms distractedly. I felt unsettled and knew it was because I didn't like disappointing Sam. He was always so good-natured and willing to give me anything I needed. It made me feel twice as bad for having turned him down about accompanying him to the fund-raiser tonight.

As I walked across the Fosters' family grounds, it was hard not to be in awe of how impressive in scale and beauty the property was. Everything was so perfectly groomed, I felt underdressed just taking a walk in my T-shirt and shorts. I couldn't imagine living with so many people around all the time serving my needs. My dad had made good money and we'd lived a good life, but his wealth hadn't been anything like the Fosters' level. And yet, Sam had never seemed arrogant about his family's money. He definitely took it for granted, but he'd never come off like a spoiled, rich brat.

I walked until the sun went behind the hills to the west and the big white moon lifted slowly into the sky. I entered the quiet cottage and sat on the couch, feeling bored. There were some photo albums tucked on the bottom shelf of the coffee table, and I decided to look through them. The first album was filled with pictures of Sam's family at political rallies. Sam was younger in the photos, and his hair was longer. As I flipped through the pages and then moved on to the next album, I noticed that gradually Sam's bright-eyed enthusiasm seemed to fade.

When I came to the pages that had Terry in them, my stomach clenched with distaste. Although there were no photos of them holding hands or kissing, the obvious familiarity made my skin crawl. There were several photos of Sam and Terry laughing and sharing a smile that had me gritting my teeth with jealousy. I didn't love seeing Sam looking at Terry the same way he sometimes looked at me. Logically I knew I had no right to feel territorial about Sam when we hadn't even known each other back then, but it was hard not to.

I stuffed the books back where I'd found them and stood, feeling restless. I knew it would be hours before Sam came home, and I needed to figure out how to amuse myself. When my phone buzzed on the coffee table, I picked it up, kind of hoping it was Sam calling to check in. But I didn't recognize the number, and I hesitated answering. Eventually, I decided I had nothing better to do, so I accepted the call.

"Hello," I said.

There was silence.

I thought about hanging up, but for some reason I didn't. There was obviously someone on the other end of the line because I could hear them breathing softly.

After a few more moments of silence, I asked, "This is Harper. Is there anybody there?"

"You're Harper?" A soft voice came over the line.

"Yes." I frowned. "Who's this?"

There was more silence.

"Did you call the wrong number?" I asked.

"No."

"Okay." I gave a gruff laugh. "Well, phones work best when you talk into them." I hoped I didn't sound too harsh. The voice was so shy and hesitant, I didn't want to be too hard on them.

There was a long sigh. "It's me… Allison."

I almost dropped the phone I was so shocked. My heart began to pound, and I struggled for words. Allison? Allison was calling me? It took me a few tries to speak, but finally I rasped, "My God, Allie?"

"It's me."

My eyes stung and I sat on the couch because my legs had given out. "How are you? *Where* are you? Are you okay?" I had so many questions I fumbled over my words.

"Y... Yes. I'm okay." There were little sniffling sounds. "I can't believe it's you."

There was so much to say, I didn't know where to begin. "God, Allie, is it really you?" How old was she now, eighteen? I still had a mental picture in my head of her eleven years old with her hair in pigtails.

"Yes."

"Where are you calling from?"

"I'm in Utah."

"Really? Utah?" I clenched my phone, almost surprised it didn't break into a pieces. "God, I don't even know what to ask you." I wiped at my eyes, feeling so emotional it was hard to talk. "How did you get my number?"

"Your friend."

I frowned, uncertain of whom she could mean. "Which friend?"

"Sam."

Astonished, I gaped at my phone. "Sam gave you my number?" How the hell had Sam even found her? Why would he have done that? *How* would he have done that?

"He had a detective come talk to me."

"A detective?" I repeated, feeling dazed.

"Yeah. The detective asked me a bunch of questions, and then Sam called when I guess he was sure it was really me."

"Sam did that?"

"You're not mad, are you?"

"Mad? God, no, I'm not mad."

"Okay. Good." She gave a little hiccup of a sob. "It's just that… you've been avoiding us."

"Not you, Allie. Never you."

She sniffed. "Really?"

"I'd never avoid you."

"I wasn't sure…" Her soft voice trailed off.

"It was complicated. When I left things were a mess."

"Yeah." She cleared her throat. "Sam sent me a plane ticket to come see you."

I hung my head, pinching the skin between my eyes. My eyes blurred with unshed tears, and a lump the size of a golf ball burned in my throat as I struggled to talk. "You really want to see me, Allie?"

"Of course I do, Harper!"

My hands trembled as I held the phone to my ear, trying to pull myself together. "I… I wasn't sure if you would. You were so little when I left."

"I do want to see you," she whispered. "I've missed you."

"I've missed you so much. I… I can't even believe this is real." I choked on my words.

"I know." She gave a tearful laugh. "It feels surreal to hear your voice."

"You sound so much older."

"I am older. I'm eighteen. I'm an adult."

"God. I can't even believe that." I wiped at my wet eyes. "Are Mom and Dad cool with you seeing me?"

"I don't need their permission."

So then, no.

"I don't want you to get in trouble with them."

"I want you in my life. They can't stop me from seeing you. I… I love you, Harper. I want my big brother back."

That did it. The tears started streaming down my cheeks, and I lost my fucking shit. I started crying, although I still tried to hide it. But she'd have had to be deaf not to know I was losing it on the other end of the phone.

"Don't be sad, Harper."

I gave a broken laugh. "God, Allie, I'm not sad. I'm happy."

She gave a jagged laugh too. "Okay. Good."

"I'm still in shock."

"Me too. I tried to find you a few years ago, but I didn't know where to begin."

"Dad wanted me to disappear."

"You did." She sniffed and her voice wobbled. "You were there and then you weren't."

"I didn't want to go. You have to believe me, Allie. But it was complicated." I clenched my jaw, wondering how much she really knew.

"I wished you'd said goodbye."

I winced, remembering how scared I'd been at the time. "I should have. I was a kid myself. I didn't really know what to do."

"Well, that's the past. Let's focus on the future."

"Yeah." I wiped my eyes some more. "That sounds good." My voice was raspy.

"I'm in Utah for school. But I have spring break in a few weeks. I... I want to come see you then, Harper." I heard her swallow. "Does that work for you?"

I widened my eyes. "Of course. Of course, Allie. I want that more than anything in the world."

She blew out a shaky breath. "Okay. Okay, good."

I loved hearing her voice so much I didn't want to hang up. "When you know all the details of your flight, text me. I want to come meet you at the airport."

"Sam said he'd send a car."

"He did?" How had he handled all of this without me knowing anything?

"Yeah. Sam seems nice. He said you might be upset that he did this without telling you."

I shook my head. "I'm shocked, but how could I be mad? This is the best thing that anyone has ever done for me. I still don't even believe it."

"Me neither," she said softly.

"I don't want to hang up. I just want to hear you talk some more."

She laughed. "I can't believe I was afraid to call you."

"Why?" I widened my eyes.

"I don't know. I thought maybe you'd forgotten about me."

"No. No way. I've never forgotten about you, Allie. And I never would. I thought about you every day. Every single day. I can't believe Sam would do this for us. I just can't get my head around that."

"He said he wanted to make you happy. I thought that was sweet."

I bit my lip as my emotions swelled again. "I've never met anyone like Sam."

She sighed. "I can't wait to see you."

"God, me too, Allie. Me too."

"I have to go to class in a few minutes, but I'll talk to you soon, Harper." Her voice was hushed. "I can't believe I get to say that to you."

"I know."

"Bye for now."

"Bye, Allie."

After she hung up, I stared at my phone for what felt like an hour. I'd been so afraid that I'd never see Allison again. I'd promised my dad I'd disappear, and that was what I'd done. It had never occurred to me she might want to find me. I'd still lived in fear she thought I was a horrible monster. But she didn't. And she was coming to see me because Sam had found her for me.

I felt like I was in a stupor as I got ready for bed. I wanted to thank Sam, but doing that over the phone didn't seem right. Plus just saying thank you felt like it wasn't nearly enough. He'd given me the best gift in the world, and I wanted to repay him.

Feeling emotionally drained, I got into bed and lay there thinking about how grown up Allison had sounded. She'd lived so much of her life without me. I hadn't been able to be there to protect her from school bullies or help her with her homework. Of course, I'd protected her from the worst bully of all: my dad. And in doing that, I'd thought I'd lost her forever. But I hadn't. I hadn't lost Allison because Sam had brought her back to me.

When Sam finally came home it was late, but I was wide-awake. I sat up when he crept into the room. "How did it go?" I asked.

He faced me. "Shit. Sorry. I didn't mean to wake you."

"You didn't." I wanted him to hurry and get in the bed. I wanted to hold him in my arms and thank him for what he'd done for Allison and me.

He stripped quickly, tossing his clothing over a chair. Then he crawled under the covers in his boxers. He immediately pushed up against me and started kissing me. I tasted whiskey on his breath, and I wound my arms around him tight.

"James Bond is ready for you to fuck him," he whispered. "Should I have kept my tux on?"

I'd forgotten about our little joke earlier, and I laughed. "No."

"Good. I don't want to have to squeeze into that thing again." He kicked off his boxers and kissed me again. His erection pressed into my thigh as his tongue pushed between my lips. He seemed desperate to fuck, and I wanted to please him so much I wasn't about to say no.

I wanted him too, but I was also distracted by my need to thank him for what he'd done for Allie and me. But it was obvious this was not the time for talking. I rolled over on top of him and nudged his legs apart.

He tugged at my hips. "Fuck me. Fuck me, Harper."

I laughed. "Let me get the condom."

"Hurry."

"Somebody's horny."

"Oh, yeah."

"And maybe even drunk?"

"How else would I get through the fucking night?" He smoothed his hands over my backside. "I want you inside me now."

"Pace yourself, my little horn dog." I grabbed a rubber and lube from the side table.

"All I could think about tonight was this moment. There's nothing like you inside me, Harper. I feel so complete when your cock is in my body. It's like we're truly one."

His words spilled out in a passionate, jumbled mess, and he slurred slightly. My heart tugged at his raw emotion. I rolled on the condom and lubed my cock. Even though he grumbled I was taking too long, he moaned with pleasure as I prepped his hole carefully, making sure he was nice and ready.

"I love you so much," he whispered.

I covered his body and kissed him as I pushed into his ass. He groaned into my mouth. and we shared hot breaths as I sank in balls-deep. He clutched me and I thrust deep, the squeeze of his channel so delicious I felt like crying. God I loved Sam. I loved him so much it was scary. He'd given me the greatest gift by bringing Allison back to me, and I was going to try and return the favor—just as soon as I was done fucking his brains out.

He arched his back and begged me to fuck him harder. I snapped my hips back and forth, my eyes almost rolling up in my head the friction was so perfect. "Oh, God, Sam." I clenched my teeth and tried to hold back my orgasm.

Sam's hands roamed my body as my cock rammed in and out of his tight ass, coaxing ragged groans from both of us. I held his gaze as I took him hard, and suddenly he gasped and shuddered, his cock jerking between our bodies and spilling hot seed. Our abs were smeared with his sticky release as I thrust, seeking my climax. His ass quaked and tightened on my dick as his orgasm rolled through him.

Then with a grunt, I fell over the edge and came, filling the condom deep inside his ass. "Oh, *fuck*."

"Yeah, yeah," he hissed, clamping his muscles on my cock.

I shivered as my body flooded with warmth, my muscles slowly relaxing and then tensing with my climax. I found his mouth with mine, and I kissed him as my orgasm rippled through me. Once I'd caught my breath, I whispered, "I love you, Sam."

Without a word, his arms clamped around my waist, and he buried his face into my sweaty throat. His breath was hot against my bare skin, and I shivered as we lay wrapped around each other, joined intimately with my cock still inside him.

Holding each other was so perfect. I didn't feel scared or weird at all about telling him how I felt. There was no point in pretending I didn't love him. It was stupid to even try. And after what he'd done for me and Allison, he deserved to know how I felt. Why would I hide my feelings from him when he was everything in the world I needed? I finally, truly believed Sam was mine. I was going to give him anything he wanted from this point on. And I knew exactly what that was too.

I pulled out and we cleaned off. Then I wrapped my arms around him, and we held each other. "Sam, I meant what I said. I love you."

He sighed. "God, I was afraid I'd imagined it."

"No."

"I'm so happy." He laughed and tightened his grip on me.

I cleared my throat. "Allison called me tonight."

His body tensed. "Oh?" He sounded breathless. "How... how did she find you?"

I looked down at him. "Sam, I know it was you."

He grunted and struggled to sit up on his elbow. "Now... don't be mad, Harper. I... I had the ability to find her, and I knew it killed you that you didn't have her in your life. I'm sorry, but I'd do it all over again. It was the right thing to do."

"I'm not mad."

His expression changed to shock. "Really?"

"How could I be? You gave me my baby sister back." I pulled him back down and held him close. "I can never thank you enough for that. I can't even believe it's true."

"So you guys talked and it all went well?" His voice was muffled against my chest.

I laughed and let go of him, and he sat up on his elbow again.

"It went really well. I was shocked as hell, but it's a dream come true." I shook my head. "I can't believe you did that."

"What good is money if it can't fix shit like that, right?" He smiled weakly. "God, I was afraid you'd want to strangle me for butting in."

"Maybe there was a time when I would have been mad." I wrinkled my brow. "But not now. It just makes me love you even more that you would do that for me."

His expression softened. "Harper, I'd do anything for you."

I swallowed against the lump in my throat. "I know."

He smiled hesitantly. "I'm so glad it worked out."

I touched his cheek. "And I've decided that I'll do anything for you too."

"Yeah?"

"Which is why…" I cleared my throat. "Which is why I'm going to go with you to the big fund-raiser you wanted me to go to."

He bugged his eyes. "What?"

"I'll go with you if you still want me to."

"Seriously?" His voice squeaked.

"Yes."

He sat up and raked a hand through his hair. "I can't believe you're willing."

"That makes two of us." I sat up too. "I've made no bones about the fact that I suck at relationships. But I'm gathering that if this thing between us is going to work, I need to be as willing to fall on my sword for you, as you are for me."

"I don't expect that from you."

I frowned. "Well, you should, Sam. You deserve a man who will take a bullet for you just the same as you would for him."

His eyes seemed to glitter. "I don't know what to say."

"Look, I know nothing about how to be a good boyfriend, but if I do this… will it make you happy?"

He hesitated, and then he nodded slowly. "But I wouldn't force you."

"I know."

He exhaled and rubbed his face. "God, I don't even know what to say."

"I understand. I feel the same about Allison."

He shifted and studied me. "My dad was such an asshole tonight. I tried three times in the limo to talk to him about coming out and he shut me down every time." His voice was hard. "Does he just not give a shit that it's killing me to lie all the time? Does he just really not care?"

"He's selfish."

"Yeah." He hung his head. "I've done it his way long enough. I've tried talking to him in private, and he won't listen. This has gone on for fucking *years*." He slid his gaze to me. "I need to live my life openly with you. I'm not staying in the closet anymore. He won't listen to me in private? Well, he won't be able to ignore me anymore when the whole world knows."

"I'm sorry you have to do it that way."

"Me too." He sighed. "Kara thinks bringing you to the fund-raiser and just letting people see us together will start tongues wagging. Then the news will slowly spread. I think it might be less dramatic than making some big announcement."

"Okay. Yeah, maybe she's right."

"My dad probably will want to kill me, but what choice do I have?"

"He already wants to kill me."

He laughed and moved to me. "Thank you, Harper. I'd don't know if I'd have had the courage to do this without you by my side."

"You're sure you really want to do this? Things are going to change big-time."

"Good. I've run out of patience. He just won't listen." His face tensed. "He'll always have some reason why I need to keep my sexuality a secret. There will always be a new election or a new person he wants to impress. I'm angry that for my whole life he made me feel like I wasn't good enough—that there was a part of me that embarrassed him. He was so convincing I think subconsciously I thought there *was* something wrong with me too. Well, that's bullshit and I'm done hiding."

"Fair enough." I pulled him down, and he rested his head on my chest. I fluttered my fingers softly over his back. "I don't know what most relationships are like, but for me it means we have each other's backs no matter what. Okay? I've never trusted anyone to do that for me, so this is a big deal to me."

He nodded, his stubbly cheek rubbing my chest. "Yes. You can trust me, Harper. I have your back."

I probably had no business even trying to pursue an actual relationship with Sam. But I couldn't seem to stop this forward momentum and turn back. Something about his love made me feel hopeful that something wonderful waited for me if I just trusted Sam enough. I had no choice but to go forward because I loved him.

And hopefully, those lights I saw at the end of the tunnel weren't the headlights of an oncoming train.

S.C. Wynne

Chapter Twenty-One

Harper

The night of the big fund-raiser, I had the overwhelming urge to tell Sam I'd just been kidding and that I wasn't going to accompany him after all. But then he'd walked into the room in his tux, exuding a happiness and confidence I'd never seen before, and I decided to strap my balls back on. If he could do this, then so could I.

I hadn't been to a black-tie affair since I was fourteen. I felt uncomfortable in my tux, and my shoes were too tight. I longed to have this over with so I could come home and change into my shorts and T-shirt.

Sam had insisted on driving us to the party, rather than taking a limousine like his dad wanted. He said in case we needed to make a quick getaway it was better if he drove. I really hoped he was just kidding.

I was sweating like a pig as we walked up the twisty path that led to the big hotel where the gala was being held. I hated that the first time I was going to meet Sam's mom it had to be at something like this. As we neared the doors, there was a group of photographers snapping pictures of everyone who entered the party.

Big, burly guys in black tuxes stood outside the doors, and I knew immediately they were security. Sam hooked his arm through mine and whispered, "Here goes nothing."

There was a loud flurry of clicks, and a ton of bulbs flashed, making it hard to see where I was walking.

Sam pressed closer as we entered the actual building. Once inside, two of the security guys patted me down, although they let Sam go through untouched. I guess that was the perk of being the guest of honor's son.

Kara was already at the door when we walked up, and I was relieved to see her. She had the same calm demeanor Sam usually had, and it was nice to see a familiar face. She wore a figure-hugging black gown, and her green eyes stood out against her creamy white skin. "Anyone else feel like throwing up?" she asked, giving a breathless laugh.

"Yes." I grimaced.

Sam rubbed my back, and I tried not to feel self-conscious as people turned to look at us and then whisper to one another. I felt conspicuous at their curious stares and had to remind myself that this was why I was here, to help Sam be true to himself. I lifted my chin and grabbed two glasses of champagne from a waiter as he walked by with a tray. I handed one to Sam, and we clinked glasses.

"I'm too young to be having a stroke, right?" I muttered as I sipped my drink.

Kara laughed tensely.

"Oh, shit. Here comes my mom." Sam's voice shook, and he looked like he wanted to dive under the nearest table.

I recognized the approaching blonde woman from Sam's photo albums. She smiled warmly at her children, and they exchanged kisses on the cheek. She then turned her attention to me. Her expression was welcoming and also curious. "I don't believe we've met. I'm Valerie Foster." She held out her hand.

I shook her hand, embarrassed at how calloused mine felt against her smooth skin. "Hello." I was so tongue-tied I didn't even say my name.

"Mom, this is Harper," Kara said smoothly, giving me an encouraging smile.

It took a few seconds, but slowly she seemed to recognize my name. "Oh." She frowned. "You're Harper?" She laughed uneasily, looking confused as she turned to her daughter. "The boy on the bike?"

"The same," Kara said brightly.

"Oh…" Her puzzled gaze returned to me. "How… how are you? All healed up I hope?"

"Yes, thank you."

She bit her lower lip and whispered to Kara, "I'm sorry. I'm confused about why he's here?"

Sam cleared his throat. "He's my date, mom."

Something close to panic rippled through her gaze. "Your… your *date*?"

"Yes." Sam's jaw was set stubbornly.

She gave an uneasy laugh. "Honey…" She looked around. "What are you doing?" She plastered a fake smile on her face as she spoke through clenched teeth.

Sam swallowed. "I've tried talking to Dad. He won't listen."

"Oh, God, Sam… does that mean your dad doesn't know you've brought Harper?" She looked around again, and I suspected she was trying to find her husband in the room. I didn't get the feeling that was so she could call him over to greet me warmly either.

"I'm sick of pretending for the cameras." Sam lifted his chin.

She grimaced. "Well, okay." She lowered her voice. "But this isn't a good way to make your point."

"Why not? Every time I try to talk to Dad about coming out publicly, he shuts me down. Well, he won't be able to do that to me tonight."

She turned to Kara. "Did you know your brother was going to pull this stunt?" She sounded angry now.

Kara nodded slowly. "Actually… it was my idea." She held her mom's livid stare. "And it's not a stunt."

"This was your idea?" Mrs. Foster squeaked.

"Sam has been ignored long enough," Kara said. She had the same sulky glower Sam sometimes got.

My stomach hurt and I was really wishing the champagne guy would come by again. I needed about two more glasses of bubbly to help me deal with the stress. The tension was crackling between the three of them, and I was afraid if I spoke up I'd just make things worse.

Mrs. Foster leaned toward her son. "You know we love you, honey." She licked her lips. "But this is not the time or the place to be doing this to your father."

"When will it be the time, Mom?" he asked gruffly. "And I'm not actually doing anything to my father. I'm simply bringing a date to an event. Just like any other person would be allowed to do."

"You know your father has very conservative constituents." She gave yet another nervous glance around. "I'm not telling you anything you don't already know."

"Senator Larry Foster has a gay son. It's just a fact, Mom." Sam crossed his arms.

I put my hand on the small of his back, trying to lend him some silent support.

"Sam, you're trying to make tonight about you, and it's supposed to be about supporting your father." She scowled.

"I'm here supporting my dad. How about you guys support me too for a change?"

"We do support you." She pulled her light brows together. "We don't mind that you're gay."

"You don't mind?" He widened his eyes.

She grimaced. "You know what I mean."

Sam turned to me, looking frustrated. "You see what it's like? They don't hear me."

I gave him an empathetic look. "I'm sorry."

"I might as well talk to a wall," grumbled Sam.

A woman with her hair in a bun and bright pink lipstick approached and touched Valerie's shoulder. "Hello, hello!"

Valerie jumped and then plastered on a phony smile. "Lydia, it's so wonderful that you could come." She steered the woman from our immediate area and chatted with her a few feet away.

"See?" Sam looked furious. "I knew they wouldn't listen. They just want me to stay in my closet and shut up."

"It ends tonight, Sam." Kara patted his back. "Mom is in denial at the moment, but pretty soon she won't be able to ignore the questions she'll be getting from the guests."

I downed my champagne, and when I looked across the room, I was horrified when I locked gazes with Sam's dad. He didn't recognize me instantly, but gradually I could see recognition set in. His jaw hardened and the older man began to push through the crowd in our direction. "Incoming," I muttered, feeling weak in the knees.

"Oh, God." Kara's eyes bugged. "Dad's headed our way."

"Shit." Sam's voice shook.

I straightened my back and sucked in a steadying breath. I had no idea what was about to happen, but from the furious look on Senator Foster's face, I knew it wasn't going to be pleasant.

Chapter Twenty-Two

Sam

"What the hell are you doing here?" he growled at Harper the second he was close enough to us.

My mom disengaged from Lydia and hurried over, looking around nervously. Through gritted teeth she muttered, "Lower your voice, dear."

Dad's face was beet red, and he was eying Harper like he was the devil. "What game are you playing at?"

Harper flushed. "I'm just your son's date. I have no agenda."

Dad's face was stony. "Right. If you say so."

"Sam invited me and I said yes. I'm not here for you."

"Bullshit. You're here to make trouble for me. Did McTarn put you up to this? How much is he paying you?"

Harper recoiled. "What? I don't even know McTarn."

I couldn't take the bullying stance my dad had toward Harper another second. I stepped forward. "He's here as my date. Harper's just trying to help me."

"Bullshit. This punk has been milking you for money ever since the accident." My dad sneered. "What's the matter? The money not coming in fast enough? I'll bet you think you've found the golden goose with my son, don't you, Harper?"

Harper stood his ground, even though my dad looked like he was ready to take a swing at him. "You want to make this about me? Go for it. But you should be talking to your son. He's the reason I'm here."

I wedged between the two of them. I wasn't sure what Harper would do if my dad threw the first punch.

Dad gave me an impatient glance. "What is he yammering about? I talk to you all the time."

"Yeah, but you don't actually listen to me," I grumbled. My heart pounded so hard as I held his scowl I felt ready to pass out.

He scrunched his face. "Says who?"

"Me. You don't hear me. You ignore every word that comes out of my mouth."

"Sam, don't get dramatic." Dad sighed.

"I'm not being dramatic. I'm telling you how I feel. I'm not happy with the status quo. I'm sick of being a secret."

"And I've told you a million times that it's only temporary," Dad snapped. "Why are you being such a pain in the ass about this lately?"

Kara chuffed. "Because he's miserable, Dad. Stop lying to him. This has gone on too long to say it's temporary."

"Yeah, Dad. You've been saying to be patient for years." I held my dad's angry gaze. "I... I can't do it anymore. I'm done."

Dad widened his eyes. "What does that mean?"

I swallowed hard. "It means I'm not hiding anymore. I'm gay. You have a gay son. You need to deal with that. Your voters need to deal with that."

"Shhh." Dad shifted his eyes around at the people in the room. "Keep your voice down."

I narrowed my eyes. "No."

"We can talk about this later." He glared at me. "Leave now and we can talk tomorrow."

"I'm not going anywhere." I shook my head. I could see we were drawing some funny looks from people, but I tried to ignore them.

"Dad, you need to stop this nonsense," Kara hissed at our father. "How can you think it's cool to make your son pretend he's straight for the cameras?"

"I'm helping the country," he snapped. "There are far more important things in this world than my son's sexuality."

"Not to me," I said, with my voice breaking. "How would you like to live a lie your whole life?" I guess I shouldn't have been shocked at how uncaring my dad seemed, but his callous dismissal of my feelings always still surprised me. Even after all these years.

Dad's gaze flickered. "It's not your whole life."

"It's been years. Do you think it's been easy to guard every thought and word?"

Mom leaned closer and whispered, "Honey, if you feel this strongly about it, then yes, it needs to be addressed. But there are some of your father's most important donors here tonight. This is too important of a fundraising event to pull this now."

Harper grabbed another glass of champagne as the waiter passed and downed it quickly. He looked like he was struggling to control his anger as he clamped his jaw and met my gaze. "This is your moment, Sam. Don't let them shut you up."

His protective tone gave me courage, and I turned to my parents. "Harper and I are in love. He's staying with me at the cottage, and that's not something we'll be able to hide. The truth is going to come out whether you like it or not. I would think we should control how and when the news breaks. Don't you, Dad?"

Dad looked like I'd slapped him. "You're in love? When the hell did that happen?"

"We've spent a lot of time together while Harper healed. We fell in love. People fall in love, Dad. Even gay people."

"Why would you bring him to your house?" Dad's face was flushed and sweaty.

"My apartment building burned down," Harper said quietly.

Dad turned his furious gaze on Harper. "I guess good fortune just follows you around, doesn't it?"

Harper curled his lip. "I didn't burn the damn place down."

"Are you actually trying to destroy me, Sam?" Dad faced me. "How could you do this to me?"

I flinched. "Not even close. I've always supported you. How about you do the same for me now?"

Dad widened his eyes. "You don't think I've supported you? You live rent-free, have a company car, and a high-paying job at my company. We give you everything you could ever ask for."

I grimaced. "I'm not talking about material things. I need your emotional support too."

Dad scowled at Harper. "I knew you were trouble the first day I met you in the hospital. Have you put this crazy idea in Sam's head? What's the matter, not getting the cash from my kid fast enough?"

"I don't want your son's money."

"Bullshit." He scowled. "I've seen your kind come and go. You're not fooling anyone."

Anger swept over Harper's features. "I love your son. I'm sorry if that's a problem for you."

The color drained from my dad's face. "You make me sick."

I moved closer to Harper. "I just want to be treated like everybody else. I want my boyfriend with me when I go to these functions. Why does my sexuality have anything to do with supporting you? We don't want to have sex in the middle of the room. Why is who I love such a god damned problem for you?"

"Sam, *language*," my mother hissed.

"Oh, good Lord. I've heard you and Dad use far worse language." Kara rolled her eyes.

"Sam, you're missing the point." My dad rubbed his hand over the back of his neck.

"In what way?"

He leaned toward me as he jabbed his finger against his own chest. "I'm not the problem. I don't care who you love or if you're gay." Surprisingly, he sounded sincere. "But some of the people who support me sure as hell have issues with homosexuality, and I have to tread carefully."

"And I've been very patient about that," I muttered. "But I can't do it anymore. I just can't hide for the rest of my life because you want me to."

"Besides," Kara said glancing around. "It's too late. From the looks we're getting, people already suspect that Sam and Harper are more than just friends. By tomorrow more and more people will know the truth." Kara gave our dad a wary look. "And yes, you'll lose some people. But you'll also gain some because I can guarantee there are plenty of conservative voters out there who also have gay children."

"Of course there are," Harper said.

Dad still looked angry, but he also looked almost resigned. It had to be obvious to him by now that I wasn't leaving or backing down. "If I lose this election because you pulled this stunt—" He shook his head.

"It's not a stunt. I'm your son, and I happen to be gay." I hardened my jaw.

Mom looked worried as she addressed me. "I don't know why you'd want to do this to yourself. You know, people are going to be mean. Twitter will probably have all sorts of horrible things to say about you tomorrow."

I scowled. "Do you honestly think I don't know that?"

Harper put his hand on the small of my back. "That's just how it is. You learn to shut it out over time."

"Dad, if you and Mom will just back off, the people in the room will take your lead. But if you continue berating Sam and turn this into a big family drama, McTarn and the newspapers will love that." Kara spoke firmly.

Mom's expression fell, and she nodded. "She's right, Larry. It's too late. The truth is coming out tonight whether we like it or not."

Dad glared at Harper. "I hope you're happy with the trouble you've caused my family."

"You've got me all wrong," Harper said, taking a step back from Dad's obvious anger.

"Yeah, right. I won't forget this." He turned and strode across the room with Mom following behind.

I was happy to see him go but still shaken by the level of anger he'd directed at Harper. He hadn't seemed to understand my side of things at all. I suspected he'd have been happy to keep me in the closet the rest of my life. And for some reason he wanted to blame Harper for my newfound independence. Obviously my desire to be with Harper had influenced me hugely, but this had needed to happen no matter what. It was time.

I blew out a shaky breath. "I'm still in once piece, right?"

Kara widened her eyes. "Holy fuck. That happened."

"Wow." Harper ran a trembling hand through his hair. "I was very close to wetting myself."

Kara and I laughed.

I gave Harper an apologetic look. "I thought you two were going to hit each other for a second there."

"Yeah. I was trying to figure out what to do if he punched me in the face." He rubbed his jaw. "I didn't think it would go over well if I got into a brawl with the guest of honor. His security detail would probably take me out back and beat the crap out of me."

"Probably." Kara smiled weakly at him. "Have you seen those guys? They're like Neanderthals in tuxes."

"I hope you two will forgive me if I don't vote for your dad in November?"

Kara smiled and surprised Harper with a kiss on his cheek. "Thank you for being here for my brother."

"Of course." He laughed awkwardly, giving the people around who stared curiously a wary glance. "There's a lot more of that sort of unpleasantness ahead of us. Hope you know that, Sam."

I ran a finger under my collar. "I do."

Kara sighed. "But at least you don't have to pretend anymore, and that's the most important part."

"Yeah." I nodded.

Kara eyed the people nearby. "Mom and Dad are so worried about what these people think, but I once caught two girls kissing in the bathroom at one of these functions. So many of dad's supporters wants to act like being gay is the ultimate sin, and yet you know some of the people here tonight have gay kids."

I shrugged. "That's what Dad doesn't seem to grasp. There are lots of people who vote for him who have gay kids. This could even help those voters connect with Dad more."

Harper grimaced. "While that may be true, realistically, he's going to get some pushback."

"Sure," I agreed. "There will be plenty of that too." Stress made my gut ache because I knew there was plenty of negativity coming my way also.

Someone at the front of the room tapped a microphone, and a few people got up and made some announcements. The first few hours after the run in with Dad, every muscle in my body felt tense. But as the evening progressed, I slowly began to feel like a weight had been lifted off me. I couldn't seem to stop smiling. Even Harper looked happier and more relaxed as the night wore on. I felt so lucky to have him in my life. Maybe we'd met under crazy circumstances, but he was everything to me now. As unpleasant as that scene had been with my dad, the fact that I would be allowed to live my life openly made me giddy. The thought of holding Harper's hand in public or kissing without fear of discovery seemed almost too good to be true.

For the rest of the night, other than furtive glances from people nearby, nobody did or said anything to me or Harper that made us uncomfortable. A few people I knew came up and chitchatted with me, but they didn't address the elephant in the room. I was emotionally exhausted by 11:00 p.m., and so we snuck out with Kara then.

As we waited for the valet to bring our cars around, Kara gave me a huge hug. She squeezed me so tight I could barely breathe. "I'm so proud of you, Sam."

I smiled. "I didn't really do much."

She bugged her eyes. "What? You did too. You stood up to Dad, and now you get to show the world who you really are."

Harper shot me an encouraging smile. "It was time."

"Definitely."

Kara moved toward her car as the valet drove up. "I mean, I'm not foolish enough to think this is the end. I know there is lots of work ahead. But at least now Mom and Dad can't keep you in the closet anymore." She blew us kisses and waved. "I love you and I'll call you tomorrow."

"Okay." I waved back.

By the time we made it home and crawled into bed, I could barely keep my eyes open. Harper held me in his arms, and the feeling of contentment that warmed me brought tears to my eyes. I couldn't remember ever being so happy.

"Thank you for tonight," I said quietly.

"Of course." He nuzzled my hair and sighed. "Hey, Sam?"

"Yeah?" My voice was husky with sleep.

"I'm proud of you too."

"Thanks, Harper." I pressed my lips to his chest, inhaling his clean scent. "Thanks for having my back."

"Always will."

"I know," I whispered. He tightened his hold on me, and I drifted off to sleep with a smile on my lips.

Chapter Twenty-Three

Harper

The next day our happy little world exploded.

Someone had done their homework and managed to get our cell numbers. Both of our phones rang incessantly, and we finally had to turn them off. It seemed that social media and the regular media were fascinated that super-duper conservative Senator Larry Foster had somehow kept his gay son under wraps.

I'd had little doubt there would be some fallout, but I hadn't expected it to be so aggressive. I could tell Sam hadn't expected that strong of a reaction either. I hated that I could sense him questioning his decision to do what he'd done. He withdrew from me a little and wouldn't really talk, which wasn't like him at all. The very fact that I was the one trying to get him to open up was ridiculous. I texted Kara, hoping she could get him to talk, but even she couldn't get him to articulate what exactly was making him clam up.

Before we'd realized just how bad it was, we'd run out to grab breakfast. Sam had hoped to enjoy our first public meal together where we wouldn't have to hide and worry about discovery. But when we got mobbed at our table by guys with cameras and reporters screaming questions at us, we figured out we needed to stick close to home for a while. We hadn't been so naive we didn't know there might be some interest, but neither of us had expected to be besieged by press. It was so bad, I wasn't sure how I was going to be able to go to work

Monday morning. That was kind of a problem for me and my plans of independence.

It was after that disastrous breakfast that Sam clammed up. I didn't push Sam to talk even though I wanted to. I forced myself to back off and let Saturday pass by, giving him his space. He was still cuddly in bed, which comforted me, but when we woke up Sunday morning he was back to not talking much. When I asked him for the hundredth time if he was okay, he said he was. I knew he was lying, but I wasn't sure how to handle his silence. Midafternoon, I went for a jog on the grounds of the Foster estate, needing to burn off some pent-up stress. When I got back to the cottage, I found Sam on the back patio with a beer. I sat near him without a word, and he glanced over.

"Feel better after your run?" he asked.

"Definitely." I lifted my T-shirt and dabbed my face. "I was feeling a little claustrophobic."

He fell silent and sipped his beer.

His reticence to talk was starting to get to me. Sam usually talked a lot. Not in an annoying brainless way, but he often had stories to share and he was usually very open with his emotions. But ever since we'd been inundated by the press, he'd been like a vault.

"The beer making you feel any better?" I asked hesitantly.

He avoided my gaze, but the muscles of his jaw clenched. "Who said I wasn't feeling fine already?"

I rolled my eyes. "Come on, Sam. It's obvious something is eating at you."

He didn't respond.

"You know you can talk to me about anything, right?"

"I know."

"So talk to me. Tell me what is bothering you." I leaned toward him, and he slid his wary gaze to mine. "You know I'm the last person in the world who'd usually want to have a heart-to-heart. But it's obvious something is going on with you."

He pressed his lips tight. "What is there to say?"

I chuffed. "Um… I would say a ton."

He hung his head. "I wish we'd never gone to that damn fund-raiser."

I scowled. "You can't mean that. You didn't do anything wrong. Your dad did when he hid your sexuality all those years ago. If he'd just been honest from the first, none of this would have had to happen."

"Or if I'd just kept my mouth shut."

"Right. If you would have just kept up the masquerade, you're right, everything could have gone on the way it was." I gave a hard laugh. "You did nothing wrong."

"Have you seen those vultures? They're ripping my dad to shreds in the media."

"It will blow over."

"When?"

"Give it a week. Something else will probably happen, and they'll lose interest. You know how this works better than me."

"Yeah. I know how this shit works. But I've never been the reason they came after my family before." He swallowed loudly. "It makes me sick to think I'm responsible for possibly losing my dad the election. All because I was being selfish."

"Selfish?" I squeaked. "You're the least selfish person I've ever known, Sam. You did nothing wrong. Don't start second-guessing yourself. You're free, Sam. You're finally free to be who you are. There's nothing wrong with you that needs to be hidden."

"Then why are the media outlets all acting like I said I was a fucking Martian or something?" He took a big swing of his ale, then wiped his mouth with the back of his hand. "I knew there would be interest. But I didn't expect them to act like my dad is the Antichrist because he hid that his son was gay. I thought there would be curiosity aimed toward me. I figured homophobes would come after me. I didn't think they'd be so horrible to my dad."

"I've seen a lot of support on Twitter for you and your dad. Are you even noticing that a lot of people are on your side?"

He shrugged and finished off his beer.

I stuffed down my frustration because it made me want to yell at him. Instead I sucked in a calming breath, and I spoke softly. "I don't understand why you're shutting me out, Sam. We're going through this together. Shouldn't we lean on each other?"

He set the beer bottle on the ground at his feet, and he slid his gaze to mine. "Can we lean on each other, Harper?"

I frowned. "We should be able to."

"That takes a lot of trust."

I twisted my face, trying to figure out what his point was. "Yeah. Obviously."

He studied my tense face for a few moments, and then he exhaled, dropping his chin to his chest. "I need to ask you something." He glanced up. "And I need you to be a hundred percent honest."

I frowned. "Okay."

His mouth was a straight line. "I've been struggling with something my dad told me yesterday morning."

"About me?"

He nodded, and an uneasy feeling came over me.

"Great. What did my biggest fan have to say about me?"

He licked his lips and hesitated.

"Shit. Is it that bad?"

He moved, and his foot knocked over the empty beer bottle. The jarring sound made me jump, and he grabbed the bottle and said, "I'm not sure how to even ask what I need to."

My heart pounded as I studied his pinched face. "Just get to the point, will you?"

He licked his lips. "My dad said…. he said you tried to extort money from him."

My gut clenched. "What?"

A hint of suspicion hovered in the green depths of his eyes. "He said you called him the night of the fundraiser, before it started, and said you would talk me out of coming out publicly if he'd pay you twenty thousand dollars."

The blood drained from my face, and I felt sick to my stomach as I stared at him. It was as clear as day on his face that he didn't think his dad would lie about something like that. That meant that he actually believed I was capable of something as despicable as extortion. Shock radiated through me as I struggled to control my confusing emotions. I couldn't wrap my brain around the fact that Sam, who I trusted more than anyone in the world, might believe something that horrible about me.

You can trust me, Harper. I have your back.

I wanted to stand and tell him to fuck off. But my legs were shaking, and I was afraid I'd fall. "You believed him?" My voice was like sandpaper.

His face was flushed, and he didn't answer me.

My heart felt cracked in two as I gazed on the face I'd grown to love. I barely recognized him in that moment as he stared at me like I was his enemy. I tried twice to speak, but I couldn't get the words out. Finally I managed to growl, "You honest to God think I would do that to you?"

His gaze faltered. "I... I don't know what to believe. He's my father."

"And therefore he couldn't lie?"

He winced. "Well... he's many things... but usually he's at least honest."

"And I'm not?"

"I didn't say that."

"You just asked me if I'm an extortionist." I gave a jagged laugh. "Have you forgotten I've spent our entire relationship telling you I didn't want your money?"

"I know." He wrinkled his brow.

"But you still believe I would do that?" I asked hoarsely.

His face was red, and he looked ashamed. He dropped his gaze. "I told you I don't know what to believe."

"If I'd actually done that... asked him for money... would he have looked so shocked last night when you showed up to come out?" I gave him a frigid stare. "He was obviously taken off guard last night. How could he be if I'd called him and offered that?"

He wrinkled his brow. "That's probably true."

"Probably?" I snapped.

"Harper..." His voice trailed off.

I was so hurt I could barely breathe. I managed to stand, and I walked into the house, just so I get away from him. I was so wounded and angry I didn't trust what might come out of my mouth. I ended up in the kitchen and leaned both hands on the counter, and stared out the window at the cheerful sunny day that seemed to mock me.

Sam followed me into the house, and he stood in the doorway of the kitchen.

I turned my head and gave him an angry glare. "What do you want?"

"I had to ask." He sounded defensive.

My eyes stung. "No you didn't."

"I didn't say I believed him."

"Yeah, you did. Just by asking me that question."

He moved closer to touch my arm, and I jerked away. "Don't you fucking touch me." I backed away from him, hurt and furious.

"Harper—"

"I don't want to talk to you," I yelled, the muscles of my face quivering with anger.

"He's my dad." His voice trembled. "Am I supposed to not believe my own family?"

"He's *lying*," I growled, clenching my hands into fists. "He's never wanted you with me. It didn't occur to you he might try and make up shit about me to turn you against me?"

"Harper… I didn't know what to think. He's my dad."

I curled my lip. "How the hell could you fall for his stupid lie?"

"He was very convincing."

"What happened to having each other's backs?" I croaked.

His face paled and he looked nauseated. "I do have your back—"

I pointed my finger at him. "Don't you fucking *dare* say that. You have no right to say that to me." My voice shook.

His lower lip trembled, and he stepped closer. "I believe you. I believe you, Harper."

"Better late than never," I said coldly.

"Shit, Harper," he groaned. "He was so convincing, and I was distraught thinking I'd fucked up his career. He got me at my weakest. I'm sorry. I'm sorry I even believed him for a second."

"It doesn't matter." I stared at him blankly, feeling numb. Two days ago I'd actually believed that I had a happy future in front of me. I'd bought his bullshit about loving me and having my back. Had it all been a pack of fucking lies? God, had he laughed at me at night? Had this all been some twisted game to him? I felt sick and I needed to get away from him.

"Harper…" He took a step toward me.

I pushed past him and headed toward the front door.

"Where are you going?" he called after me, sounding panicked.

I stopped in the middle of the living room, feeling confused. I knew there were reporters at the front gates. I couldn't just walk out there and ask for a lift into town.

"Harper, talk to me." He spoke from behind me.

I faced him. "There's nothing to say."

"That's crazy. There's almost too much to say."

I swallowed against the lump in my throat. "For a day and a half you've harbored the thought that I'm the kind of person who'd extort money from your family. We've slept in the same bed, and all the while you've actually believed I'd take money and rob you of your right to come out. You can't talk through that, Sam."

He grimaced. "Look, I'll admit I shouldn't have even entertained my dad's story for one second. But I did because he's my dad. I see now I was wrong to trust him. He's obviously not the man I thought he was. But now we just have to move past this."

I scoffed. "There's no moving past."

"Why?" He hardened his jaw. "I'm not allowed to fuck up?"

"I guess not."

He scowled. "I didn't think my dad would lie to me about something like that. I really didn't. But I can see from your reaction that he did. He must have. Now I know better."

"And it only cost you our relationship."

He winced. "That's not fair. Jesus, Harper. People screw up sometimes."

"Now you know why I avoid people whenever possible."

"Cuz that's healthy." He walked toward me. "You need to cut me some slack. We've known each other a little over a month. Forgive me for entertaining the idea that my dad, a man I've known my whole life, wouldn't lie to me."

"Really? Even though he's the same man who urged you to lie about *yourself* to further his political career?"

He hung his head. "Yeah, but… but he's still my father."

"We're going in circles. I can't stay here."

"You go out there and the vultures will pounce." He wrinkled his forehead.

"I'll figure it out." I started toward the guest bedroom.

"Harper. Where are you going?"

"I need to think." I slipped into the bedroom and locked the door behind me.

He knocked on the door. "Harper, this is ridiculous. Talk to me."

"Not now," I muttered. I sat on the bed and stared at the door. I heard his exasperated sigh through the wood, and then the floor creaked as he walked away.

I needed to figure out a way to get into town and away from Sam. It hurt too much to be near him. My pain was way too raw to just pretend everything was fine. I needed distance between us right now. I was tempted to wait until dark and try and walk back to the city. But Sam's family lived a ways outside of town, and it would be a long walk.

I tried to think of anybody I knew who might be able to give me a ride and a couch to sleep on for a few days. Unfortunately, most of the people I knew might have had couches, but they didn't have cars. The only person I could think of who would have both was my ex, Peter. But I was reticent to reach out and ask him for a favor. We'd parted on rather rocky terms, and we hadn't exactly kept in touch either. But a hotel was out of the question since my new credit cards and license hadn't arrived in the mail yet, and I had hardly any cash on me.

While I cringed at the thought of calling Peter, I felt like I didn't have any other option, and my desire to get away from Sam was stronger than my embarrassment. I sucked in a shaky breath and made myself text Peter. He didn't answer right away, and so I continued to sit on my bed, staring into space as the sun went down. My heart ached with Sam's betrayal, even as a part of me wanted to go to him and let him comfort me. But I couldn't let go of the fact that he'd allowed his dad to poison his mind against me. I couldn't shake the memory of the look in his eyes when he'd asked me those hurtful questions.

Sam knocked on my door a few times trying to get me to talk, but I ignored him. Around 10:00 p.m. Peter finally responded. He was understandably shocked to hear from me, but, thankfully, Peter had always been a kind soul and he agreed to pick me up. I knew Sam would try to stop me if he knew I planned on running. So I watched the light under my door, waiting until Sam went to bed. When the house went dark, I knew Sam had gone to bed.

I waited a half hour, and then I grabbed my small duffle bag and opened my door slowly, praying it didn't creak. I crept silently across the wooden floor and slipped silently out of the little cottage. I hurried down the long driveway to a small side gate that wasn't near the main entrance. Peter's red car waited a few feet away, and I trotted to his vehicle.

When I slipped into his car, he gave me a funny look and shook his head. "I can't believe you called me to help you escape your current boy toy." His voice was gruff as he started his car.

I stared forlornly out the windshield. "I had literally no one else to call."

"You always were great for my ego, Harper." He sighed and pulled out onto the deserted road to help me make my getaway.

Chapter Twenty-Four

Sam

When I discovered Harper was missing the next morning, I felt like puking. I had no idea where could he have gone, and that terrified me. He no longer had his apartment, and I knew he had no money or credit cards, so where the hell would he have run to? I was so worried I called Kara and told her everything that had happened the night before. She came over immediately to give me moral support, just like I'd hoped she would.

Kara came out of the kitchen carrying a steaming mug. "Drink this." She handed me the cup. "It's hot, so don't burn your mouth."

I took it from her but then just stared at the tea blankly. "God, Kara. I fucked up so bad."

"I know, honey."

I set the cup down on the coffee table because my hands were shaking so badly. "I'm gonna murder Dad when I see him. I can't believe he lied to me. I just can't believe he'd do that. What the hell was he thinking?"

"He wasn't thinking. He was pissed at Harper, and he just wanted to hurt him."

I closed my eyes, feeling sick when the memory of Harper's wounded expression came to me. "Oh, God. He was so hurt."

She sat next to me and put her hand over mine. "He'll forgive you. He loves you."

"You didn't see his face." I swallowed against the lump in my throat. "He looked like he hated me."

"That was a shocking accusation for him, I'm sure." She squeezed my chilled fingers. "But hopefully if you can find him, you can talk this out."

"The night of the charity thing, I stupidly thought everything would get better. I really thought I would get to be happy finally." I leaned back against the couch feeling sick. "I should have known Dad wouldn't want to let that happen."

She winced. "Dad loves you. He wants you happy. I think"

"Yeah, I can tell." I covered my face. "God, I don't know what to do. Harper has no money, and he's out there all alone."

"We'll find him." She bit her lip, a deep line between her brows. "I'm sure of it. Besides, Harper is not a delicate flower. He knows how to survive."

"I know. But he doesn't have any money. Where is he going to sleep and how will he eat?"

"We'll figure out where he is. Don't worry."

"Why did I listen to Dad even for one second?" I asked hoarsely. "Why?"

"Because he's your dad." She scowled. "You should be able to trust him. Who the heck expects their dad to make up lies?"

"I should have. Like Harper said, Dad has encouraged me to lie about myself my whole life." I felt like crying when I thought about Harper running from me. I loved him more than anything, and he'd thought he had to flee my house in the night like I was his worst enemy.

There was a knock on my front door, and Kara and I looked at each other.

"Maybe it's Harper," she said softly.

"Please, God." I leapt to my feet and ran to the entrance. I prayed it was Harper, but when I flung the door open, I found my dad standing there looking uneasy. My face fell and I glared at him. "What do you want?"

He held out his hands in a placating gesture. "Now son, I know you're upset. But I only did what I did to get that shyster away from you before he could do any more damage."

I started to slam the door shut, but he blocked me.

"Go away!" I growled. "I can't stand the sight of you."

"Now, Sam—"

"No. I don't want to hear it." I stepped back from the door. "I don't need protection from Harper. I need protection from you. Harper has never done anything to hurt me. Ever."

Dad stepped into my house, and he met Kara's frosty stare. "Kara," he said softly. "I didn't know you were here."

"You really stepped in it this time, Dad." She scowled.

"What is wrong with you two?" Dad shook his head. "Harper isn't anyone we need in our family. He's nowhere near worthy of you, Sam."

I clenched my fists. "Say one more word against him and I'm going to punch you."

Dad widened his eyes. "Sam. Why are you being like this?"

"Why? Because I love Harper. You chased him away, and I have no idea where he went. He has no money and no place to go. He could be hurt and in a ditch somewhere. I hate the sight of you. Go away."

"Oh, come on, he must have some money." He looked skeptical. "You're telling me he's been hanging out with you, but he has no money?"

I leaned toward him angrily. "He hates taking my money. See, that's what you just don't get about him. He's not trying to steal from me. He's always telling me to stop spending my money on him. You've got him all wrong."

He looked puzzled. "Well… that's odd."

"Not really." Kara scrunched her face up in a frown. "He's been telling you since day one he didn't want our money."

"Well…. of course he would *say* that."

I exhaled, feeling demoralized. I sat back down on the couch, wanting to punch something. "All he ever took from me was living expenses and some money so his boss wouldn't give his job away. He didn't want gifts or new cars. He just wanted me." My voice broke. "And now you've gone and screwed that up for me too."

Dad looked completely confused as he crossed his arms and studied me. "Let me get this straight… he didn't ask you for extra cash or gifts?"

"No," I grumbled. "He just wanted to get well so he could go back to work. He wanted to be independent."

Rubbing the back of his neck, Dad perched on the arm of a chair. "That makes no sense. Then why was he with you, son?"

Kara chuffed. "Did you seriously just ask that?"

I squinted at him. "Yeah. What the heck kind of a question is that?"

He grimaced. "I just mean… the kind of person he is… it makes no sense that he wouldn't want to get stuff from a rich kid like you."

"You don't know the first thing about what kind of person he is," I snapped.

"Yeah, Dad. He's a good person. If you'd bothered to get to know him instead of treating him like dirt the second you met him, you might have known that about him." Kara sat beside me, and she put her arm around me. "You need to make this right. I don't know how you're going to do that, but you need to fix this, Dad."

Pulling his salt-and-pepper brows tight, he looked muddled. "What is going on with you people? Even your mother is mad at me. Don't you see I did it to protect the family?"

"Liar," I hissed. "You didn't like that I was finally standing up for myself. Well, I deserve to be happy like anybody else. Why shouldn't I stand up?"

"You think I don't want you happy?" Dad looked shocked.

"So long as I stay quietly in the closet, maybe." I huffed.

Dad studied me. "You actually love him?" He looked like he didn't understand how that could possibly be true. "You're sure it's not just some physical thing?"

Kara laughed gruffly. "Yes, Dad, gay people love each other. It's not all about sex."

"I know that," Dad muttered. "But you didn't know each other very long. How can you be in love?"

"We spent every day together for over a month under very intense circumstances. We got close." My voice was hard. "Whether you like it or not, we love each other. Or at least he loved me until you ruined it. Or I ruined it because I was so stupid I trusted you enough to ask him if he was an *extortionist*." I groaned again. "God, he must hate me now."

"I can't believe he didn't ask you for money," Dad mumbled. "I thought for sure he'd have shaken you down for cash."

"Not once."

He blinked at me, looking uneasy. "Wow. That's surprising."

"Not if you knew Harper it isn't."

He rubbed his chin, frowning. "I suppose it's possible I might have… misjudged him." He looked like he couldn't believe the words coming from his own mouth.

I gave him an angry look. "Not maybe. You did. You completely jumped to conclusions from the first second you met him. Actually, even before you met him. You walked into that hospital room assuming all kinds of things about Harper that were wrong. He was the best thing that ever happened to me. He helped me find myself. I love him, and I hate you for ruining things between us." I stood and stalked from the room, wincing inwardly at Dad's gasp.

I closed the door of my bedroom and leaned against it. I never lost my temper with Dad. I hadn't yelled at him since I was eight and we'd had some stupid argument over me playing in the sprinklers or something. I'd always held my tongue when he got me mad and trusted that Dad knew best. But he'd failed me horribly this time. I'd trusted him to always tell me the truth, and he'd utterly and completely fucked me over.

And then *I'd* failed Harper. I'd betrayed him just as he'd finally begun to trust me. I knew enough about Harper to know that trusting me had gone against every instinct he'd had. I'd seen his fear of being hurt at times. I'd felt his hesitation. But then he'd always got control of his doubts and kept moving forward with me. Trusting me. Believing in me. Giving more of himself to me every single day.

And his reward was me accusing him of being the kind of scumbag who'd extort my family.

S.C. Wynne

Chapter Twenty-Five

Harper

On the drive to his place, Peter didn't grill me for information about what had happened between Sam and me. After thanking him for picking me up, he allowed me to sit in embarrassed silence. When we reached his home, I was struck by how cozy and welcoming it was. It didn't give off the bachelor vibe like it had in the past. We'd done a lot of clubbing when we were together, but now Peter seemed more settled and less like he was on the prowl.

I guess he could see how emotionally exhausted I was because he led me straight to the guest room. "Do you need a toothbrush or any essentials?" he asked.

I held up my bag. "I've got that covered."

"Okay." He nodded and moved to the door. "We can talk in the morning."

"Sounds good." I gave a weak smile.

He shook his head. "This is super weird."

"Yeah." I frowned. "Thanks again."

He shrugged and left the room, closing the door behind him.

I was thankful the guest room had a private bathroom. I stripped down to boxers and brushed my teeth. Then I crawled under the sheets and curled into a ball. I still felt numb about what had happened. I think it was self-protection because if I'd allowed myself to feel all the pain and anger I was stuffing down, I'd have wanted to punch a wall.

My argument with Sam kept swirling around and around in my head. I tried to think if there was any way I could find it in myself to forgive him. But I couldn't forget the distrustful look he'd given me when he'd asked his question. His lack of trust had hurt so deep, I didn't see how I could just let my feelings go. Eventually my lids became heavy, and I fell asleep.

When I woke, it took me a second to remember where I was. I sat up, taking in the small yellow room and the sheers moving in the breeze from the open window. But then all the depressing memories of my fight with Sam came seeping back. I groaned and threw back the covers so I could sit on the edge of the bed.

My depression made it hard to want to get up and dress, but I forced myself to brush my teeth and shower. Then I dressed and left the room, heading straight to the kitchen where I smelled fresh coffee.

Peter sat at the kitchen table with his feet up on a chair and a newspaper in front of his face. When he heard me enter the kitchen, he lowered the paper and dropped his feet to the ground. "Good morning."

"Morning." I hesitated and gestured toward the coffee maker. "Do you mind if I have some coffee?"

"Help yourself." He folded his paper and set it on the table.

"Thanks."

"You're lucky I didn't go out dancing last night. I wouldn't have wanted you here." He smirked and lifted his cup to his lips.

"I really appreciate you doing this." I poured myself some coffee and sat across from him at the table. "I know we didn't exactly split on great terms."

"We weren't meant to be." He shrugged. "And it's been long enough now my feelings aren't hurt anymore."

"You always were a better person than me."

He chuffed. "Are you saying if I'd called you to come save me from my current boyfriend, you wouldn't have done it?"

"I like to think I would."

"I guess the difference is, I wouldn't have asked." He tapped his finger on the side of his china cup. "So why the dramatic exit?"

"It's a long story."

"Hey, I've got all day." He studied me. "Did you have a big fight with your boyfriend or something?"

I sighed. "It wasn't quite that simple."

He didn't respond; he just watched me expectantly.

I rubbed my eyes tiredly. "I fucked up and fell in love."

"Really?" He lifted one smooth brow. "Wow."

"Yeah." I winced. "And surprise, surprise, the guy let me down."

He twisted his lips. "Let me guess… he wasn't perfect?"

"What does that mean?"

"Never mind."

I scowled. "No. You can't just throw that out there and not follow up."

He grimaced. "You really want to get into this?"

"Well, yeah. You're implying that I'm the problem in this situation and you don't even know what happened."

"Maybe I should have kept my mouth shut. It's just I know how you are."

"There you go again." I set my coffee cup down. "Stop alluding to things and say what you want to say."

He shrugged. "Let's just say you're not very forgiving of people's flaws. When people let you down, you don't forgive easily."

"That's kind of a blanket statement."

"I'm just going by your track record."

"You think I just bolt without trying to work stuff out?"

"Yep. You just disappear." He made a *poof* gesture with his hands. "Like a phantom in the night."

I flushed. "Bullshit."

He rolled his eyes. "It's your MO, dude."

"Hold on." I leaned toward him. "You dumped me."

He grinned. "True. But you'd have probably started ghosting me anyways. You told me enough about your past relationships that I could see the writing on the wall. You'd have dumped me soon."

"You don't know that."

"Come on, Harper. We were going nowhere. You wouldn't let me in at all. I got tired of banging my head against a wall with you. So I left first. I have pride, you know?" He winced. "Well, I mean other than coming the second you called me last night. *Fuck.*" He scowled.

I couldn't help but laugh at his muddled expression. "You were doing a friend a favor."

"Aww, we're friends now?"

"Shit. You're not cutting me any slack, are you?" I shook my head and got up to add more cream to my coffee.

He studied me in silence for a moment, then asked, "So how did this guy let you down?"

"It's complicated."

"Things usually are with you, Harper."

"Yeah, but this really wasn't my fault." I sat back down with a grunt.

"What happened?"

I sighed. "The nuts and bolts of it are the guy I fell in love with thinks I'm a scumbag who would extort his dad for money."

"Ouch." He widened his eyes. "Why would he think that?"

I narrowed my eyes. "You really want to hear all this?"

"Yes." He laughed. "I've got nothing better to do."

"Do you know Senator Larry Foster?"

He looked confused. "Um, I've heard of him. I've never voted for him. Why? What does he have to do with this?"

I clenched my jaw. "The guy I'm in love with... Sam... Larry Foster is his dad."

Peter held up his hand. "Whoa. What the hell? How did you get involved with anybody like that?"

I laughed gruffly. "Yeah, I know. We aren't exactly a typical couple."

"I'll say. How'd you meet him?"

I winced. "Sam hit me with his car while I was on my bike. Then he insisted on taking care of me." I exhaled, trying to push away the painful memories.

"Seriously?" He squinted at me like he suspected maybe I was kidding. "Are you pulling my leg?"

"Nope. Sam stayed with me, and he basically nursed me back to health and paid for everything the insurance didn't cover." I swallowed hard. "And somewhere along the line we fell in love."

"I'm speechless." He laughed.

"Sam's a special guy," I said softly.

"So if he's such a saint, why did he suddenly accuse you of being a crook?"

"His dad hates me. Thinks I'm just using Sam to get money from the family." I glanced up. "But I'm not. I really fell for Sam."

"Okay." Peter looked confused. "You still haven't told me why Sam thinks you could be an extortionist."

"His dad lied to him and said I tried to get money to stop Sam from coming out publicly." I grimaced. "It's complicated. Sam's dad has pressured Sam to hide that he's gay most of his life. But Sam wanted to live openly and be in a relationship with me. He even stood up to his dad so that we could be together. But I guess his dad wasn't having it," I said bitterly.

He leaned back in his chair. "Holy fuck. That's like a soap opera."

"Yeah." I shrugged. "So his dad made up that lie about me, and Sam believed him. He actually had the nerve to ask me if what his dad said was true."

Peter nodded. "Yeah, that would hurt. But it's not like he took the word of a stranger. It was his dad who told him that story. Of course he'd probably entertain the thought for a minute. I mean, why would he think his dad would lie to him?"

I scowled. "Are you serious? You see nothing wrong with him doubting me? He's supposed to love me."

"Yeah, but according to what you've said, he knew you a little over a month. He's known his dad his whole life."

"Still—"

"No, Harper, a lot of people would probably entertain the idea for a split second. At least he came to you and asked you for the truth. It's not like he just dumped you. He came to you."

I tensed my jaw. "You don't get it."

He scoffed. "No, you don't get it because you have no relationship with your dad. Most people find it hard to believe their family would lie to them."

I held his gaze stubbornly. "If he loved me, he would have known I'm not capable of that."

He leaned toward me and snapped, "People aren't perfect, Harper. You need to get that through your stubborn head, or you'll never be happy."

I was surprised at his impatient tone. He was usually easygoing. "Shit, Peter. Don't you understand he *hurt* me when he accused me like that?"

His expression softened. "You're like a little kid, Harper. You think the world shouldn't ever let you down. Well, news flash: people let you down sometimes, but it isn't because they don't care or want to do better. It's because we're all just doing our best."

"I know people aren't perfect. But he betrayed my trust."

"He was caught between two people he loves. He came to you, Harper. He could easily have just shut you out and believed his dad. But he didn't. He asked you to tell him that he was wrong. But you got so hurt you ran."

"What was I supposed to do?"

"Stay and talk it out. He was probably horrified he hurt you. I gotta say I feel for the guy. He was in a terrible position."

"He might hurt me again if I go back," I said quietly.

"Yeah, he probably will. And you'll hurt him too because love is messy and emotional. It doesn't come with instructions, so we all just fumble along hoping it works."

I studied him. "You're telling me if someone you loved accused you of extortion you'd just forgive them because people aren't perfect?"

"Well…" He grimaced. "I'd be hurt too. We'd probably have a huge fucking row, and then, if he seemed truly sincere, I'd forgive him. Because why would I want to lose someone I love?"

I opened my mouth to respond, but I couldn't think of what to say.

"Do you still love him?"

I nodded slowly. "Of course. I'm wounded, but I can't just magically stop loving him."

"That's good at least."

I slumped in my chair. "Is it?"

"Yes. How did you leave it with him? I mean, before you ran."

I sighed. "He said he believed me. But I was too upset, and I didn't want to talk to him. Then I texted you."

"Aww, Harper. You should have stayed and worked through this. You said he stood up to his dad for you. That's huge. He was probably freaked-out and second-guessing his decision to defy his dad. His dad probably knew he was weak and knew that was a good time to try something."

I scowled. "That's despicable."

"The guy's a politician. He's used to smear tactics and shit."

I covered my face and groaned, and then I let my hands fall limply to my lap. "Can you even picture me a part of a political family? That's so not me."

"Sam isn't the politician. He's just involved by default." He tipped his cup and drained his coffee.

Leaning back in my chair, I studied his face. "So you think I overreacted?"

"I think you had every right to be hurt." He narrowed his gaze. "But the bottom line is do you want to be with Sam, or do you want to be hurt forever?"

Thoughts of Sam filled my mind. "I just wish this had never happened."

"But it did."

I exhaled and nodded.

The doorbell rang, and he looked at me. "Are you expecting someone?"

I frowned. "No one knows I'm here."

He stood and moved to the front door. I heard him speaking to someone, and then he returned with a funny look on his face. "Um… you have a visitor."

When Senator Foster walked in the kitchen, my stomach dropped like a brick off a high-rise. I stayed where I was, frozen with shock. He approached and his face was stiff. "We need to talk."

I found my voice. "What about?"

"Sam."

I scowled. "How the hell did you find me?"

He sighed tiredly. "I have my ways."

"I'll bet," I muttered.

"Like I said, we need to talk."

I hardened my jaw. "What is there to say?"

He glanced toward Peter. "Do you think we could have some privacy?"

Peter arched his brows. "Uh… sure… even though this is my house, I'll go in my bedroom and let you two chat." He gave me an apologetic look as he left the room.

Mr. Foster pulled out a chair and sat. Then he clasped his hands on the table and leaned toward me. "Why did you just run off without a word? You've upset Sam."

I bugged my eyes. "*I've* upset Sam? Oh, that's rich coming from you."

He twisted his lips, and his eyes dark were hard to read. "I've been in politics a long time." He cleared his throat. "It's possible it has made me somewhat... jaded."

I held my tongue because the only comments that came to me weren't nice.

Rubbing his big hand over the back of his neck, he grimaced. "I can put up with the bullshit from the media, but when my wife and my kids won't speak to me, that's not something I'm willing to have continue."

"You ruined everything with me and Sam. I'm not sure what the hell you want from me."

He winced. "I was mad." He shifted uneasily. "Regardless of what you must think, I love my son."

"Great. I'm happy for you."

"Harper, I'm not a bad man." He sighed. "I'm a little self-centered, and I made the mistake of looking at you as if you were my enemy."

"I wasn't." I narrowed my eyes. "But I'll probably give a big donation to your opponent given the chance."

"I'm not here as a politician. I'm here as a father." His mouth drooped. "I've never seen Sam this upset. It's unsettling to say the least. It's like he hates me."

"You lied about me to Sam. I'm not sure why you expect sympathy."

He held his hands out. "Look, I don't know you. I'm a suspicious guy, and in my world everybody has ulterior motives. I see now that I might have misjudged you. If I'm honest with myself, you've never done or said anything inappropriate."

"And yet you hate me."

"No. I don't hate you. I don't know you well enough to hate you. But I saw you as problem to be dealt with, not as a person."

"Well, it worked."

He held my gaze unblinkingly. "I misjudged you. You affected Sam profoundly in a way that made him different, and that upset me."

"Different how?"

His cheeks had a hint of pink. "Well… to be perfectly frank, you made him less malleable. He fought me more and stood up to me more. That pissed me off."

I huffed. "Wow."

He shrugged. "I'm being honest."

I squinted at him suspiciously. "I'm not sure what you need from me. I'm not going to help you get Sam back in line."

He frowned. "No. I know that." He sighed and leaned toward me. "You and I will most probably never like each other. But I love my son, and he loves you. So while I think you're kind of a punk, that's not the point."

"I'm a punk?"

"You're very opinionated."

"If this is you asking for a favor, you suck at it."

He gave a grudging smile. "That's because I'm not used to groveling."

"It shows."

He straightened and pressed his palms to the tabletop. "I'm here to bring you back."

I gave a confused laugh. "Excuse me?"

"To Sam. I'm here to bring you back to Sam."

I scowled. "I'm not a runaway puppy."

He smirked. "I know. If you were, I'd just buy Sam a nicer puppy and be done with it."

"There you go charming me again." I wasn't sure what to make of Mr. Foster's visit. It was obvious he wanted to fix his relationship with his son. But I wasn't sure I was ready to see or forgive Sam. Sam had said I could trust him and that he'd always have my back. But he hadn't. He'd believed his dad when he said those despicable lies about me. Sure, when he saw how upset I was he'd backpedaled, but I wasn't sure I'd ever be able to forget the look on his face when he'd thought I was capable of trading his coming out for money.

Maybe Senator Foster could see my emotions on my face because he said, "Don't hate my son for trusting his dad. I misused his belief in me to further my agenda. But for the record, he fought me and denied you would ever do anything like that. You think he just swallowed my lie without question. But the truth is he argued with me on the phone for over an hour, defending you."

My chest squeezed when he told me that. I had assumed Sam had just believed his father without question. "Really?"

"Oh, yes." He scowled. "That pissed me off all over again."

I watched him, uncertain of what to do.

"But then he asked you if it was true, and the shit hit the fan between you two. Now Kara is furious with me, and even his mother chewed me out. My wife is usually always on my side." He threw his hands up. "Sam won't even look at me."

I got some pleasure hearing how miserable Mr. Foster was. "I'm not a scam artist. Sam hit me with his car, and that's the truth."

He nodded. "I know. I believe you. Sam wouldn't love you if you didn't have redeeming qualities. But there really are a lot of shysters around."

"Well, I'm not one of them."

"Fine. Fine."

I hardened my jaw. "How can I be sure you won't pull something like this again? You don't really want Sam with me. You could easily just keep trying to undermine us."

He winced. "Jesus. Are you serious? My family would skin me alive." He sighed. "Sam loves you. Even I can see he's happier these days. Part of me is annoyed with him for standing up to me, and part of me is proud."

I studied him in silence. He actually seemed sincere. It was rather surreal that Sam's asshole dad was sitting at Peter's kitchen table begging my forgiveness. "So you're not mad at Sam for coming out and causing such a stir?"

"I wish he'd have done it differently. But to be honest this emotional hoopla has given me a bump in the polls. McTarn tried to spin it as a tragedy that I had a gay son, and it seems to have backfired on him a little." He snorted. "Who knew?"

"You're saying your voters don't care?"

"Oh, well, not exactly. There are plenty of people who are being disgusting and hateful toward Sam too."

"Obviously. This is America, not Wonderland."

His slick expression slipped, and I got a glimpse of the real man beneath, the concerned father. "I don't apologize often but I wholeheartedly apologize for what I did. Please come back with me. My son hates me right now, and Sam doesn't hate anybody." His mouth drooped.

I frowned. "Sam didn't trust me, and that still stings."

"He loves you. He's human. Please just talk to him."

I didn't want to get my hopes up and believe that Sam and I could work this out. But after talking with Mr. Foster, I felt a little less angry. I figured I could talk to Sam and go from there. "Okay. I'll talk to Sam."

Mr. Foster slumped with relief. "Thank you, Harper. You won't regret this decision."

I hoped he was right.

S.C. Wynne

Chapter Twenty-Six

Harper

I hunkered down in the back seat next to Mr. Foster as we drove through the front gates of his home. Bulbs flashed like little explosions as we rolled past, and I stared straight ahead nervously. Once we were safely behind the walls of his property, I relaxed a little. His chauffeur parked, and I got out of the car.

"He doesn't know you're coming." Mr. Foster met my eyes over the roof of the limo. "Please don't be mean to him."

I frowned. "That wasn't my plan."

"Just keep in mind that I tricked him and used his trust in me to my advantage."

I nodded and headed off down the drive toward the cottage. The gravel crunched under my shoes, and my heart pounded as I neared the house. I sucked in a steadying breath and walked up to the front door. I knocked, feeling like I was about to hyperventilate.

Sam opened the door, his face a stony mask. When it sank in that it was me on the doorstep, his expression changed suddenly. He widened his eyes and stepped back. "Harper? You're back?"

"I… I thought we should talk."

"Yes. Come in." He waved for me to enter the cottage. "God, where were you? I was so worried." He started to reach out to touch me, but he pulled his hand back, looking uncertain.

"It doesn't really matter where I was." I cleared my throat. "Your dad came and got me. He brought me here so we could talk."

He bugged his eyes. "My dad did that?" He appeared as if I'd told him I could travel to the moon without a ship. "No way."

"He did."

"My dad?"

"Yes."

"I'm shocked." He crossed his arms, looking confused. "Really shocked."

"He even apologized." I chuffed.

"My dad? Senator Larry Foster hunted you down and apologized?" He scrunched his face.

"I was as surprised as you."

"Wow." He inched closer, his eyes bright. "Well, I told him I never wanted to speak to him again. Maybe it got through."

"I think it did." I wanted to touch him, but I was still confused about my feelings. It still upset me that he could so easily have believed the worst of me.

"Well, I'm just glad you're back. I was worried about you." His voice wobbled. "I know I fucked up. I need you to know that first off."

I hardened my jaw. "I can't believe you thought even for a second I'd try and stop you from coming out for any reason, let alone money. I wanted you to come out."

His face crumpled. "I was so rattled after that fund-raiser. I felt like I'd probably ruined my dad's political career, and I got inside my head too much. I'm so sorry, Harper. I know in my soul you'd never do anything like that. But I wasn't thinking straight. I was just scared, and my dad was so convincing. I argued with him. I called him a liar and told him I didn't believe him. But then a tiny doubt crept in."

"Why?" I shook my head. "Why would you doubt me at all?"

"I was so guilty about my dad. I wasn't myself at all. Harper… shit. I'm so sorry. I know I screwed up. I feel like complete shit. I love you. I know you'd never do anything like that to me. I swear I do know that. It was a paranoid moment, and I fucked up."

I shook my head. "I don't know what to do, Sam. You really hurt me."

"I know." He squeezed his eyes closed for a second. "Just give me another chance. Please. I swear I'll have your back." He hung his head. "I've gone over what happened a million times in my head. Why did I even entertain the thought of you doing something that despicable?" He scowled. "I think I've just always been afraid that you don't really want to be with a guy like me."

I scowled. "Why?"

He shrugged. "I'm the kind of guy you'd probably have mocked with your buddies in the past—the spoiled rich kid who's had everything handed to him on a silver platter."

Guilt nudged me. "Trust me, more people understand why I'd be with you than why you'd be with me."

"Maybe we don't need to worry what those other people think. If we love each other, and I do love you,

Harper, then I don't really care what anyone thinks. I've never connected with anyone like I do you. Perhaps we come from different worlds, but you get me better than anyone in my own circle ever has." He swallowed. "And I understand you too. I don't blame you for being hurt or pissed or whatever you are. I deserve that. I let you down. But it wasn't because I don't love you enough. It's because I felt insecure and scared."

His raw emotion got through to me. It was impossible not to move toward him slowly. "When I say we have each other's backs, I mean always." My voice was hushed. "Always, Sam."

He nodded and his eyes were dark with pain. "I agree. I won't let you down again."

"You sure?"

"Yes. I swear. I know who you really are, and I was an idiot for listening to my dad."

I sighed. "I don't want to lose you. That I do know."

"Really?" he asked softly.

"I don't want to say goodbye."

"Can you forgive me, Harper?" His voice wobbled.

I slipped my arms around his waist, and he melted into me. His warm breath was against my throat, and he hugged me back. I found his mouth with mine, and we kissed passionately for a few moments. It felt so amazing to have him back in my arms I almost couldn't believe this wasn't a dream. His familiar taste and touch made my heart ache with need.

"Harper," he whispered. "I'm so sorry I hurt you."

I thought about what Peter had said. "I'm sure I'll hurt you too someday. But I want this to work. I don't want to run. I want to stay and fight for this."

"That means everything."

I held his affectionate gaze. "It's a weird feeling to need someone as much as I do you. It makes me feel vulnerable, and I'll be honest, I don't love that feeling."

"I know. I get it." He tightened his grip around me. "But you're mine. You've always been mine. You just didn't know it." His smile was tentative.

My lips twitched. "Did you have to run me over to make your point?"

He winced. "Maybe I'm more like my dad than I realized."

I bugged my eyes. "Oh, God. Don't say that."

He laughed, and then the smile slowly faded from his face. "I'm so glad you're home. You're back where you belong."

"I think maybe I am."

I'd never felt like I'd belonged anywhere before. Not really. Not until Sam. He'd crashed into my life and then rebuilt it piece by piece into something wonderful. Something meaningful. I wasn't afraid to trust him because I had no choice. I'd been running most of my life. Running from my dad. Running from fear. Running from feelings. But maybe it wasn't the running that was the problem, as much as the direction you chose.

And from now on, the only running I'd do was toward Sam.

S.C. Wynne

Epilogue

Harper

When Allison came into the baggage claim area, I recognized her immediately. She was so tall and grown-up-looking, but she had the same warm smile she'd had even as a kid. I guess I looked similar to how she remembered too because she didn't even hesitate when I approached, and she flew into my arms.

Once I had her in my embrace, it was hard to let go. I laughed and did my best to suppress my tears of joy. But it felt so surreal to have her in my life again. I finally let go of her and held her at arm's length. "You're so tall. And so pretty." I wiped at my eyes. "God, this is insane."

She nodded, and her cheeks were streaked with tears. "I know." She gripped my arm as if she didn't want to lose that connection. "You look so much like you always did." She sniffed. "More muscles and your hair is longer."

I tugged at my hair. "Yeah. I need a haircut."

From behind me, Sam cleared his throat. "I'm Sam."

Allison looked at him and immediately moved to hug him. "Sam! I'm so happy to meet you."

He smiled at me over her shoulder. "It's great to finally meet you too."

She straightened and returned her gaze to me. "I can't stop staring at you."

I laughed. "Same here." It was weird how familiar she seemed after not having seen each other for so many years.

Sam grabbed her suitcase. "Shall we get going?"

"Oh, yeah." Allison laughed. "I guess we don't need to hang out in the baggage claim all day."

As we made our way to the car, Allison chatted cheerfully about her flight. It was weird how her mannerisms and her laugh were so familiar. I couldn't stop staring at her and putting my arm around her shoulder. I felt protective of her and eager to hear about her life.

Sam had insisted on driving to meet Allison, and he'd decided she'd stay with us for the week she was here. He'd wanted us to have as much one-on-one time with each other as possible. Allison insisted on sitting in the back seat, and so I turned to talk with her on the trip to Sam's house. Once there we got her situated in the guest room, and then Sam went to make lunch. Allison and I sat out on the back patio with ice-cold lemonade to keep us cool.

"I'm so happy this day has finally arrived." She grinned, tucking a strand of blonde hair behind her ear. "My roommate is sick of hearing about you."

I was still surprised that she was so affectionate toward me. She wasn't guarded or resentful in the least. For so long I'd feared that she would think I was a violent monster lowlife. But it was obvious she just wanted to be closer to me. "Did you tell Mom and Dad you were coming to see me?"

Her face hardened. "Yes. But I knew they wouldn't be supportive about it. They're negative about everything."

I nodded. "Yeah, I remember."

She sighed. "Mom's better than dad but…" She shrugged. "I don't care. Nothing was stopping me from seeing you."

My chest ached. "I'm so glad. I really didn't think I'd ever see you again." My eyes stung, and I sipped my lemonade to distract myself.

"What?" she squeaked. "Why?"

"I didn't know if you'd want to see me. I was too scared to reach out to you."

"Harper, why wouldn't I want to see you?" She squinted at me. "I never even understood why you went away. Mom said it was because you were on drugs, but I didn't believe her."

"She said that?" I scowled. "I was never on drugs."

"I know." She gave me an encouraging smile. "I remember the night you and Dad got into that fight." She swallowed hard. "I remember he slapped me and I fell. Then you went after him, and there was a lot of blood. I didn't understand what was happening. I was so confused."

"I was protecting you." My stomach clenched, and I avoided her gaze. "I didn't just go crazy and start attacking for no reason."

"I figured that out a little later. After you'd gone." She winced. "I was scared that night because I'd never seen that side of you. But I knew you were fighting for me. I always knew that, Harper."

"I wasn't sure. I didn't know what to do because Mom and Dad didn't want me to come home. Dad promised to keep his hands off of you if I'd get out of town. Mom had always been repulsed by me the minute she knew I was gay. Dad gave me a thousand dollars and told me to go. He said if I took off he wouldn't try to press charges. I was confused and scared. It was easier to just leave and do what they wanted."

Her face was pale. "I didn't know they made you leave. They said you ran away."

I shook my head. "Not willingly."

Her eyes glittered with tears. "They lied to my face my whole life."

"Dad didn't try and hurt you ever again, right?" My heart pounded as I waited for her answer.

"No. Mom was protective of me." She frowned. "I don't know why she was so awful about you."

"She was always kind of distant with me. But when she figured out my sexuality, she seemed disgusted." I watched Allison's face closely. "She seemed to think I was gay on purpose just to annoy her."

"Oh, for goodness' sake." Allison sounded appalled. "She makes me nuts with her bible verses and rosary beads, when all the while she's so unloving to so many people. I don't get it."

Tension drained from me as she spoke. I'd been afraid for so long that my parents would have twisted her and made her just like them. But she wasn't like them at all. She was loving and warm. I was so proud she was my sister. "It's so good to see you, Allie."

She stood and moved to me. We hugged and laughed tearfully.

Sam came out right then with plates of chicken and potato salad, and he grinned when he saw us. "Awww, look at you two."

Allie sighed. "Just making up for lost time."

"Good." He set the dishes down. "I hope you like chicken. It's nothing fancy, but it's food," he announced cheerfully.

"It looks delicious," Allie said.

We sat at the patio table, and I inhaled the honeysuckle-drenched air. I couldn't believe I was sitting there with Allie across the table from me. Sam put his arm around my shoulder and kissed the side of my head. Then he ruffled my hair and helped himself to some chicken.

I met Allie's warm gaze across the table, and we both smiled. If anyone had told me a few months ago I'd have found the love of my life and be reunited with my sister, I'd have said they were crazy. I'd have been positive they had a screw loose. And yet, here I was, happier than I probably had a right to be.

I sighed. "Life is pretty good right now."

Allie nodded. "I agree. It's just about perfect."

"Now if we could just do something about that jackass you work for." Sam licked his fingers as he spoke.

"He is a jerk," I said.

Allie frowned. "Really? Do you have to stay there?"

I shrugged. "I make better money there than if I started new somewhere else. But Jack is definitely an asshole to work for."

"You know, Harper, I was serious about loaning you the money to start your own messenger service," Sam said.

I gave him a startled glance. "Sam, I don't see myself as an entrepreneur."

He gave me a patient smile. "I know. But you didn't see us together either. Sometimes I have to see this stuff for you first, and then you see it too."

I laughed gruffly. "This is different."

"No it's not."

"Your dad would blow a gasket if he knew you want to throw even more money at me."

Allison gave me a curious glance. "Why is that?"

I grimaced. "It's a long story. I'll tell you how Sam and I met after we eat. It might give you indigestion."

"What?" Sam laughed. "It's a great story."

"It's a crazy story." I winced.

"Pfft." Sam grinned as he turned to address Allison. "I ran Harper over on his bike, and then I nursed him back to health."

Allison's eyes widened. "What?" she squeaked.

I couldn't help but laugh at her shocked expression. "He's telling the truth."

"You ran him over?"

"Well... not on purpose," Sam said. "And we will discuss me loaning you the money to go out on your own later, Harper. This conversation is not over."

"If you say so."

"So... he actually hit you with his car?" Allison laughed.

"Yep." I met Sam's warm gaze. "First he ran me over, and then he made me fall in love with him."

"Oh, my goodness." She wrinkled her brow. "Why would Sam's dad be mad if he loaned you money?"

"We didn't get off to a great start. He thought I was a con artist." She bugged her eyes, and I grinned. "We're better now. Not great. I don't think we'll ever be close. I'll tell you everything later if you want to hear about it."

"Of course I do." Allison grinned. "I love dramatic love stories."

I smiled. "Then you'll love this one."

Sam sat up straighter. "Oh, did you see my dad actually answered a reporter's question directly the other day about me being gay?"

"I didn't." I frowned. "What did he say?"

"He said that yes, his son is gay, but that his son isn't the one running for office, he is. The reporter looked like he wasn't sure what to do with that." Sam laughed.

"That actually is the truth."

"Yep." Sam nodded. "But I'm just happy he didn't try and dodge the question like he used to. I want to give him the benefit of the doubt, but truthfully, I think he only answered the reporter because he was trying to distract the guy from asking about that Russian oligarchy money story. That rumor has reared its ugly head again and Dad is slipping in the polls."

"He's losing?" I raised my brows.

"Looks like he might."

"Wow." I frowned.

"He might catch back up. But he might not. I guess we'll see how it all plays out in November."

"It's fascinating that your dad is a senator," Allison said.

"Is it?" Sam laughed.

"You must have lots of stories."

Sam twisted his lips. "Oh, I have a few."

"I'll bet." She turned her gaze to me. "I still can't believe you two met because Sam ran you over." She smiled weakly. "That's a very unusual love story."

I nodded. "We're an unusual couple."

Sam grinned and helped himself to more potato salad. "Yeah. But we have each other's backs, no matter what." He nudged my shoulder with his. "Isn't that right, Harper?"

I met his trusting gaze, and my heart squeezed tight. "Back. Front. Sides. I've got you covered from all angles."

I sometimes got choked up when Sam looked at me like that. Maybe because I'd felt worthless for so long I'd never have believed someone like him could love me. But thanks to Sam, I was gradually accepting that maybe I was a tiny bit valuable after all.

Other Books by S.C. Wynne

Hard-Ass is Here
Christmas Crush
Hard-Ass Vacation
The New Boss
Guarding My Heart
The Cowboy and the Barista
Damaged Heart-Rerelease coming soon!
Up in Flames
Until the Morning
Falling into Love
The Fire Underneath
Kiss and Tell
Secrets from the Edge-Rerelease coming soon!
Hiding Things
Home to Danger
Assassins Are People Too #1-Rerelease coming soon!
Painful Lessons
Assassins Love People Too #2-Rerelease coming soon!
Believing Rory
Unleashing Love
Starting New
The Cowboy and the Pencil-Pusher
Memories Follow
Shadow's Edge Book #1
Shadow's Return Book #2
My Omega's Baby (Bodyguard & Babies Book #1)
Rockstar Baby (Bodyguard & Babies Book #2)
Manny's Surprise Baby (Bodyguard & Babies Book#3)
Strange Medicine (Dr. Maxwell Thornton Mysteries #1)
Doctor In the Desert
Redemption
Married To Murder

Buy Links for all my books are available at

www.scwynne.com